HARD EXIT

J. B. TURNER

HARD EXIT

A JON REZNICK THRILLER

THOMAS & MERCER

Text copyright © 2023 by J. B. Turner
All rights reserved.

Published by Thomas & Mercer, Seattle

www.apub.com

Amazon, the Amazon logo, and Thomas & Mercer are trademarks of Amazon.com, Inc., or its affiliates.

ISBN-13: 9781542039796
eISBN: 9781542039802

Cover design by @blacksheep-uk.com
Cover images: ©Peshkova, ©AvDe / Shutterstock;
©Dusica Paripovic / ArcAngel

Printed in the United States of America

To my sister, Sarah

Prologue

It was nearly midnight. The street was cloaked in darkness.

Hans Muller was wrapped up in multiple layers as he headed to his work for the last time. Snow crunched underfoot. His breath turned to a white vapor amid the deathly quiet. Not a soul in sight. Backpack slung over his shoulder, he approached steel security gates. The harsh floodlights bathed the entrance in an icy glow. His boots trudged a slushy footpath toward the barriers. And all the while, surveillance cameras watched his every move.

He approached the turnstile and tapped in the six-digit security code on a metal panel. He pushed the steel bars and walked into the floodlit courtyard entrance. He headed through the secure outer checkpoint. His was such a well-known face, he figured even though he was being watched, they wouldn't give him a second glance. They knew who he was. He was part of the senior team.

Muller walked up to the first guard. He reached into his jacket and held up his ID card, hung on a lanyard around his neck. House keys, cell phone, and backpack were all checked. But not thoroughly.

"Guten Abend," Muller said.

A second security guard frisked him. The guard rechecked his backpack. He seemed bemused when he looked inside Muller's bag. He opened his plastic lunch box and peered inside. The box contained two thickly smeared peanut butter sandwiches Muller had carefully prepared that morning. The guard sniffed the contents and winced as if the spread was off. Then he clicked the lid shut. He rummaged inside the backpack. But it contained only a bottle of water, a packet of disposable wet wipes, and a bar of Muller's favorite Swiss chocolate.

Muller was waved through the initial checks and walked through an airport-style metal detector. A cursory glance from a third security guard on the other side. In an adjacent booth, a supervisor scanned a bank of surveillance cameras.

The supervisor looked up briefly to wave him through.

Muller continued to the elevator and headed to the fourth floor. He stepped out into the open-plan office. Big screens on the wall displayed real-time footage of major rail stations and airports in Switzerland. The place was deserted, as he had predicted.

He knew three coworkers were on an NSA intelligence-sharing course, training in America. New hacking tools. New techniques. Backdoor entries to encrypted cloud servers. It was a cool junket. It would be fancy hotels, wining and dining, and talking shop with US cybersecurity specialists. It was a working holiday for making connections. He had undertaken similar courses. The team wasn't due back until the following night. So, it was just Hans on the fourth floor for the night shift.

He finally reached his desk and sat down, placing his backpack carefully at his feet.

Muller was ready. His work was highly classified. He worked for Switzerland's leading intelligence agency, Nachrichtendienst des Bundes (the NDB), also known as the Federal Intelligence Service.

It had been nine long years. He was diligent and much admired for his work ethic.

Muller lived a sober, quiet, and archetypally Swiss life. He minded his own business, he paid his taxes, he was respectful of his neighbors. He didn't play his music loud, choosing to listen with headphones. He attended an upmarket gym in the center of Bern. He hiked in the summer. He visited his widowed mother when he could. And as the years passed, his advanced cybersecurity skills, attention to detail, and adherence to blending in had granted him the highest security clearance.

He was one of only a handful of employees at the NDB afforded unrestricted access. To the most classified data imaginable, including the files of Switzerland's Defense Ministry.

Switzerland was supposed to be neutral. At least that's what it told the world. That was a lie. The country was aligned to the West, no matter what anyone said.

Muller could also access Echelon, a network of spy stations around the world, operated and used by the Five Eyes. He wanted to know everything. What crossed his desk was a treasure trove of the finest intelligence data. He analyzed and sifted through what mattered.

Switzerland had long been a target of espionage by countries from around the world. It hosted the headquarters of numerous international and nongovernmental organizations, including the United Nations, the International Committee of the Red Cross, the World Trade Organization, the International Labour Organization, the World Intellectual Property Organization, the World Health Organization, the World Economic Forum, the Geneva Centre for Security Policy, and CERN, not to mention numerous banking conglomerates, biotechnology firms, pharmaceutical giants, multinational insurance firms . . . The list went on and on.

He had access to top secret memos from the CIA, emails from heads of state, financial reports, medical records of tech billionaires, information about visits from leaders of several mineral-rich African countries looking to buy properties in Switzerland, Five Eyes intelligence briefings, the latest geopolitical analysis of terrorist threats and groups in Western Europe, the movements of Russian sympathizers in Geneva linked to ultraright-wing and left-wing causes and, of course, Islamists, under covert surveillance in every mosque and prayer center across Switzerland. The levels of activity of foreign intelligence services, friendly and otherwise. He had access to it all. At his fingertips.

Muller had counted down the months to this night. His last night. The night he would disappear.

He adjusted the height of his seat until he was comfortable, his huge screen in front of him. He tapped a few keys and quickly logged on to the highly secure server. He checked his heart rate on his Apple Watch. It was rising. He took a few deep breaths, gathering his thoughts. He felt calmer. He was ready.

He tapped in a few keys. Within a split second, he had secured access to highly sensitive intelligence shared by the CIA, Mossad, and Britain's MI6, starting with names and assumed identities of Russian operatives active in the country. Moscow had been building a pan-European hub for operations in Geneva and Bern. He also accessed years of raw intelligence data accumulated by the NDB, both at home and abroad, including suspected foreign sleeper agents in Switzerland.

He was the main contact in Switzerland for the NSA, allowing him to access the hundreds of millions of intercepted phone calls, emails, and text messages into and out of Switzerland. They went through the Leuk satellite listening station in Switzerland, beamed back to 33 Thomas Street, a windowless skyscraper in Tribeca, Manhattan. It was the most important NSA facility on the East

Coast, outside of Fort Meade in Maryland. Switzerland was neutral in name only. It had been an integral part of the Western intelligence axis since the days of the Cold War.

It was time.

He picked up his backpack and headed to the bathroom. He went into a stall and locked the door. He opened up his plastic lunch box and carefully took out one of the sandwiches. He peeled back the top slice of rye bread and pushed his thumb and index finger into the thick peanut butter. He immediately felt the hard plastic. He carefully extracted the SD data storage card wrapped in plastic. He threw the sandwich in the trash can. He placed the card, still wrapped in the thin plastic film, on the toilet tank. He reached into his backpack and pulled out the wet wipes. He wiped his hands clean, then flushed the wipe down the toilet.

Muller took another wet wipe and cleaned the plastic wrapped around the SD card. He flushed that wipe down the toilet too. Then he carefully took the card out of the plastic and put it in his pocket. He headed back to his desk, backpack across his shoulders.

Muller inserted the card into the side of his computer and tapped a few keys. A few moments later, he was downloading state secrets from secure cloud servers. The servers themselves were hidden in a sprawling underground data center in Wolfhausen, a village one hundred and fifty kilometers from Bern.

Huge reams of data downloaded before his eyes. A digital deluge began as hundreds of megabytes transferred. Then gigabytes. The SD card was ultra-high capacity, one terabyte, favored by professional photographers. It could hold a quarter of a million photos. But it could also hold, at a conservative estimate, six million pages of documents. All he knew for sure was that he was going to download the crown jewels.

He sat and watched. Hour after hour. He only paused it when he went to the bathroom. Then he resumed the monster download.

When it was finished, he carefully took out the SD card and put it in his pocket.

Then he went back to the bathroom, locked the door of the stall, wrapped the card in a bit of plastic wrap. He took out his second sandwich and pushed the card, protected by plastic, into the middle of the peanut butter, pressing down the thick slice of bread. He clicked shut the plastic lunch box. When he was finished, he cleaned his hands with a wet wipe again and flushed it down the toilet.

Muller placed his lunch box back in his backpack and headed back to his desk. He logged off the server.

He enjoyed a long coffee break and a bar of his favorite chocolate.

Muller scanned numerous encrypted messages sent by the NSA asking for information on Swiss residents, including owners of tech firms and banks. His country had the strictest privacy laws, but there were ways around that. He set up the reciprocal protocol.

He counted down the minutes. Then, as dawn broke, Muller got up from his desk and took the elevator to the ground level. He was once more patted down. God knows what they were hoping to find. Then the guards gave a cursory look in his bag before waving him through.

Muller headed through the security gates for the final time, backpack slung over his shoulder, and composed himself as he walked out into the harsh wintry glare of the sun, knowing he would never be back.

One

It had reached the low nineties, the sky cobalt blue. The road south cut through mangrove swamps, isolated white beaches, and azure seas. Total isolation.

Reznick drove hard, fierce sun on his face. The BMW convertible he had rented in Miami tore up the miles. He began to relax. It was great to get away from the icy roads and snowdrifts in Maine.

The hot, sticky air felt good. He was in the far south of Florida in the middle of a winter heat wave. The guy on the radio said it was near-record temperatures for mid-January.

Reznick had driven over the Seven Mile Bridge on the overseas highway, past Marathon, the Atlantic Ocean on one side, the Gulf of Mexico and Florida Bay on the other. Then over Shark Key. Mile after mile of sleepy hamlets dotting the highway. Seafood sandwich shacks, beach bars by the road.

He loved this part of the country, with its slower way of life. More laid-back than Miami's frenetic South Beach party scene. Down here time seemed to melt away.

Reznick saw a sign up ahead. A shooting range. He hadn't done any shooting in weeks. He turned off down a dusty road. The Stars and Stripes fluttered high up on a metal pole cemented into the ground. A few pickup trucks with NRA bumper stickers on the back windows were parked facing out in the small lot.

He got out of his car, shirt already sticking to his back. Once inside the range, though, it was cold as hell. Jon felt an icy blast on his neck, heard the sound of rapid gunfire. The air-conditioner units rattled.

The owner, cigar at the corner of his mouth, introduced himself. "Chuck Rayner, pleased to meet you."

Reznick shook hands and exchanged a few pleasantries. Rayner asked about his gun training.

"Extensive," Reznick replied.

"I got you, buddy. So, you'll know your way around."

Nevertheless, Reznick was given a few quick lessons in gun safety and shooting etiquette before he was handed a pair of Peltor earmuffs.

Rayner showed him to lane three.

Reznick took out his 9mm Beretta handgun. He pulled back the slide and took careful aim at the target. Gun held tight, just like a million times before. The target was sixty feet away. He flicked off the Beretta's safety. Then he squeezed off fifteen rapid-fire rounds. The muffled sound of gunshots bounced off the concrete walls. The smell of smoke and lead floated thick in the air. Slowly, the lingering smoke dissipated.

Reznick pointed his gun at the ground.

He depressed the magazine release button. Then he thumbed on the safety and checked that the chamber was empty.

Reznick looked down the lane at the bullet holes in the target. The middle was nearly shredded. Perfect.

He clicked in a fresh magazine and pushed it into the pistol grip. He flicked off the safety again. Then he took aim. He fired off his rounds into the target, emptying the magazine in double-quick time.

He did the same over and over again for the next twenty minutes. Satisfied he was still sharp, he holstered his handgun.

The owner dragged on his cigar, turning to blow the blue smoke away from Reznick. He shook his head and smiled. "Who the hell taught you to shoot like that, bro?"

"The United States government."

The guy laughed. "Good one. Military?"

"A little while back."

"Let me ask you something: You ever think of doing some instructing in the use of firearms? If you do, just holler. I could use some help in here."

"I'll keep that in mind. I'm just passing through."

"You from up north?"

"That obvious, huh?"

"Everybody and their dog down here at this time of year is from up north. Great weather. Low taxes. And guns! What's not to love about Florida?"

Reznick smiled. "Any good bars around here?"

"Are you kidding me? We have plenty of good bars. I recommend Jimmy's. A little place, couple hundred yards due south, just off the highway. Tell them Chuck sent you."

Reznick strode inside the weather-beaten shack and pulled a stool up to the bar. He ordered a cold pitcher of beer and cheese fries. The small TV was airing a Dolphins game. At the end of the bar sat two burly guys in golf shirts. Reznick overheard their loud conversation about retirement, fishing, wives, falling police numbers, and the spiraling levels of crime in New York City. They sounded like cops. One of them wore a Mets cap.

The younger of the two looked over at Reznick. "You believe this place, bro?"

Reznick looked back. "What was that?"

"I mean, half a foot of snow on the ground in Queens, and we're enjoying this life. What could be better? I mean, come on. Tough choice, right?"

Reznick didn't like getting drawn into conversations, no matter how benign. "Nice place."

"You live here, pal?"

"Me? Vacation."

"Where you from?"

"A little place. Up north. Even colder than New York."

"Where?"

"A small town in Maine. You wouldn't know it."

The other guy smiled. "I love it up there. Let me ask you something: When you retire, you headed down here to Florida, or staying up in Maine?"

"I hadn't really thought about it."

"Yeah, but if you had to choose."

"I don't see why I can't do both. Live down here in the winter, summer up north."

The guy snapped his fingers. "Now we're talking. The best of both worlds. I'm telling you, I'd miss seeing the Mets."

Reznick nodded.

"So, you staying nearby?"

"Just passing through."

"Is that right? We brought the wives down. Rented an Airbnb a couple blocks away, right by the beach. Phenomenal. A friend of my brother's recommended it."

Reznick's cell phone rang. He got up from his seat and walked past the two guys in the bar. "Excuse me. Got to take this."

"Sure thing, buddy."

Reznick walked out into the blazing sunshine, shielding his eyes. He checked the caller ID but didn't recognize the number. "Jon speaking, who's this?"

"I'm so sorry to bother you." A woman's voice. "Is this Jon Reznick?"

"Who's this?"

"My name is . . . Marjorie Jameson. I'm Brad's . . . wife. Brad was in Delta."

Reznick took a few moments to process the faltering words. "Brad Jameson?"

"That's right. I'm his wife."

"Marjorie, how the hell are you?"

"Not great, Jon. He asked me to call you. I hope you don't mind."

Reznick had been close to Jameson when they were in Delta together, many years back. He was classically tough, stoic, like all the operators he worked with. "Is he OK?"

A sigh. "No. Brad is dying, Jon. He has stage four cancer."

Reznick scrunched up his face. He couldn't picture the guy who could run marathons for fun, do push-ups in the hundreds, ever dying. "Oh God, no."

"He wants to talk to you. Just to say his goodbyes."

Reznick felt his throat tighten, the news like a hammer blow, out of the blue. "I'm so sorry. Yeah, of course, where is he?"

"I feel bad imposing. But he did specifically ask to speak to you."

"You're not imposing. Where is he, Marjorie?"

"He's in the hospital. I think he's scared, Jon. Scared of dying. He said he wants to talk to you. He begged me to get in touch with you."

"Where exactly is he?"

"He's at a hospital in Manhattan."

11

Two

Soft white surfaces, wooden floors, and modern art on the wall made the hospital feel like a five-star hotel.

Reznick rode the elevator to the nineteenth floor and headed along a carpeted corridor. It was far removed from the veterans' hospitals or care rehabilitation facilities he had visited over the years.

A nurse showed him to a spacious room overlooking the East River. The door was ajar, but Reznick knocked anyway.

"Come in."

Reznick opened the door, and his heart sank.

Brad Jameson looked up from his bed, rheumy eyes bulging. His bone-white skin clung to his skeletal face. His emaciated arms were limp on the white bedsheets. His right hand reached out and pressed a button attached to a machine. Reznick assumed it was a patient-controlled pump to administer morphine.

Reznick walked around the bed and sat down in an easy chair. He reached over and held Brad's hand. It was cold and clammy to the touch.

Brad's eyes filled with tears. "I knew you would come. I didn't doubt it for a minute."

Reznick forced a smile. He was dying inside. It was unbearable to see his former Delta buddy this way. Brad had fought alongside

Reznick in the hellhole that was Fallujah, street by street, down filthy alleyways, house to house, side by side. He was as tough and smart as they came, known for his black sense of humor. But now? Skin and bones, close to death.

Brad licked his parched lips, eyes rolling around his head. "Our Father, who art in Heaven, hallowed be thy name."

Reznick poured a glass of cold water and placed a straw in it. He handed it to his old Delta pal.

Brad's shaky hand gripped the glass, and he sucked the water down in a few gulps. "Thanks. So, here we are."

Reznick nodded and took Brad's hand again. "I wish I'd known earlier."

"Sometimes it's best not to know. Stay in the dark. But I'm glad you're here, man."

"Glad to be here."

"Who told you I was here?"

"Marjorie called me. She said you've known for a while. I wish you'd told me."

"What's the point? Stage four, Jon. Endgame time. Nothing you could have done. Nothing anyone could have done. Way it goes."

"Is there anything I can get you?"

"No. I just want to talk. They say I might lapse into unconsciousness before I go, but they don't know when. So, while I'm still here, I want to say a few things."

"Of course."

Brad's eyes rolled back in his head for a few moments. "Shooting the breeze. Just like old times. You believe this place?"

"The hospital?"

"Yeah, the fucking hospital. The best in America, they say."

Reznick nodded. "It's more like the goddamn Plaza."

Brad smiled for a few moments before he grimaced. "They say I've got weeks, if I'm lucky. Realistically, maybe days."

"Why isn't Marjorie here?"

"Her? We got divorced three years ago."

"I'm sorry to hear that."

"Forget it. It was all my fault. She had to put up with a lot from me, truth be told. But she's a good woman. A very good woman. Better than I deserved."

"Is there anyone I can contact for you besides your ex-wife? Family, friends?"

Brad closed his eyes and shook his head. "The Lord is my shepherd . . ." He seemed to drift off again for a few moments. "They've already cut out pieces of my lung. Biopsies came back. I ain't got long. Whatever the fuck a biopsy is."

"What about your sons?"

"They're due in tomorrow. Flying in from California and Seattle."

"They work out there?"

"Fuck knows, bro. Never hear from them."

Reznick bowed his head and nodded. He felt the anger in his dying friend's voice. The hurt.

"What about your daughter, Jon?"

"Lauren?"

"Yeah, Lauren. You talk to her?"

"I do. I'm lucky."

"That's good, Jon. That's real good. Try and keep in touch with her. I never did with my kids. And I regret it. Too busy working abroad, making money, disappearing for months, years, who the hell knows. I think the divorce was the final straw for them."

"Forget it." Reznick wanted to change the subject. "The last I knew, you were in Riyadh, trying to persuade me to head out there."

"Trust me, you dodged a bullet. Don't get me wrong, the money was sensational. The hotel was out of this world. But who the hell wants to hang out there?"

"When was that?"

"Eighteen months ago, I don't know. I can't even remember. I do remember who I was there with."

"Anyone I know?"

"Usual reprobates. A few ex-Delta guys like us, former SEALs. And one guy from the Agency."

"Sounds like a fun crowd."

"Not quite. Paid big fucking bucks, though. That job is how my insurance can afford to put me up here. Apparently I can order any meal from any restaurant in the city. But I can't eat, throw up all the time."

Reznick smiled uncomfortably.

Brad gripped the pump attached to the morphine drip and pressed a button. He closed his eyes as the opioid took the pain away. "Motherfucker. It's eating away at me."

"You want me to get a nurse?"

"I ain't got long now."

"I wish there was something I could do for you."

"You being here is nice. I said to the doctor, I said, *Jon Reznick will turn up. You'll see.* And here you are."

"I wish it was under different circumstances."

"You ever been to Yemen, Jon?"

Reznick sat back as Brad hopped between subjects. "No. Nice?"

Brad grimaced, eyes scrunched up. "I was there a few years back, advising the Saudis. Don't ever go there."

"It's not top of my list for vacations."

"I told one of the guys I was with about you."

Reznick smiled. "Who was it?"

"You don't know him. He worked for the Agency. I've known him for a while. But it was the first time I had talked about knowing you. And that's when it got weird."

"I don't understand, Brad."

15

"It's probably the fucking morphine . . . Mind is like a fog."

"You said it got weird?"

"The Agency guy asked about people I had worked with in the past. He runs a security consultancy. I talked about you."

Reznick wondered what exactly Brad was getting at. "It got weird?"

"That's right, when I mentioned your name. The strangest thing. I couldn't for the life of me figure out what he was saying. I always meant to talk to you about it. Never got around to it, I guess."

"I don't understand."

"The guy. CIA, right? I met him in Yemen."

Reznick nodded. His friend sounded like he was just rambling, reminiscing in a drugged haze.

"I've known him for years. He always worked at Langley, in and around DC, sometimes in New York, and after I mentioned your name, he said way back, he knew your wife before she died."

Reznick took a few moments to absorb the information. "He knew Elisabeth?"

"Said she was very pretty. Smart too."

"Did he meet her in college?"

"Nope."

Reznick shifted his weight, suddenly uncomfortable. "She's been dead more than twenty years."

Brad went quiet for a little while. "Dead?"

"Elisabeth died on 9/11."

"Yeah, right. Of course. Sorry, my brain is fogged up like shit."

"It's OK. Do you want some more water?"

"He said he met her twice. Nice lady. The last name rang a bell to him when I mentioned you. The moment I said *Jon Reznick*. He said he met your wife in New York."

"She did work in New York. But it must've been a long time ago."

Jameson sank further into his pillow. "Yeah . . . Three months before 9/11. Guy's super bright. He's got like a photographic memory. I also remember he said she worked in the World Trade Center."

Reznick patted the back of Brad's bony hand. "That's right, she worked there. She was a tax attorney. Senior partner. I might have mentioned that way back."

"Tax attorney?"

"Yeah. Was he getting advice on his tax situation?"

"Tax situation? Nothing to do with that, Jon. Let me think. He said she worked on the twenty-fifth floor. Yeah, the twenty-fifth floor. He was very precise."

"Elisabeth didn't work on the twenty-fifth floor. He must be mistaken. It happens."

"Maybe I made a mistake. Are you sure?"

Reznick nodded. "I would know. She worked on the eighty-ninth floor of the World Trade Center. Couldn't have been Elisabeth."

"Jon, my memory's not too good. I apologize for that."

"Forget it."

"But I can't. I swear, Jon, he said he met your wife at a meeting on the twenty-fifth floor of World Trade Center Building 7. He definitely said that."

Reznick felt his ire rising. "Who said that?"

"Ken."

Reznick sighed. "You want to explain to me who Ken is?"

"He worked at the Agency. Ken McGill."

"I don't know a Ken McGill."

"I think he worked in Europe too, station chief in Helsinki or something."

Reznick glanced at the door, willing a nurse to ask him to leave. "Whatever, it doesn't matter. It's all ancient history."

"Ken said she was smart. High-IQ type. The youngest boss he'd had."

"Elisabeth worked for Rosenfeld and Williams as a tax attorney. She was a partner. You remember Mike Leggett?"

"Sure."

"Mike's sister Angie worked with Elisabeth in the same office on the eighty-ninth floor. They both died on 9/11. Those are the facts. I don't like talking about stuff like that. It's personal."

Brad grimaced and shook his head. "They both died . . . I don't understand."

"Memory is a funny thing. Plays tricks on you. It was a long time ago."

"I was sure that's what he told me. Ken's a straight shooter. He's a stand-up Montana guy. And he said the office was on the same floor as the IRS."

"Well, that might make sense, her being a tax attorney."

"No, Jon. She wasn't a tax attorney."

Brad closed his eyes. He drifted into a morphine-induced sleep. It was the last time Reznick saw him alive.

Three

A week later, Brad Jameson was laid to rest under a slate-gray Montana sky. The cemetery spread in the shadow of the snow-covered Boulder Mountains range.

Reznick felt the bitingly cold wind on his skin as it buffeted the mourners. Close family, security industry colleagues, school friends, and a handful of former Delta operators gathered around the grave to pay their final respects.

Reznick watched as the mahogany coffin was lowered into the frozen earth. He bowed his head as the minister quoted from the Bible. After the ceremony ended, he looked over at the graveside and saw Brad's ex-wife. He walked over and shook her hand. "I'm so sorry for your loss, Marjorie."

"Thanks for coming, Jon. He always talked about you. Meant a lot to him that you managed to see him before he passed away."

"He was a brave man. A great patriot. A great American."

Marjorie blinked away the tears. "He was a lousy husband, God rest his soul."

Reznick said nothing.

"I still loved him. He was a crazy son of a bitch, that's true. He drank too much. He chased women. But I still loved him. Go figure."

"He would try the patience of a saint. And he did, let me tell you. But he was the sort of man you wanted by your side when the bullets were flying. He was a tough guy. He knew sacrifice. He was like a brother to me."

"He was a bastard, Jon. Too hard on the kids. Discipline-wise."

"It's how he was trained. How we were all trained. It's drilled into us."

"They were children, Jon."

"What's done is done."

"I guess. He left me two million dollars. You believe that?"

"That's a nice amount."

Marjorie closed her eyes as the tears spilled down her face. "Oh, Jon, I couldn't bear to see him in his final days. I wish I had."

"I'm glad you didn't. It wasn't pretty. Brad was in a great hospital, and the pain medication would have taken him away well before he finally passed. He wasn't suffering."

Marjorie hugged Reznick tight. "That's a comfort, Jon. And thanks for coming. Thanks for being there for Brad."

"He was always there for me when I needed it."

Marjorie smiled through the tears. "Before I forget, there's coffee and sandwiches and drinks at the Fairfield Inn across town."

"I'll see you there, Marjorie. If you need anything, just let me know. You have my number."

The room in the hotel, on the outskirts of Butte, an old mining town, was packed with former Delta operators.

Reznick nursed a Scotch on the rocks when a bearlike man approached.

"I've been told that you're Jon Reznick," the man said.

"Guilty as charged."

20

The man shook Reznick's hand. "Frank Fitzpatrick. I worked with Brad in the Middle East. He told me a lot about you. My partner and I would love to have someone like you as part of our team. As a consultant, directing operations."

"I don't know. I'm sort of out of the game now."

"Like hell you are. I keep my ear close to the ground. You've been working with the Feds for a few years, am I right?"

Reznick sipped his drink. "I'd rather not talk about it right now, if you don't mind."

"Sure, I get it. Do you mind if I introduce you to my partner? He worked a lot more closely with Brad than I did."

"Not at all."

Fitzpatrick signaled to a silver-haired guy in the corner. "This is Ken McGill. He's a longtime Agency guy."

Reznick shook the guy's hand. He had a viselike grip. "Nice to meet you, Ken. Brad mentioned you when I visited him in the hospital."

"We're going to miss him. His contacts with current and former Delta operators were second to none."

Fitzpatrick leaned closer. "I was just telling Jon that he's exactly the type of guy we're looking for."

McGill handed Reznick his card. "Please, when you have some time, give me a call. I'd love to hear from you."

Reznick slid the card into his jacket pocket. "Maybe another day."

"We pay top dollar. And I mean seriously top dollar, for the best people. Brad raved about you."

Fitzpatrick said, "Jon, if you'll excuse me, I'm just going to talk to Marjorie, if you don't mind."

"Sure, sure."

Fitzpatrick stepped away as McGill and Reznick made small talk for a few minutes. Everything from the situation in Ukraine to reminiscences about daylong drinking sessions with Brad in Miami.

McGill exuded a quiet confidence. He lowered his voice to a whisper. "Jon, I know this might not be the best place and the best circumstances. But we sure need someone like you to fill Brad's shoes for our operations. We have a new contract about to start in Kyiv. Military advisors."

"Ukraine's a mess."

"We know."

"Let me ask you something, Ken. And I hope you don't think I'm being too direct."

"Direct is always good with me."

"I don't know if Brad was hallucinating or under the heavy influence of morphine, but he mentioned that you had heard about me before, and that you told him you met my late wife, twice."

McGill frowned as if thinking back. "Yeah, I remember. That's right, I did."

Reznick took a few moments to absorb the information. "Do you mind explaining where you met her?"

"World Trade Center in New York. That was a long time ago."

"He said that. And if you don't mind me asking, Ken, in what capacity did you meet her?"

"Let's see now. I had been with the Agency for about ten years or so. And there were a couple of meetings in Manhattan. The name Reznick stuck with me. And that's how your name rang a bell with me, and I mentioned it to Brad all those years later."

"Let me get this straight. You were working for the CIA and you met her at a meeting at the World Trade Center in New York?"

"Right."

"The thing is, Ken, my wife was a tax attorney."

"A tax attorney?" McGill shook his head. "Not my recollection."

Reznick shrugged.

"If my memory serves me correct, the meetings were in the office. And she wasn't a tax attorney. WTC 7. We were on the twenty-fifth floor. You don't look convinced."

"Here's the thing, Ken. I was trying to figure it out. Her office wasn't on the twenty-fifth floor. So, why was she there?"

"Why was she there? I don't follow."

"My wife worked on the eighty-ninth floor in One World Trade Center. She showed me the office once at a meet-and-greet for husbands and wives."

McGill shrugged. "I only met her twice, like I said, couple of months before 9/11. But it was definitely WTC 7. I didn't see her again after that, obviously."

"I don't mean to badger you, Ken, but are you sure?"

"Quite sure. Elisabeth Reznick. It was right after she joined the CIA."

Four

The Cessna jet was cruising at 35,000 feet as it entered Saudi airspace.

Hans Muller stood in the plane's tiny bathroom and peered at his reflection in the mirror. He looked pale. Gaunt. Gray. It was good to be on the move, finally. He had been cooped up in a safe house for days. No natural light. He hadn't fled the country as he had imagined. Instead, he had hunkered down in the basement of the Belarusian Embassy in Bern.

His disappearance had sparked a massive manhunt across Europe. But the whole time, Muller was sitting it out underground in a quiet residential street in the Swiss capital.

Now? He was relieved to be on the move again. He had escaped Europe. It was all going according to plan.

His handlers had smuggled him out in the dead of night. An ambulance backed onto the embassy grounds. Men dressed as paramedics and wearing surgical masks carried him on a gurney into the back of the ambulance. Then he was whisked to a remote landing strip fifteen miles from Bern.

Muller's stomach knotted as he imagined the world of possibilities awaiting him. He would get to start his life again. A journey to who-knows-where. He was being disappeared. And he was confident the plan, wildly audacious and almost counterintuitive, was going to work.

The more he thought about it, the more he wondered if his theft of huge amounts of highly classified intelligence data meant his name would become more famous than any other hacker. Would he become as infamous as Edward Snowden? Maybe Kim Philby? Would he be talked about in years to come in reverential tones by cybersecurity experts? *He was the guy who pulled off the biggest hack of Western intelligence in history, then disappeared off the face of the earth!* Is that how he would be talked about? Hated in some circles, lauded in others. The maverick. The antihero. Maybe a libertarian cybersecurity genius outlaw like John McAfee.

He scanned his features once more. Cropped hair, pale blue contact lenses, paler complexion. The old look, with shiny, shoulder-length wavy hair, was gone. The glasses, gone. He looked like a different person. It was surface. But it would do. For now.

Muller headed back to his seat and gazed out the window, the endless sands of Arabia below. His work record was impeccable. His work and diligence had intercepted six major terrorist plots in Zurich, Bern, and Geneva in the last three years. He worked long hours. He had been content to do whatever it took to protect his country and its economic interests. Over the last eighteen months, however, he had grown just that little bit more disaffected. Small issues became larger problems. He wanted to reform and implement new systems and techniques. But there was pushback. Slowly, his loyalty receded.

The problems were exacerbated when his father died. He struggled to cope. He took Xanax. It numbed the pain. He slept more. He began to drink at home. He saw a therapist. Nothing worked.

He began to feel suicidal. He found himself in debt. He couldn't foresee a way out. He had asked for a raise. That was rejected. He showed his worth by launching a new biometric encryption system the NDB had belatedly rolled out. Still, he didn't get a raise. No recognition apart from a pat on the back.

Muller had considered leaving. He thought long and hard. He thought about setting up his own consultancy. He thought about moving to America. Maybe become a contractor for the NSA. He could get a job there easily. Highly paid too. Then he changed his mind. He came up with a plan. A daring plan that would rock the complacent Western intelligence establishment and make him filthy rich.

He had already seen that fifty million dollars had been deposited in secret offshore accounts. He alone could access the funds anywhere in the world, moving his millions in seconds, whenever he wanted. But he had been promised another fifty million more if he handed over the keys to all the data he had stolen. The codes. When they got that, he would have a new identity, be a citizen of whatever country he wanted. New passport, new biometric data uploaded. Whatever he desired.

Muller was snapped out of his reverie as a blonde waitress handed him a glass of chilled French champagne.

"Sir?"

Muller took the glass. "Thank you."

"Anything else, sir?"

"I'm all set, thanks."

The hostess smiled as she turned to serve the handful of other passengers at the front of the plane their drinks and snacks. His minders making sure he was safely delivered.

The plane began its slow descent. He took a couple of large gulps of the champagne. His vision became blurred. He felt a rush to his head. His world turned upside down as if he were looking through a fish-eye lens.

Then everything went black.

Five

It was still dark, and the snow was falling when Reznick's cab pulled up outside Bozeman Yellowstone International Airport in Montana.

He quickly checked in at the ticket counter. A voice announced that the early morning JetBlue flight to New York was running thirty minutes late. He slung his bag over his shoulder and sat down for a cup of coffee, crunching down on a couple of Dexedrine pills.

Reznick believed McGill was telling the truth. He had appeared genuine. The more Reznick thought about it, the more the conversation unsettled him. He was usually a good judge of character. But maybe McGill was just a lying piece of shit. It was the CIA, after all. Was he fucking with Reznick? Was this some mind game he was playing?

The revelation, whether it was true or not, had stirred the ghosts of Reznick's past. Ghosts he had confined to the darkest recesses of his mind. Memories he wanted to forget. He never wanted to look back. It was just too painful. But there it was, swimming around his head. The scab had been picked.

He wondered why his wife would have been leading a double life. It seemed like a flight of fancy to imagine his solid tax lawyer wife working for the CIA. It would mean that she had concealed her true self from him. It didn't seem plausible, or even possible. But what if it was?

Reznick felt a lingering sense of emptiness slowly giving way to simmering anger. He wondered if he was angry with Elisabeth for the deception or with himself for not seeing the truth. The reality was, he had been away before 9/11, thousands of miles away. He had been focused on deployments with Delta. He wasn't at home most of the time. And it would have been perfect cover for Elisabeth to begin a role working for the CIA. But what he couldn't get his head around was that she had been working in WTC 7.

That was the point that stuck out the most. That meant she hadn't been working in the towers that fell that morning. WTC 7 had lasted a lot longer. The building fell at 5:20 p.m. that day. She would have had hours to escape. None of it made sense.

She knew what he did for a living. Not all of it, but enough to know that he was not CIA, but directed by them. The sense of betrayal gnawed at him.

The voice said the JetBlue flight to JFK would be boarding soon.

Reznick headed across to the gate and waited in line. He needed more information. And he knew just the person to help him.

He took out his cell phone and called Trevelle Williams. Reznick had known the ex-NSA computer genius for a few years. A guy he had grown to rely on. A guy he could trust. If anyone could help, it would be him.

"Yo, Mr. R., you out in the Wild West?"

"Montana, yeah. Trevelle, can you do me a favor?"

"You name it."

"This sounds crazy . . ."

"I'm used to it. What do you need information on?"

"My wife. Rather, my late wife, Elisabeth, was a tax attorney. She worked for Rosenfeld and Williams in New York more than twenty years ago."

"Where are you going with this?"

"Bear with me. So, she worked for the company in the World Trade Center. That's what she told me. I actually attended a social function with her there once. So, I had no reason to disbelieve her. She was my wife, right?"

"I'm listening."

"Here's the thing. I'm looking for a quick-turnaround favor. Can you access Rosenfeld and Williams's files, in double-quick time, just to confirm she was employed there?"

"What brought this up?"

A voice over the loudspeaker again announced his flight was boarding.

Reznick pressed the cell phone tight to his ear. "Conversation I had last night with a guy. He said he remembered her at the CIA in New York in WTC 7."

"CIA?"

"None of it makes sense. But anyway, this guy, he worked for the Agency, I think he was mistaken. Badly mistaken."

"Leave it to me. I'll find out all about that company in New York. And we'll take it from there."

"I'll call you when I land in New York."

"Don't worry, man, we'll sort it out. Probably just a case of mistaken identity. It'll be fine."

About four hours later, Reznick's flight landed at JFK. He picked up his bag and caught a cab to meet up with his daughter.

"The Mercer Hotel, Soho," he said to the taxi driver.

The cab headed through heavy traffic in Queens en route to downtown Manhattan.

Reznick called Trevelle. "I'm back in New York. Any news?"

"I accessed the Rosenfeld and Williams company files, including tax returns and IRS documents and God knows what else."

"Wasn't that all lost?"

"It was all lost at the time. Apparently Microsoft sent over a few engineers to the Rosenfeld and Williams office in New Jersey, cabled up huge amounts of new connections, and managed to retrieve everyone's lost passwords. So, the files were not lost—all retrieved and restored about two weeks later."

"Interesting."

"Your wife was on their payroll, and their offices were located on the eighty-ninth floor at One World Trade Center."

"That's what I thought."

"However . . . I'm sorry to say there's a kicker. Elisabeth Reznick left the company on Friday, May 18, 2001."

Reznick felt as if he had been hit by a truck. "Can you verify that?"

"I've got her resignation letter from February giving notice."

"February?"

"February 2001. Her last working day was May 18, 2001. I have a letter from Charles Rosenfeld, the managing partner, thanking her for her work."

The cab inched toward the Queens Midtown Tunnel.

"I met him. So, she wasn't there on 9/11?"

"That's what it looks like."

"But that doesn't make sense. I got a letter from the chairman of the company, Max Williams, expressing his condolences for my loss. The company lost thirty-two employees. What you're saying doesn't line up with that. No, I can't accept that. Listen, I'll call you back."

The cab entered the tunnel. Reznick turned this information over in his mind as the driver changed lanes and traffic picked up.

The Manhattan skyline of the twenty-first century opened up before him as the cab emerged from the tunnel under the East River. A skyline that had changed dramatically since 9/11. He dialed the last number.

Trevelle launched in as soon as he answered. "You mentioned that this Agency guy said he was sure she was working for the CIA in New York, right?"

"That's right."

"I did some checking on this. I don't have a list of CIA staff in New York, not yet."

"Would you be able to get that?"

"I'm working on it. But I can confirm there was a CIA office on the twenty-fifth floor of World Trade Center 7. It all got destroyed along with the rest of the building on 9/11."

"Later in the day, though, right?"

"Exactly. WTC 7 was located north of Vesey Street. I have a list of tenants from 9/11. The Department of Defense, the IRS, and the CIA were all on the twenty-fifth."

Reznick's mind flashed back to the conversation with McGill. It was starting to make sense, the pieces of the crazy jigsaw falling into place.

"While WTC 7 was hit by debris from the north tower after it collapsed, fires broke out, but crucially, no injuries or lives lost. It was evacuated in plenty of time."

"It did collapse, though."

"It did. I checked, it collapsed at 5:20 p.m. on the same day."

"What about Max Williams? The chairman. The guy I got the letter from?"

"I have a newspaper clipping in front of me from 2006. A double suicide at their home upstate. He killed himself; so did his wife. So, Williams won't be able to explain why he sent that letter to you. Maybe it was an administrative error."

"So, did my wife get out?"

Silence.

Reznick sat in the cab, wondering if he was losing his mind. "Is she alive?"

"She was working in WTC 7, it seems. And everyone got out. So, I can't answer whether or not she's alive, but if she died that day, in WTC 7, she'd be the only one who did."

Six

It was a short cab ride from the Mercer Hotel in Soho to Puffy's Tavern in the heart of Tribeca.

The bar was a favorite haunt of Reznick's any time he was in Lower Manhattan. An old-school New York bar. Great drinks, no crazy loud music, a couple of TVs showing baseball or football.

Reznick ordered a cold Heineken and waited for his daughter. The sixtysomething bartender wiped down the bar and gestured up to the TV. "You a Knicks guy?"

"Not really. You?"

"I can take it or leave it. You been in here before?"

"A few times."

"You want something to eat?"

"I'm fine."

Reznick nursed his drink for a few minutes, glancing occasionally at the game, still wired after his trip to Montana and his conversation with Trevelle. Lauren walked in, smiling broadly. His dark thoughts were banished, at least for now.

He got up from his stool and pecked his daughter on the cheek. "Good to see you, honey."

"You too, Dad," she said. "Sorry I'm late."

"I just got here. What are you having?"

Lauren surveyed the bottles of white wine in the glass cooler. "A Pinot Grigio, please."

Reznick grinned. "Very fancy." He ordered his daughter a drink as she pulled up a stool beside him. "So, tell me, how's work?"

"Hectic. And you? How was Florida?"

"What's not to like? I love it down there. Especially down in the Lower Keys. Nice, slow pace for an old guy like me. But I just flew in from Montana."

"What were you doing there?"

"Funeral. Brad."

"Of course. I'm sorry about your friend, Dad."

"It was a tough one. He was forty-nine."

"God, that's awful."

"He packed more into his short life than most people fit into three lifetimes."

Lauren smiled and curled some hair behind her ear. "You OK?"

"Me? Sure, why?"

"I don't know. You just look distant. A bit distracted."

Reznick gulped some beer and smiled. "Hey, I'm fine," he lied. "Nothing a few drinks and a meal with my daughter won't fix."

He chatted with his daughter for an hour before they walked over to a Michelin-starred Italian restaurant on Battery Park City Esplanade.

Reznick looked around. "Fancy."

"Martha recommended it."

"Did she?"

"I'm paying."

"The FBI must be paying you too much."

Lauren rolled her eyes. "Yeah, right."

"Forget it, my treat."

Lauren leaned over and pecked him on the cheek. "You don't have to."

"You're my daughter. That's the rules, right? Besides, when I'm old and decrepit, you can pay for my meals."

Lauren smiled. "That'll never happen."

After the meal, Lauren suggested they head over to the nearby 9/11 Memorial.

Jon reluctantly agreed. He walked in silence with his daughter as they strolled through the streets of Lower Manhattan to the sacred site. A few tourists were taking photos. He always felt uncomfortable with that. He didn't know why. Maybe because it was a place where thousands had died. But he knew they were just paying their respects.

He stared into one of the reflecting pools of the memorial and wrapped a protective arm around Lauren. "Long time ago," he said.

"I know."

Elisabeth's name was carved into the bronze parapets surrounding the twin memorial pools. He went over and touched it. Then he kissed it. He felt conflicted. He wanted to tell his daughter. But he couldn't bring himself to say anything until he knew more, a lot more.

Lauren hugged him tight and began to sob. "I wish she was still here, Dad. I wish I had known her."

Reznick looked up at the empty space where the Twin Towers once stood. "So do I, honey. So do I."

Seven

It all started to go to shit on Monday morning. Major General Chuck Gronski strode along a highly polished corridor in the Eisenhower Executive Office Building, briefcase in hand. Director of special programs in the Department of Defense, he was escorted to a conference room by a fresh-faced staffer. The kid tried to make small talk, but Gronski's mind was elsewhere, annoyed that his busy schedule was being interrupted.

He had far better things to do than waste his time on some White House national security advisor. But he had still prepared thoroughly ahead of the face-to-face meeting.

Gronski sighed as he was shown into the conference room for his meeting with Philip Hudson.

Hudson glared across at him like a displeased teacher who hated being kept waiting.

Gronski took his papers out of his briefcase and arranged them on the table. He had seen Hudson's type before. Rosy-cheeked New England Ivy League smart kid. The guy was forty-two years old, got a degree in international studies at Harvard, then a master's in international relations from Cambridge University, then it was back to good old Harvard, where he graduated with a JD from

Harvard Law. He was extraordinarily bright, no question. He was the debate champion at the elite Phillips Exeter Academy in New Hampshire, debate champion at Harvard, European debate champion at Cambridge. Bottom line, the fucker liked to talk. A lot.

He also liked to write columns for the *New York Times* on geopolitical problems America was facing. But the little brat didn't know shit about the real world. How it really worked. Real life wasn't academia, that was for sure.

Gronski had read Hudson's file. He had learned that, three years earlier, Hudson parachuted into a DC think tank set up by a tech billionaire. Hudson's father was an early investor in the tech firm when it was launched in the 1990s. Quid pro quo, so to speak. Hudson's father had made his wealth in hedge funds and derivatives in the 1980s. Leveraged buyouts. And from there he became a big-time investor in tech startups in Silicon Valley.

"How are we this morning, Charles?" His voice was as irritating as always. A hint of superiority.

"Busy."

"I seem to be in the dark on a matter pertaining to national security."

"We have a lot of compartmentalized programs, many of which must remain secret. I'm sure you understand."

"I understand. But my job is to advise at the highest level of government on matters our political overlords need to know about. I can't have people like you dragging your heels, not divulging what they know."

"I appreciate that."

"Do you?"

"Of course."

"You see, I didn't know about a pressing intelligence matter until an aide of mine brought me up to speed. I had to learn about it from my fucking aide. Do you think that's a proper way to conduct business?"

"What are you talking about?"

"A Swiss intelligence expert has gone missing, vanished into thin air. Western Europe is my area of responsibility."

Gronski nodded but remained quiet.

"So, you know about this?"

"I was briefed a few hours ago."

"I had to reach out to the CIA personally, who tell me that the guy is believed to have stolen classified information."

"You reached out to the CIA?"

"They also mentioned a keylogger found on the guy's equipment at his apartment before he disappeared. Swiss intelligence is going crazy. This is problematic. But so is the fact that I'm learning all about this bullshit second-fucking-hand."

Gronski said nothing. He knew the guy wanted to get this shit off his chest.

"Hans-fucking-Muller, that's his name. Do you know it?"

"Yes, sir, I have heard the same name."

"The CIA and the Swiss intelligence services are working hard to get to the bottom of this. I'm asking you now, is there anything else I need to know about, Charles? Operations we are running?"

"I'll find out everything you need."

"More like it."

"Which city was Muller working in?"

"Bern. Where do you fucking think?"

Gronski shifted in his seat, his blood pressure rising. He had knocked out insubordinates for less. But this kid was no subordinate.

"I don't want any bullshit about need-to-know. I've heard a ton of your lectures. So, I'm telling you now, I need to know. And by that, I mean the President. Are we on the same page?"

"Absolutely."

"Good. Now I'm going to ask you straight out. Should I be aware of any special Pentagon programs covering Switzerland?"

"I'm sure we have them."

Hudson leaned back in his chair and smiled. "Well, that's just great. So, we might have assets compromised."

"I hear what you're saying. I share your sense of frustration and concern. I'll look into this as a matter of urgency."

"I don't like being kept in the dark, Charles."

Gronski nodded and sighed, pretending to be listening intently to the brat.

"I need clarity. Clarity of thought, clarity of purpose, clarity that cuts through all the bullshit."

"Understood."

"Is it really? I live for clarity."

"I'm sure you do."

"What does that mean?"

"It means, I understand you believe in clarity. You need intelligence and defense experts to give it to you straight."

"Your tone bothers me, Charles."

Gronski sighed. "I apologize. Thirty years in the military does that to a man." He looked at Hudson's hands. Manicured fingernails. Soft hands. Soft man.

"I want names of American contacts and secret agents we're running across Switzerland."

"I'll get it. Hans Muller is not a lone wolf. He's not acting alone."

"Russians?"

"Makes sense. The Russian Foreign Intelligence Service is very active in Germany and Switzerland, with a lot of connections. Academia, industry, trade unions, politicians."

Hudson scribbled on his legal pad. "That's what worries me. Now I want answers. And I want them in the next forty-eight hours."

Gronski was driven back to his office at the Pentagon across the Potomac. He couldn't abide academics masquerading as national security experts. He was sick to death of them. *I demand this*, and *I demand that*. He operated under Department of Defense protocols. He served as the principal staff assistant and advisor to the secretary of defense under the authority, direction, and control of the deputy secretary. And he was responsible for all programs protected under special access controls. It was his solemn responsibility and duty to protect the most classified of programs.

When he got back to his office, he called Ramon Diaz, his second-in-command.

"I know the gist about Switzerland. I just had a glorified college kid reading me the riot act. So, I want to know the latest."

Diaz answered, "I just got off a briefing with the station chief in Bern. And they're mad."

"Tell me something I don't know."

"The CIA apparently told Hudson they don't have the full picture." Gronski leaned back in his seat as he listened. "So, they're stalling too."

"We have secrets, Ramon. We deal in intelligence. It's the nature of the beast."

"But I have a name from the station chief."

"A name?"

"The name of an American asset, deep-cover agent. Long term. Her name is Anna Bruckmann." Gronski was well aware of the name. "Do you want me to determine if her name is listed among the special access programs?"

Gronski shook his head. "Don't mention a word to anyone about that name."

"Why not?"

"Don't question me, Ramon. You need to know when to follow orders."

"Yes, sir. Won't happen again. I was just eager to help out the Agency."

"I know a little about this. Let me deal with this personally."

Eight

The sun peeked over the glistening New York skyscrapers.

Reznick limbered up with some stretching on this bitterly cold day. He glanced across the Hudson to Jersey City. He wondered if Elisabeth had run the same route all those years ago. It was hard to believe that his beloved wife had lived a secret life. It was so at odds with the warm, vivacious, and open personality he had fallen in love with.

He set off at a light run along Battery Park City Esplanade.

As he ran, he cut his eyes across the water toward Ellis Island. The fabled place where immigrants had arrived in the new world. A new life. Had his wife really started a new life without him after 9/11? Had that been the catalyst for her to disappear? Had she used that atrocity as the cover for her disappearance, with the connivance of the CIA?

The more he thought about it, the more outrageous it sounded. It appeared that she might very well have been a CIA operative. Then she had vanished.

Reznick had somehow managed to pick up the pieces and had immersed himself in the work of Delta Force. The sharp end of the spear in the hunt for those responsible for 9/11. Thousands of miles from home. *What had she done? What had she become?*

When he had finished his workout, Reznick slowly walked back to his hotel room in Soho. He showered, changed, picked up his backpack, and headed down for a hearty breakfast of scrambled eggs, toast, and bacon, washed down with black coffee.

Reznick strode out of the hotel. He took the subway to Twenty-Third Street and walked three blocks to the underground shooting range. It was a place he used often when in New York. The only public gun range in Manhattan. A refuge for gun nuts, ex-military, cops, and security guards keeping their skills honed. Most of all, it was a place to do what he was trained to do.

He fired off countless rounds using his trusty 9mm Beretta, but he also used an assortment of rifles provided by the range. Afterward, he made small talk with a few regulars, including an off-duty US Marshal and a celebrity bodyguard.

His cell phone rang. "Hey, Mr. R." The voice of Trevelle, hacker extraordinaire.

Reznick headed outside to get some privacy. "You got anything for me?"

"I do."

"So, what is it?"

"I would prefer to talk face-to-face. In New York."

"Why can't you tell me over the phone?"

"I need to talk face-to-face. Do you trust me?"

Reznick wondered what Trevelle was getting at. "Yeah, I trust you."

"I'm in the city. Let's meet up. Where are you exactly?"

"I'm near the Flatiron."

"You're not far from me. Do you know the Old Town Bar on Eighteenth?"

"Sure do."

"Meet you there in an hour."

The bar was from a bygone age of old New York. It was all dark wood and brass.

Reznick felt right at home. He spotted Trevelle sitting at the end of the bar, checking his cell phone. He wore shades and a wool hat, and he was nursing a club soda. "You look like fucking Serpico. All you need is a great big shaggy dog."

Trevelle grinned. "Nice to see you too, Jon."

Reznick ordered a cup of coffee and another club soda for Trevelle. "Let's get down to business."

"Good idea. So . . . you're probably wondering what brought me out into the open, so to speak."

"It did cross my mind."

"Sometimes face-to-face feels better. I didn't want to risk texts or emails."

"I thought you were an end-to-end encryption guy?"

"I most certainly am. But this feels right. I don't know why. Besides, I believe this is the sort of stuff you need to hear face-to-face."

Reznick shifted on his stool. "What've you got?"

"I've reached out to some very close friends of mine. People in the same field as me. People I've worked with in the past."

"NSA?"

"Contractors, staff, all IT experts of the highest level. One guy I messaged had an interesting story to tell."

Reznick shrugged. "About?"

"About a guy in Switzerland."

Reznick took a sip of coffee, intrigued. "What does this have to do with my wife?"

"Hear me out. This Swiss guy, name's Hans Muller, went missing. He's a Swiss IT expert. He disappeared. He's wanted by everyone, and I mean *everyone*. CIA, Pentagon, Swiss intelligence, the Russians, you name it."

"Why?"

"He was an expert in the field of biometrics, facial recognition in particular. According to my friend, he was developing a world-beating facial recognition system."

"Immediate red flag."

"Exactly. Now he's missing. The question is where he is and what happened. But here's the kicker. The Swiss have alerted the United States that Muller stole a ton of classified data, highly sensitive intelligence. State secrets. The most classified diplomatic cables. Lists of agents, secure facilities, terrorist targets, you name it. It's a nightmare."

"How did you get all this information?"

"I'm getting to that."

"And you haven't answered my question: What does this have to do with my wife?"

"I quietly reached out to a close friend of mine who used to work with Muller at the NSA."

"NSA?"

"Muller is one of the top guys in Europe. He was asked to be part of an NSA-led intelligence-sharing program, and my friend mentored Muller in some of our little-known techniques. They became quite close while Hans worked at the NSA."

"How close?"

"They were gamers. They spent all their waking hours together. They were close. But at the end of the program, Hans went back to Bern. My friend hadn't heard from Hans for a couple years. You know how it is, right?"

Reznick nodded.

"Then suddenly my friend got an end-to-end encrypted email, totally out of the blue. Personal account. My friend hadn't given him his new email, but Muller obviously found it."

Reznick eyed the bartender as he listened. "Go on."

Trevelle leaned in close, his voice nearly a whisper. "The Swiss guy, Hans, needed help. And he wanted my friend to run this face that had pinged on the Swiss intelligence system run by the NDB."

"Swiss intelligence?"

"Correct. He thought the results from the scan were an anomaly. And he wanted to run this face through the NSA's full database, just on the off chance it set something off."

"He get a match?"

"I don't want to get ahead of myself. He said it's a woman. Late forties. But there is no name that corresponds to any legal identity in the United States. Not one who's alive anyway. That's all he said."

"Does your friend think this might actually be Elisabeth? Seriously?"

Trevelle went quiet, head bowed. "Jon, he believes this image, from Zurich, may be of your late wife."

"How does he know that?"

"He ran it through American intelligence databases. This guy is a brilliant analyst."

"When was the image taken?"

"Three days before Hans disappeared."

"Are you saying this is connected?"

"It's a possibility."

"I want to see for myself. I want to see the picture."

Trevelle finished his club soda. "He never sent me anything. He's the only one who's seen it."

"Put me in touch with your friend. I need to know the truth, no matter what happens."

Nine

It was nearly dark when the flight from New York touched down in Aspen. It had been a particularly bumpy journey.

Reznick was lost in his own dark thoughts throughout most of the flight. Trevelle slept, having crunched on a Xanax washed down with a large Scotch on the plane.

He came to as the passengers began to disembark.

"What happened?" he said.

"We landed," Reznick said. "You OK?"

Trevelle rubbed his bloodshot eyes. "Are we there yet?"

"You shouldn't drink with Xanax."

Trevelle nodded meekly. "Very good point."

Reznick and Trevelle retrieved their bags and headed over to Avis to pick up an Audi. He switched on the navigation, but it wasn't really necessary for the short drive to Woody Creek.

Trevelle groaned. "It's freezing."

Reznick grinned. "Nearly there."

In the distance, the setting sun dipped over the snow-covered mountain peaks.

"You sure I'm not wasting my time?"

"Jon, this guy is smart. He's reclusive. But he's a good guy. I trust him."

They headed through the village. Past old mining shacks, log cabins, a rusting old bridge, a ramshackle trailer park, past the Woody Creek Tavern. A couple of hardy old-timers bundled up, drinking beers on the deck.

"Tough bunch up here, Trevelle," Reznick said.

"I like it."

"Me too."

"Mountain air is good."

"Wait till the wildfire season starts, you won't be saying that."

Trevelle gave a rueful smile. "True."

They headed past another trailer park on the edge of the village. A mile later they saw a wooden sign for a ranch.

Trevelle began to doze off again.

Reznick turned onto an icy gravel road. He drove for a few hundred yards until he got to steel gates, a metal keypad on the stone wall. He rolled down his window and pressed the buzzer.

"Yeah, who's this?"

"My name is Jon Reznick. I'm here with my friend, Trevelle Williams."

"Head on through, guys."

The steel gates opened, and Reznick drove for another couple hundred yards to a sprawling log cabin, shrouded in snow-covered pine trees.

Reznick prodded Trevelle awake. "Wake up, sleepyhead, we're here."

"What is it?"

"I said we're here."

Trevelle's tired face broke into a wide grin as he saw his friend emerge from the house. The guy wore a Van Halen sweatshirt, faded jeans, and cowboy boots.

Trevelle got out of the car first. "Hey, Gabriel, how's it going?"

"I'm OK. How the hell are you? You look like shit."

"Xanax and booze, not a good combination."

Gabriel winced. "That's crazy, man. I used to do that, seeing as I'm terrified of flying. But then my doctor told me never to mix that shit. So, I can't fly anymore. It's too scary without being loaded."

Reznick walked up and introduced himself, shaking Gabriel's hand. "I believe you might have something that would interest me."

"Let's talk inside, man."

Reznick followed Gabriel inside as Trevelle shuffled behind them.

"Can I get you anything to eat first?"

Reznick stamped the snow off his shoes in the hall. "A couple of strong coffees will be fine."

"Coming right up." Gabriel headed through to the kitchen. "Make yourself at home in the living room."

Reznick and Trevelle walked into a huge space and sat down on a sofa adjacent to a roaring log fire.

A few moments later, Gabriel returned with a tray containing two steaming mugs of coffee and a tray of cookies, a MacBook under his arm. "There you go." He handed a cup to each of them.

Reznick's attention drifted past the huge windows. Long shadows spread as the sun dropped lower in the sky, pine tree tops burnt orange. "This is a beautiful place."

Gabriel opened up the MacBook and tapped a few keys as it booted up. "I used to work in Utah, and I loved it there too. Utah Data Center, I helped set that up. Then I came across this place when I was on a hiking trip. Decided I had to live here. It's peaceful."

Trevelle nodded. "Glad to be out of there?"

"The NSA? Couldn't fucking wait."

Reznick looked at the thirtysomething computer guy. "What was the problem?"

"They're spying on everyone. I went in all idealistic. But I quickly realized what was going on. They spy on everyone. Me, you, the man in the street. They have eyes and ears everywhere, intercepting every call, email, text, we all know it. There comes a time and place when you begin to ask: What the fuck is my purpose in life? Is this what I'm all about? You begin to question things, right?"

Trevelle nodded. "My friend Jon is interested in what you know about Hans."

"Total shocker. Can't believe he disappeared. Stealing classified files? That could get a man killed."

"You want to tell me what you know?" Reznick asked.

Gabriel tapped a few more keys. "Check it out."

Reznick leaned forward and studied the screen, a grainy spectral figure in frame. "There's no detail."

"Right. But that's the raw photo Hans sent me. What I'm about to show you should be highly classified, you know the drill. In light of the circumstances, after Trevelle explained your story, I thought you needed to know this."

"Got it."

"Trevelle said you served in Delta."

"A while back, but it's true. I work for the government from time to time."

"My father, God rest his soul, never made it back from his third tour of Iraq. Blown to pieces. What a waste."

"I'm sorry to hear that, man. That's tough to take."

"My mother, she never recovered. She overdosed as a result. But anyway, I'm here, and I want to help. Even in a small way."

"Appreciate that. So, what've you got?"

Gabriel pointed at the screen. "Hans sent me this from Switzerland. It's a poorly taken image from a fixed camera position. Resolution, accuracy, it's a mess. But despite that, he believed, from this almost unrecognizable photo, he might have identified someone."

"He did?"

"Here's the thing: the blurred image kept on returning false positives. He cleaned up the photo the best he could. Then I got to work on it with some new software Trevelle coded. The photo cleaned up. And it kept on coming back with the name *Anna Bruckmann*."

Reznick scanned the slightly blurred image. "Where was the photo taken?"

"It was taken in Zurich Old Town. And it was the only person he couldn't identify on the Swiss database. His new system is going to become the gold standard once it's ready in a year or two. But this was a glitch. Or so I assumed."

"What do you mean?"

"The name assigned to the face returns an identification as unknown. So, it was regarded as unidentified. Which contradicted the cleaned-up photo."

Reznick looked at Trevelle, who was sipping his coffee, eyes on the floor as if averting his gaze. "So, what I'm looking at now is the raw footage, not cleaned up?"

"Correct."

"And from there you worked your IT magic, cleaning up the picture, which returned the name *Anna Bruckmann*?"

"Exactly."

Reznick evaluated the blurred image. "I'd like to see the cleaned-up picture."

Gabriel took a deep breath and tapped a couple of keys.

Reznick perused the screen. The figure was identifiable. A woman wrapped up in a winter coat, cropped black hair, scarf covering her chin. He let the image be absorbed. The shape of her face, the eyes. The woman bore an uncanny resemblance to his late wife.

But this woman's hair was shockingly different from Elisabeth's shoulder-length mousy-brown hair.

It looked like his late wife. But at the same time, it didn't.

Trevelle said, "Are you OK, Jon?"

Reznick analyzed the screen. "Yeah, I'm fine." He wasn't fine. He was troubled by what he'd seen. Deep within the dark recesses of his soul, he recognized the face. He sensed it was her. His rational mind might not like it. But he felt it in his heart. It was her. It was the eyes. He could never forget her magnetic eyes.

Gabriel cleared his throat. "The name assigned to that face is *Anna Bruckmann*. I sent this information back as confirmation to Hans. A matter of hours later, he downloads every piece of data on all the NDB servers, including the most classified shit, and drops off the fucking grid. It's crazy, man. I thought I knew him."

Reznick studied the haunting image again. "What else do we know about this woman?"

"Well, she works in Geneva. Heads up a technology firm. Specializes in next-generation two-stage text message verification."

Trevelle leaned over and pointed to the image. "Jon, is that her?"

"I don't know."

Reznick did know, though. He knew it in his bones. He felt it deep down in his soul. Every fiber of his being was telling him that *Anna Bruckmann* was a false name. That was Elisabeth Reznick. His wife. She was alive.

Ten

The men stood outside her lakefront home in Arth, grim-faced.

Anna Bruckmann pulled up in her car and realized they were from the NDB.

Franz Schumann, the head of the NDB, stared at her, cell phone pressed to his ear, deep in conversation.

Bruckmann locked her car and approached him. "Do you mind explaining the meaning of this?"

Franz ended his call and put away his phone. "Anna, so glad we've caught you."

"Cut the bullshit. You know the arrangement as well as I do. The strictest privacy. And now you're turning up with your officers?"

"We have a situation developing. We need to talk. Now."

"Couldn't it have waited?"

"I'm afraid not."

"So, why the urgency?"

Franz averted his gaze. "A matter of national security. Swiss and American."

"You need to talk right now?"

"I'm afraid so, yes."

Anna reluctantly showed him inside as his men waited outside. She walked through the hallway. "This is most irregular, Franz."

"I'm aware. We had to alert you to a catastrophic breach."

Anna showed him upstairs to her second-floor study, overlooking Lake Zug.

"This is a beautiful view you have," he said.

Anna indicated for him to sit down on a chesterfield sofa. She shut the door behind her.

Franz slumped down and cleared his throat.

"Are you out of your mind? Couldn't you have been more discreet?"

"Sit down, Anna."

"I prefer to stand."

"Please, take a seat."

Anna pulled up an Eames plastic armchair and sat down opposite him, arms folded. "What do you want? I thought we had an arrangement."

"You have been compromised. *We* have been compromised."

"How badly?"

"The Russians know who you are. They will want to find you."

"I don't believe you."

"It's true. Your life is in grave danger."

Anna absorbed the news. Her first thought was to get in her car and drive out of the country, due south. "After all this time?"

"It's a shock, I know."

"How did they find out?"

"One of our most trusted intelligence operatives has gone rogue."

"Shit."

"Your name is buried in the most classified files, including correspondence and cables between the State Department and the Swiss government going back twenty years. And all that information, along with many terabytes of our intelligence networks, identities of agents in the field and overseas, not to mention the names and addresses of CIA assets across Switzerland, has been stolen."

Anna shook her head. "How long have you known?"

"About forty-eight hours."

"Why didn't you tell me earlier?"

"We had to establish what had happened and why. We are now in a better position to get a handle on this."

"How was anyone able to take this?"

"A massive data theft on a memory card from within the NDB offices. He was a traitor in our midst. But he's disappeared."

"Unbelievable."

Franz turned and leaned forward, hands clasped like an earnest priest.

"You got a name?"

"We have a name. The man was under the radar for years. We're learning more and more. We believe he became compromised within the last year."

"Specifics, please, Franz."

"Specifically, a relationship with a Swiss national who is also known to us as being in a close friendship with a Russian-born woman in Zurich. This man, the spy, could be anywhere. He might be overseas, we believe. But he only recently reached out to a former contractor of the NSA before he fled." Franz took a deep breath. "I knew him well. At least I thought I did."

"How well?"

"I invited him to lunch with my family at our vacation home once."

"Jesus Christ. So, he reached out to the NSA guy in America. About what? That's quite unusual."

"Indeed." Franz reached into an inside jacket pocket and pulled out a grainy black-and-white photo of Bruckmann. "He reached out to the American about you."

Bruckmann analyzed the image. It was her.

"This is a cleaned-up version. The original photograph was just a grainy figure walking down a street."

Anna looked long and hard at the photo. "Where was it taken?"

"A surveillance camera in a private residence captured you. It was taken in Zurich Old Town."

Bruckmann felt sick to the bottom of her stomach.

"The man who stole the data was also in charge of a secret biometric project we have been developing for the last five years. It would have been Europe-wide with encryption he devised. But he ran up against a problem. You were the problem, Anna. He couldn't identify you. He needed help."

Anna buried her head in her hands.

"Yours was the one identity he couldn't figure out."

"Was that before the theft and disappearance?"

"We believe so. So, we've checked all the emails and messages he sent, and it is clear that our NDB operative has been in touch with a foreign government, via this Russian-born expatriate, offering to sell all this information and technology. He put a price on your head. He asked for Bitcoin to the value of one hundred million American dollars. Fifty million dollars of Bitcoin was the deposit. We managed to trace the address it was linked to via the Bitcoin blockchain. But the address is linked to an offshore entity in the Caymans. And from there it is wrapped up in hundreds of other related companies, mostly shell companies."

Bruckmann listened, shaking her head. "I need to move."

"That's why I'm here. We have a safe house ready until we finalize plans to get you out of the country."

"I need to get out of Switzerland right now!"

"Not possible right now. We're weighing our options with the State Department."

"I have only one option. I need to get to an American base. And then back home."

"That hasn't been approved yet. They're trying to figure out the best route."

"Are you kidding me?"

Franz shook his head.

"So, what's the plan, if indeed you have a plan?"

"You'll still be in Switzerland. It might be a few days, maybe more. But we have a place. And you'll be out of sight, trust me."

Eleven

Reznick drove to Denver International Airport and took a long overnight flight to Frankfurt. He had no idea what he intended to do when he got there. All he knew was that he wanted to contact this woman in some way. The more he learned, the stranger her story had grown. This woman who bore a striking resemblance to Elisabeth had an American passport.

Reznick sat in business class, unable to sleep, dark thoughts swirling around his head. It was a long night. He endured hour after hour of mind-numbing comedies, headphones on. He looked around. The rest of the passengers in his section were fast asleep. A stewardess asked him if he wanted any drinks. He ordered a beer and a double vodka with a splash of orange. He crunched on a couple of Dexedrine pills as he tried to come to terms with the ghostly image he had seen on Gabriel's computer. Reznick could see from the outline of her face, the figure . . . He knew that woman. It had to be her.

Was he being delusional? Some physical markers were different.

Still, the wife he thought he had lost forever, who existed only in his dreams, could be alive, and someone else entirely. He wanted it to be true. But it was too fantastical to make sense.

Maybe this woman just bore an uncanny resemblance to Elisabeth. Maybe he was projecting his innermost thoughts and longing. Maybe he just wanted her to be alive. Maybe he wanted her back. Maybe it was all just a figment of a fevered imagination.

He finished his beer and knocked back the rest of the vodka.

Reznick sat and chewed another Dexedrine, the amphetamine coursing through his veins. He didn't want to sleep. The hours dragged as he watched the screen in front of him. It showed the plane's course over the Atlantic.

His mind began to drift. The mother. The wife. The lawyer. He thought of all their times together. Sitting in the cove at Rockland, hugging her tight after an overseas deployment, staring out over the cold water. Feeling safe again.

Reznick closed his eyes as he was enveloped in a deep sleep.

The plane touched down in Frankfurt.

Reznick had a ninety-minute layover. He hung around in the terminal drinking coffee, checking his phone. Then he caught a flight to Zurich. The moment he arrived and stepped out of the airport, a blast of Arctic air nearly took his breath away.

He caught a cab and headed to a luxury hotel overlooking Lake Zurich. He checked in and was escorted to his room.

"Your first time in Switzerland, sir?" the bellhop asked.

"First time, yeah."

"I think you'll like it."

Reznick tipped the young bellhop twenty euros. He waited until the guy was farther down the corridor before he swiped the card to his room. A large-screen TV on the wall, muted pastel tones. Very clean and minimal. He opened up the minibar to see candy bars, beer, vodka, Scotch, and Swiss mineral water.

Reznick put down his bags, emotionally drained. He was running on empty, a combination of sleep deprivation, amphetamines in his bloodstream, and a growing feeling that he was stepping into the abyss. He pushed his jumbled thoughts to one side as he unpacked his bags. He put away his clothes, hanging up T-shirts, jeans, and his thick jacket in the closet, sturdy Rockport boots and sneakers lined up underneath. He showered and got changed, stepped out onto the balcony. A savage, cold wind swirled as snow flurries whipped in across Lake Zurich. The cutting chill was waking him up from the jet lag and lethargy of the long flight and lack of sleep.

He gazed out at the mountains in the distance. He wondered if his wife was really alive, using the name *Anna Bruckmann*. Was this a CIA cover story? Had she maede this city her home? Maybe she was living just around the corner from his hotel. According to Gabriel, Anna Bruckmann was an American chief executive of a Swiss-based technology company.

The more he thought about it, the more he wondered if he was crazy. He tracked back in his mind. At first, he wasn't totally convinced by Ken McGill's assertions, assuming it had to be a case of mistaken identity. But the revelation from Trevelle, that his wife had in fact left her job, gave a lot more credence to the story.

The more Jon thought about the chain of events over the last few days, the less he understood. It made no sense. Not to him. It would mean that Elisabeth had lied to him. Deceived him. But, most importantly, she had lied to their daughter.

Reznick thought of the consequences for Lauren. He wondered how she would respond. He could only imagine the devastation she would feel. Her world as she knew it would be turned upside down. The mother who had existed for her only in photographs and in Reznick's reminiscences about their time together, alive all this time. She had never known her mother. She existed only in her fragments of the past. Photographs. Now a cyber-enhanced photograph might lead Reznick, and in turn Lauren, back to the woman she never knew was alive. How the hell would his daughter react?

Reznick's mind flashed back to the last time he had returned home to Rockland, shortly before 9/11. His wife had been working for the CIA then, if what McGill said was correct. He knew something about the Agency and how it operated. He had worked for them, numerous times, off the books. She knew that. So, why couldn't she have confided in him? Maybe the nature of her position or the operation she was involved in. It was a possibility.

His cell phone rang.

"Jon, it's Trevelle."

Reznick took a few moments to gather himself.

"Hi."

"How you finding Switzerland?"

"It's very clean. Cold but clean."

"Zurich ain't Detroit, that's a fact."

"Listen, you got anything on this mysterious Anna Bruckmann? I feel like I'm losing my mind."

"Sorry to report, not yet. I'm working on it. I need to make sure I have the correct metadata from the images. I'm taking a deep dive into various intelligence databases both in America and overseas, checking and rechecking a few things."

"I see."

"So, how are you feeling?"

"Who the hell knows? I'm here, what can I say?"

"Do you think it's Elisabeth? Is that your wife in the photo?"

"I don't know. What do you think?"

"Here's what I think. I believe a woman going by the name of *Anna Bruckmann* exists. Whether it's the woman you believe it is, that's something else. I'm sorry that's not much help."

Reznick peered out over the icy waters of Lake Zurich to the opposite shore.

"Jon, I've got something to tell you."

"Shoot."

"I ran some facial recognition over this image with known images of Elisabeth. Extracted the metadata from the original grainy photograph taken in Zurich Old Town. I hope you don't mind."

"What did you find?"

"First, I've got the GPS location of exactly where the photo was taken." Trevelle gave the longitude and latitude of where the woman had been spotted. "So, as we thought, it was indeed taken in Old Town, but now we know exactly where and at what time. Second, my findings are inconclusive. I can't say with a degree of certainty it is her, with regard to the enhanced photo."

"If you were a betting man, give me a figure."

"I would say 82 percent possibility, all things being equal, it's her. But by no means can I say definitively this is her. Maybe she's had work done, not sure."

Reznick stayed quiet as he pondered the news.

"I can only begin to imagine what you must be feeling, Jon."

"What if she's not alive?"

"May God rest her soul, Jon."

Twelve

It was a ten-minute cab ride through winding, cobbled streets into the center of Zurich. He took out his cell phone and entered the GPS coordinates Trevelle had given him into Google Maps. His phone highlighted the precise location where the photo had been taken.

Reznick relayed the exact address to the driver.

The cabdriver nodded and glanced in the rearview mirror as they headed past the grand Zurich Opera House on Sechseläutenplatz. "You like the opera, sir?"

"Me, not so much."

The driver edged slowly through the twisting, medieval streets of the city's historic Old Town.

"Are you meeting a friend?" the driver asked.

"Just doing a bit of sightseeing."

The driver pulled up in the Niederdorf district, nestled in the heart of Old Town. He gave Reznick specific instructions on how to get to his destination. "So, really not far from here, sir."

Reznick paid the cabdriver. He took a few moments to get his bearings as he rechecked his cell phone. He turned and headed along a narrow, cobbled street, Badergasse. Turned right toward a gothic medieval square, walked past people wearing puffer jackets, overcoats, and wool hats, drinking as the snow fell. The pungent aroma of strong cheese wafted down narrow alleys.

His cell phone beeped again, indicating he had arrived at his destination.

He looked around. Was this the spot where the photo had been taken? His gaze was drawn to the almost imperceptible surveillance camera positioned high up on the corner of a roof of a three-story apartment building. He looked again around the gothic square and took it all in.

He reached into his jacket pocket and took out the print of the grainy image he carried with him at all times now. He saw the jewelry shop frontage as the woman passed. He was standing no more than three yards away from that very spot.

He wondered where she had been going. He wondered if she lived around here. He looked at the faces of the women dotted about the street. It was a highly cultured area of a highly cultured city, close to art, history, museums, galleries—all forms of affluence.

Elisabeth would love such a place.

He looked up again at the camera. He wondered who owned and operated it. Was it a private residence? He knew the Swiss were fanatical about privacy. He understood the need for private lives to remain just that. But it was unusual in a modern twenty-first-century European country to see so few surveillance cameras. The spy camera was a rarity.

Back home, the NYPD had access to at least fifteen thousand cameras to track individuals across the city. The same with London. Surveillance cameras were always watching, night and day.

He moved on, sauntering around the area for the next hour. He turned a corner and walked over the Rudolf-Brun Bridge, which spanned the Limmat. Heading north, he wandered to Mühlesteg. He went into a café to warm up. He had a couple of coffees and a ham and cheese sandwich. It was nice to get a feel for the place.

The pace of life was glacial compared to Manhattan. He wondered if Zurich was important to Anna Bruckmann.

Reznick stepped out of the café and felt the cold winter wind nipping at his face. He pulled down his woolen hat and tightened his scarf. All of a sudden, the skies began to darken. Clouds rolled in. A short while later, heavier snow began to fall. Reznick headed down a narrow street, wrapped up in a thick Canada Goose jacket. But still the wind chilled him to his bones.

A mustached man wearing a heavy overcoat approached with a young, smartly dressed, unsmiling blonde woman by his side. "Excuse me, sir," he said in English.

Reznick eyeballed the guy. "Yeah?"

The man flashed ID. It showed *Nachrichtendienst des Bundes*. Reznick knew exactly who he was dealing with. "Sir, we'd like you to accompany us. We work for the NDB."

Reznick knew the agency was known in Western circles as the Federal Intelligence Service.

"We work very closely with your government."

Reznick looked around and wondered if there were others watching for his reaction. "What's this in connection with?"

"Just accompany us. We have some questions, if you don't mind."

"I do mind. I'm doing some sightseeing. I haven't done anything wrong."

"We never said you had."

Reznick wondered if they had been tipped off by the CIA or the American Embassy as to his presence in the city. "Am I under arrest?"

"No, but you will be if you don't comply."

Thirteen

The windowless interrogation room was located on the fourth floor of the Zurich police headquarters. Three chairs were set neatly around an oak table, a large mirror on one side of the room.

Reznick knew he was being observed. He wondered if this was just a Swiss-level operation or if the State Department or CIA had eyes on him too. He had to assume his fellow countrymen had been alerted. An agent he hadn't seen before entered the room, followed by the NDB guy from the street.

The NDB guy smiled and theatrically took off his coat, draping it over the back of one of the chairs. He motioned for Reznick to sit down. "Please, Jon, if you will."

Reznick slumped in his seat as the NDB operative and his heavyset colleague pulled up seats opposite. The heavyset guy opened up a notepad and began to take notes.

"Do you know why you are here, Mr. Reznick?"

"I know why I'm in Switzerland, if that's what you mean."

"That's not what I mean. Please don't be so obtuse. I was hoping you could answer a simple question. I'll ask again, *Do you know why you are here?*"

Reznick said nothing.

"Have you no idea?"

Reznick shrugged. "I'm cooperating with you. And you've asked me to come here, which I have. Do *you* want to tell me why I'm here? I have no idea what this is about."

The NDB guy checked Reznick's passport. "Interesting. Jon Reznick of Maine, United States of America."

Reznick sighed, arms folded.

The agent looked up. "Can I ask you to hand over your firearm while we're conducting this interview?"

"I'd much prefer to keep it. I'm not going to kill you. I have FBI advanced firearms certification, if you want to check."

"We have checked. We'll let you keep your gun, for now. I know how much you Americans love your guns."

"Is there a point to all this?"

"I hope we can have a full and frank discussion, Jon. We're reasonable people. And we live in an orderly country, unlike your own."

Reznick sat in silence, not wishing to take the bait and show anger.

"We have rules. We like rules. And we Swiss abide by rules. We don't want anything to disturb our peaceful, prosperous, and progressive society. Mr. Reznick, what brings you to our fine city? We've checked, and you've never visited our country before."

"Sightseeing. Travel. I'm semiretired."

The NDB guy fixed his steely gaze on Reznick. "Semiretired? Is that right?"

"Correct."

"Semiretired from what?"

"My work."

"You're being somewhat evasive, Jon. What is your line of work?"

"I work, off and on, as a security consultant. Here and there, at home and abroad."

"*Security consultant* is a broad term."

"People consult with me on security issues."

"What sort of people?"

Reznick sighed. "I'm not sure what relevance any of this has."

"Just answer the question."

"My client list is confidential. But I do work for friendly foreign governments from time to time, most with dubious human rights records, if that's what you're getting at."

The NDB guy gave a wry smile. "If you don't answer my questions in a satisfactory manner, I have authority to have you deported immediately. So, I'll ask again, what sort of people consult with you? Be precise."

"You Swiss love your precision, don't you."

"Let's leave the humor for a moment."

Reznick could only give him generalities. He had to be careful. "I advise companies and governments on countering terrorist threats."

"I believe you also work for the FBI, is that not so?"

"Not true."

"Have you ever worked for them?"

Reznick folded his arms. "I can't divulge the names of organizations I work with. I'm sure you'll understand."

A knock at the door interrupted the questioning. A young woman walked up to the NDB guy and handed him a two-inch-thick manila file.

"Thank you," he said. "That'll be all."

The woman left the room, shutting the door behind her.

The NDB guy quickly perused the file. "When did you stop working for Delta Force, Mr. Reznick?"

Reznick realized the CIA in Switzerland must have received the information from Langley. "I can't comment on anything to do with American national security. I'm sure you understand that."

"This is becoming somewhat tiresome, Mr. Reznick. You are being unhelpful. These are straightforward questions."

Reznick leaned back in his seat. "I'm not at liberty to answer such questions. Besides, I'm sure you have all the details you want on my background."

"I'd like to return to my original point. What brought you to our city?"

"I like to travel. Curiosity, I guess. Not business. Not pleasure. Just passing the time."

The NDB man glanced at his colleague before fixing his gaze back on Reznick. "I've been in touch with American intelligence."

"Lucky you."

"What do you mean by that?"

"Don't be so touchy. They're a fun crowd. I should know."

"What they say about you, Jon, off the record, is unsettling. They told me a little about your backstory, as they call it. They described you as highly dangerous, volatile, deadly. A trained killer who has links to the Central Intelligence Agency."

Reznick tilted his head, unblinking.

"Are you?"

"Am I what?"

"Are you highly dangerous? We don't want people like that in a peace-loving country like Switzerland."

Reznick said nothing.

"The American Embassy in Bern is also concerned by your presence here. And they are suggesting we deport you."

Reznick shrugged. "Why?"

"They didn't give a reason."

"What do you suggest?"

"Mr. Reznick, you don't seem too concerned."

"Do what you have to do. I'm a law-abiding American tourist, learning more about your progressive country."

The NDB guy pressed his tongue against the inside of his cheek, as if pondering what to do. "My problem is that, as officials of Swiss intelligence, yes, we work closely with our partners across the Western world. But you have broken no laws."

"That's right."

"You are a private citizen. We would find it tricky, I would say, for a judge to sign a deportation order in such circumstances with no proof of wrongdoing."

"What are you saying?"

"I'm saying, Mr. Reznick, that you are welcome here, as a tourist, in this country. But that welcome is not unconditional. The condition is that you don't carry out any illegal or violent acts, is that clear?"

"That goes without saying."

The NDB man leaned forward, eyeballing Reznick. "Have you got any questions?"

"Yeah, when am I free to leave?"

Fourteen

Reznick stepped out of Zurich police HQ and into the icy cold, his breath becoming vapor. He turned on his cell phone.

A few seconds later it rang. "Where the hell you been?" Trevelle. "I've been trying to call you."

"Detained."

"By who?"

Reznick took a few moments to explain what had happened.

"You OK? They didn't start any roughhouse tactics on you, did they?"

"It's Switzerland, Trevelle. Everyone is so polite. You find out anything on this Anna Bruckmann?"

"I got an address. She lives forty minutes south of Zurich. She moved several times over the last twenty years."

Trevelle gave an address in a town called Arth.

Reznick made a mental note of the address. "So, give me a broad picture of this town."

"It's a small town, right on the southern shore of Lake Zug."

"What else?"

Trevelle cleared his throat. "This might not surprise you. The house isn't in Anna Bruckmann's name."

"Company?"

"That's right. Get this. It's owned by a shell company in the Caymans. Offshore business set up for two things: tax haven and secrecy. What does that tell us?"

"They either have a lot of money to hide or they don't want anyone to know about them. Have you managed to go back as far as 2001?"

"Most certainly. I've been scouring a few Swiss aviation data-bases. Anna Bruckmann arrived at Duebendorf, a military airfield, according to flight logs, on a private Cessna registered to the State Department. The plane touched down in the middle of the night at 0233 hours on September 23, 2001."

"Flying from where?"

"The Cessna took off from Rome."

Reznick closed his eyes. He felt hollowed out again, think-ing of his wife landing in Switzerland while he was grieving, lost, inconsolable, drinking himself half to death. He had lost count of the days and nights he had spent screaming out at the waters of Penobscot Bay. The injustice of it all. The one left behind, a baby daughter whose care he had needed to entrust to Elisabeth's parents in New York.

"Are you still there, man?" Trevelle said.

Reznick sighed. "I'm here."

"Here's an interesting detail. I noticed that, in July 2001, Anna Bruckmann asked for a line of credit. Small amount. Five-hundred-dollar limit. She got a credit card. And I started digging a bit on that."

"Synthetic identity theft?"

"A variation of it used by the FBI and CIA. Basically, fake identity. Social security numbers being issued to this identity. But I also found something else."

"What?"

"Anna Bruckmann, all of three years old, was accidentally killed on a farm in Iowa."

"You think the CIA took that name and created this synthetic new identity?"

"Possibility, can't say for sure. A woman with the exact same name appears in Switzerland as if out of thin air. Has an American passport, social security number, credit. It's all in place."

"Son of a bitch."

"That doesn't mean it's her, Jon."

"Maybe it is. Maybe it's another piece of the jigsaw."

"That's all I've got. I wish I could do more."

"You did good, thank you."

"I know this must be painful for you. I feel for you, man."

"I guess I'm better off knowing the truth, one way or the other."

"So, you're going to Arth?"

"Sounds like a logical step."

"One bit of advice, Jon."

"What's that?"

"Be careful."

Reznick gathered his belongings from his hotel room. His cell phone rang once more. He expected it would be Trevelle again. But he checked the caller ID. It was Lauren.

"Hey, Dad," she said breezily. "Just thought I'd check in on you."

Reznick felt conflicted. It was lovely to hear her voice. But it wasn't the best time.

"Dad, are you OK?"

"Hey, Lauren, how are you?"

"I was worried about you, that's all."

"Worried about me?"

"Of course."

"You're not keeping tabs on me again, are you?" he joked.

"Gimme a break, Dad."

"How's work, honey?"

"It's New York. It's manic. What can I say?"

"Anything you can talk about?"

Lauren laughed her infectious laugh, the same as her mother's. "Dad, not a chance."

"Smart girl."

"Anyway, I'm off today. Time to chill. And I thought I'd catch up with you for a bit."

"Any plans later?"

"Martha wants to meet me for lunch."

Reznick's senses switched on. "Martha? That's nice. Any particular reason?"

"For what?"

"Meeting Martha for lunch?"

"She's mentoring me, Dad, remember? She's great."

"I know. Listen, it was nice meeting up with you in New York. We need to do that more often."

Lauren was quiet for a few moments. "I'd like that, Dad."

"I know I'm not always there for you . . ."

"Dad, you've always been there for me. You're a good father."

Reznick felt his throat tighten. "I'll take that."

Lauren laughed. "So, where are you?"

Reznick sighed. "I'm out of the country, just for a little while."

"Anywhere interesting?"

"Not really."

"Working?"

"Not really. Taking a bit of time off. A bit of traveling."

"Traveling?"

"Yeah, you know, exploring places I've never been before."

"You know what? I think that's great, Dad. Spending some quality time abroad. Take time to give yourself some space. Enjoy yourself. I think you've earned it."

Reznick's mind was in turmoil. He wanted to tell her what he knew. But it was too early. "Maybe I have."

"So, you didn't answer my question."

"What was that?"

"Where are you? Which country?"

"Oh yeah, I'm in Europe."

"That's a continent, Dad. Stop being so evasive."

"What is this? It's like the Spanish Inquisition."

Lauren laughed. "Dad, I'm just asking a simple question."

Reznick's eyes cast out over the lake. His Delta training stressed and restressed the importance of accurate intel. Over and over again, especially when identifying high-value targets. All he had right now were a few fragments of information and intelligence about his wife, which in no way confirmed anything beyond reasonable doubt.

He knew better than anyone that mistakes happen. Coordinates are keyed in wrong. Inaccurate information and intelligence further down the line can lead to deaths. Accidents. It happened over and over again.

"Dad, are you still there?"

"Sorry, honey, I was miles away."

"Are you OK?"

"Just a lot on my mind. Besides, I've got a sightseeing trip to go on."

"Sightseeing? Since when do you go sightseeing, Dad?"

"Since now, I guess. Listen, got to go. Love you."

"I'll tell Martha you were asking about her."

"Do that."

Reznick went back into his hotel room, took a long shower, and changed into a fresh set of clothes. He picked up his backpack, his 9mm Beretta firmly holstered underneath his jacket. He locked his hotel room door, headed downstairs, paid his bill, and caught a cab to the bus station.

He got on the near-empty bus and sat in the back. The journey took him past little snow-covered alpine villages and towns. All he had was a lakeside address.

Reznick checked his cell phone. He entered Bruckmann's address into Google Maps. He zoomed in on the street view of the house. Window shutters painted red. The image was date-stamped five months earlier at 14:32 on a sunny August day the previous year.

The bus pulled up in the peaceful, picture-perfect town in the central Alps. He waited until all the other passengers got off before he disembarked.

Reznick walked over to a viewing area beside the lake. It was a world away from the craziness of Manhattan. Her old life. Reznick breathed in the clean mountain air. He was determined to find out exactly who Anna Bruckmann was. He needed the peace of mind. He reached into his pocket and took out his AirPods case, pressed the two buds into his ears, and voice-activated a call.

"Trevelle, you there?"

"Copy that, Jon."

"I checked the map on the way over. I know where it is. Two hundred yards or so from here. I need more intel."

"Like what?"

"In particular, surveillance cameras on the property. What do we know?"

"I'm one step ahead of you, bro. No one home. The system is all deactivated."

"Are you sure?"

"Copy that. She might've left in a hurry."

"But not in such a hurry that she didn't have time to deactivate the surveillance of the property."

"Point taken."

Reznick kicked an empty can down the road. "Sounds like she is one step ahead of *us*. How do you know if no one is home if the system isn't working?"

"A neighbor's system, directly behind, line of sight into the property. I've checked. There's no one home. No furniture. Nothing. No sign of life."

Reznick groaned. "Motherfucker! So, they did a professional cleanup?"

"Makes sense, erasing all trace of her."

Reznick's gaze was drawn to a small boat on the far shore of the lake. He squinted out over the icy waters at a glint in the dazzling winter sun. Maybe half a mile away.

"Jon, you still there?"

Reznick saw movement in the boat. A figure with binoculars trained on him. Someone was watching him.

"Still here. I'm heading over."

Fifteen

Reznick turned a corner and moved out of the observer's line of sight.

"I think I've got company."

Reznick walked toward a quiet cul-de-sac and relayed what he'd seen on the far shore.

"That's not good."

"Tell me about it," Reznick muttered.

He walked down the quiet street, up to a black iron gate with a number—14—welded to it. This was it. The rear of the house. The front of the house overlooked the lake.

"I'll be in touch." He ended the call as he surveyed his surroundings. The lakefront enclave was about a mile from the center of the town of Arth. The snow-capped peaks of Mount Rigi stood majestic over the town. It was an idyllic retreat. Or a place to escape.

Reznick figured the person with the binoculars had to be the NDB, keeping tabs on him. It was their none-too-subtle way of showing they were not going away. To unsettle him, perhaps. But it would take more than that to unnerve him. A hell of a lot more.

He figured he'd been on their radar the moment he touched down in Zurich. He had to assume the NDB was liaising with the CIA or the FBI. He had to assume that the American intelligence agencies knew that he was on to the woman known as Anna Bruckmann. And he imagined that would cause problems for them. Problems they would rather just go away.

He walked back around to the front of the house overlooking the lake. No sign of any boat or figure with binoculars.

Reznick turned and looked at the attractive house, up to a hanging basket of flowers on the second floor. A bracket adjacent to the basket revealed a tiny camera. He remembered Trevelle had said it had all been deactivated. By who? When? The questions were mounting.

Reznick pressed the buzzer three times. He knew he would get no reply. But he waited and waited. He pressed the buzzer again—five times in sharp succession.

He waited again. Ten, fifteen, twenty seconds. Still no answer.

Back through the iron gate, down the icy path, around to the rear of the property. He knocked hard on the back door. Nothing. He knocked a few more times. But still no answer.

He crouched down and peered through the mail slot. A fashionable, gray Shaker kitchen, white quartz countertops, parquet wooden floor in the hall and kitchen. It was all very upscale. But still no sign of life.

Reznick looked for ways to force entry. He had already been told by Trevelle that it was empty. Breaking in would get him deported for sure. He paced the path outside the lakefront house. Then he stood for a few moments and stared over the lake. The same dark waters she would have stared out over. Was this her sanctuary thousands of miles from home? The place for her to escape her life, her trained killer of a husband, and her baby daughter? A place to forget. A place to start again.

He began to think back, all those years ago. It was true, he wasn't the easiest person in the world to deal with. In all honesty, he was prone to mood swings. He had a hair-trigger temper. He imagined her having to tiptoe around when he was home so as not to arouse his ire. Never physical violence. But she might have sensed the malevolence within him. She was more cultured. Highly educated. In many ways, they were polar opposites. He was the blue-collar tough guy from a small, unfashionable fishing town in Maine. Elisabeth, by contrast, was a city girl, had gone to the best private schools, was a lawyer at a top New York firm and moved effortlessly in those rarefied circles. It hadn't seemed to be a problem in the early days of their marriage. But somewhere along the line, he sensed something had changed.

He wondered if he had been the problem in their marriage. Had the relationship soured with him away most of the time? Marriage breakdowns were very common in Delta and across special forces teams. It was impossible to keep up a regular life. He wasn't a regular guy. He couldn't communicate when he returned home. He sat in long silences, drinking. Then he went out, usually just walking. A cycle which he didn't escape for years.

Reznick turned and looked again at the house. He needed some assistance. He took out his cell phone and called Trevelle.

"A few questions for you."

"Shoot."

"The company that owns this house?"

"Yup."

"Do they own any other properties in Switzerland?"

"I was working that angle. Three other properties. But none in Switzerland. One in Dubai, one in Hong Kong, and one in Munich."

"Nice portfolio."

Reznick saw an elderly woman approaching him, dog in tow. She walked down the path toward him, a growling German shepherd on a thick leather leash beside her.

"You can say that again."

"Look, I've got a visitor. I'll call you back."

Reznick ended the call and smiled. "Hello."

The old woman studied him. "Can I help you?" she said in a thick Swiss accent.

"I hope so. I'm looking for the lady who lives here. I'm an old friend."

"Are you American?"

Reznick nodded as he kept an eye on the menacing dog.

"My English is not good."

"It's excellent. I was wondering if you could help me."

"Are you a tourist?"

"Yes, I'm doing a bit of traveling in Switzerland. I'm here on vacation, and I came across my friend's address in an old diary. It appears she's not in."

"You know Anna well?"

Reznick realized he had the right house. "A long time ago back in the States. We lost touch. But I'm in Switzerland, and I thought, why not meet up?"

The woman walked up to him. "I'm afraid you're not in luck. She just left, all of a sudden."

Reznick held his ground with the snarling dog. "That's too bad."

"It's not like her."

"Out of character?"

"Yes, out of character, as you say."

Reznick smiled at the old woman. "Do you mind me asking, are you a friend of Anna's?"

"No, I'm just the housekeeper."

Reznick shook her hand. "Nice to meet you. What's your name?"

"My name is Sophie Scheder."

"How long have you lived here?"

"All my life. I live just behind Anna. It's a cottage, a lot smaller."

"So, does Anna employ you or is it her company?"

The old woman's rheumy eyes stared back at him as if trying to figure out why he was asking so many questions. "You are a very inquisitive person."

"Apologies, it's just my nature."

"Seems such a shame to come all this way for nothing."

Reznick nodded as he admired the front of the house. "Lovely place. Beautiful location. How long has Anna lived here? It must be years since I saw her last."

"Eight years, maybe more."

"Eight years? Wow. A long time. Do you mind me asking if you've got Anna's number so I can message her?"

The old woman shook her head. "Sadly not, she was a very private person. I had a spare set of keys for the property. My job was to clean it three times a week. My husband, Rudy, is the handyman. He keeps the gardens neat and tidy."

"Do you know where she is? A forwarding address?"

"Anna?"

"Yeah."

"I wish I did. It's all very strange, her disappearance."

"How so?"

"A couple of nights ago, a truck came and took all her furniture and everything away. I asked if Anna was alright, and they said they were just clearing out the house, that's all. They didn't know anything."

Reznick pondered that for a few moments. He wondered if Anna Bruckmann had been told that her cover might have been compromised. "She didn't tell you?"

"No. As I said, it's strange. Very out of character. But maybe she was in a rush, new job. That's what my husband thinks. She is involved in a technology company."

Reznick turned back to the house.

"I'm sorry you've wasted your time," she said.

"I was in the country anyway. Tell me, did you see the truck when it arrived?"

"My husband did."

"Rudy?"

"Right."

"Did he know who the company was?"

"Yes, a Geneva firm. Franz Fein Removals."

"Franz Fein Removals," he said. "Geneva, huh. Has she got a place in Geneva?"

The old woman bent down and stroked her dog. "I don't know."

"Anna hasn't been in touch with you at all?"

"No. And I have no cell phone number for her. She's just disappeared into thin air."

Sixteen

Hans Muller floated on a black lake, mountains all around, billions of stars in the inky sky. He felt the water wash over his face. He struggled and thrashed. He was drowning. He gasped for air, but he was helpless, as if paralyzed. Fighting for breath. Water seeped into his lungs.

He came to in a cold sweat, breathing hard. He looked around a darkened room.

Muller took a few moments to get his bearings. He was safe. It was alright. *Everything is alright.* He reached over and switched on a bedside light. A white room, desk and chair at the far side, camera high up on a metal bracket on the wall. It was all coming back to him.

The sound of the ancient call to prayer in the distance.

Muller got up slowly and walked across to the window. He opened the blinds. Blinding sun. The silhouetted minaret no more than two hundred yards away.

He looked down onto the courtyard below. A walled compound. An armed guard smoking a cigarette. The Russian Embassy, Riyadh. He had made it.

A sharp knock at the door snapped him out of his thoughts.

"Who is it?"

"It's Jacob."

Muller opened the door.

Jacob stood smiling. He wore jeans and a polo shirt and was accompanied by a burly man in a loose-fitting white linen shirt and black cargo pants. "How did you sleep?"

"Good, I guess."

"Sorry about the sedation. We thought it best so we could get you into the country without attracting any undue attention. I hope you understand it was for your own good. We didn't want you freaking out as you landed at a Saudi military airport. So, you were concealed in a diplomatic crate."

"A crate?"

Jacob smiled. "It was fully ventilated. Besides, we had an oxygen mask on you as well. You were fine. And now you're here."

Muller felt violated. He hadn't anticipated such antics. He wondered if this was a sign of things to come. "I guess."

"You feel OK? No ill effects?"

"Dry mouth, that's all."

Jacob handed him a chilled bottle of water. "Drink up. And follow me."

Muller took a couple of large gulps. "Where are we going?"

"You're going to meet a senior intelligence attaché here at the embassy and a military attaché. They want to ask you some questions. I assume that's not a problem."

"Why do they want to question me?"

"Relax, Hans. They like you. They just want to know more about you, your motives, and obviously they are keen to get the rest of the encrypted intelligence information you downloaded in Switzerland."

Muller felt his stomach tighten. He hadn't anticipated being grilled by Russian intelligence. He thought he would just be asked to share the intelligence he had stored. And then just sit back, kill time. "Do I have anything to worry about?"

"Do you have anything to worry about? I wouldn't have thought so."

Muller followed Jacob down a series of corridors.

"What does that mean?"

"It means relax. You are in a secure place. None safer."

The elevator took them down to the basement. Cameras watched his every move. He was escorted down a long, heavily ventilated corridor, through some steel doors, then into a vast windowless room.

Muller surveyed the scene. It was like a den. It could have been the study of a Swiss industrialist high up in the Alps. Maybe an apartment in Zurich. It was beautiful. Bach piano music played softly in the background. It was as if they were trying to find a place where he would feel comfortable.

"Take the weight off, Hans," Jacob said.

Muller slumped down on a sofa and put his feet up on the coffee table. He finished the contents of the bottle of water. "So, what now?"

"What can I get you? Are you hungry?"

"Yeah, I'm starving. You're not going to drug me again, are you?"

Jacob smiled. "Absolutely not. So, what do you want?"

"Pancakes and maple syrup and coffee."

"You got it. I'll be back in fifteen minutes. Make yourself at home."

Muller sighed as Jacob left him in the room by himself. He wondered what he had gotten himself into. He had imagined that he would land in Riyadh. Then he would give the Russians the key codes to the classified information which he had wrapped up in Advanced Encryption Standard (AES) 256, a virtually impenetrable symmetric encryption algorithm that uses a 256-bit key. The balance of the money would be transferred to his offshore accounts. Then he'd get handed his new ID and papers. His new life. A private island of his own. Bothered by no one. No government. He thought he was in the driver's seat.

He had imagined being feted like a Snowden. Fuck, how could he have been so blind? He hadn't expected to be drugged. The Russians would be overseeing his security. He began to wonder if there were any other tricks up their sleeves.

The door opened. A stunning Russian woman dressed in chef's whites brought in his breakfast on a tray.

"Pancakes and syrup, sir?" the woman said with a heavy Russian accent.

Muller pointed to the desk.

She put the tray down. "Enjoy, sir."

"Thank you."

The woman left Muller alone. He sat at the desk and wolfed down his food. Then he drank two cups of coffee, feeling so much better.

Jacob returned to take the tray away. "They're on their way. Relax."

Muller nodded. His stomach knotted with tension. "How long until they see me?"

"Very soon. Don't be afraid."

It was another lie. It wasn't *very soon*. The hours dragged.

Muller paced the room as he wondered what was in store for him. The more time that passed, the more tense he felt.

Eventually, after an interminable wait, a heavy knock resonated at the door.

"Yeah, come in," he shouted.

The door opened and two men walked in, carrying files and a MacBook. Neither introduced himself as they sat down behind the desk.

"Sit down, Hans," the older of the two men said.

Muller did as he was told.

The older of the two men flicked through a thick file. Hans saw photos of himself as a boy, as a student, as well as a passport photo. "Hans Christian Muller, born 17 December, 1992. Right?"

Muller nodded. "Correct. Where did you get that?"

"Welcome to Russia."

Muller said nothing.

"This is Russian territory. Do you understand that?"

"I do."

"Excellent. So, we've got a few questions for you. You might have preconceptions about what to expect. None of what you are expecting will happen."

Muller felt a knot of tension again in his stomach.

The younger of the two men smiled, exposing excellent teeth. His eyes were icy blue, and veins bulged on his tanned neck. "I was born in 1992 as well, Hans. You can call me Sergei. Relax, it's going to be fine."

Muller studied Sergei's handsome features, perfect teeth. "Nice to meet you too."

"My colleague is Igor," Sergei said. "OK?"

Muller acknowledged Igor with a quick nod of his head.

"So, let us begin," Sergei said. "I'll lead this conversation. That's all it is at this stage. Just trying to establish some ground rules. Getting to know each other."

"Fair enough."

"First, it's great to finally meet you. We want you to feel comfortable. And so, if you need anything—and I mean anything—please just let us know, and we'll see what we can do. We want this short stay to be as pleasant as possible. And then you'll be on your way."

"That's good to hear."

"Are you hungry?"

"I'm fine. The air-conditioning in here is perfect. That was my main concern."

Sergei smiled. "I was looking over your résumé. It is incredibly impressive. My skill set is not too dissimilar to yours. I'm a specialist in cybersecurity, cryptography, and biometrics, just like you. And I very much admire your skills and high intelligence. Pleasure to meet you in person."

Muller shifted in his seat, feeling uneasy with the praise. "Where did you study?"

"Institute of Cryptography, Telecommunications, and Computer Science in Moscow. You might have heard of it."

Muller had indeed. He knew it was where the finest mathematics geniuses in Russia went to study. Hand-picked by the state.

"The same place as Kaspersky. You have heard of him?"

Muller nodded. "Who hasn't?"

"Let's get down to business, Hans. We want to make sure that we understand each other. But first, we want to find out about you."

"What do you know? I'll see if I can help you fill in the blanks."

Sergei nodded. "We'd appreciate that. Well, you graduated top of your class, didn't you?"

"Correct."

"This caught the eye of the NSA. I believe they wanted to recruit you at one stage, is that right?"

"Correct."

"But you spurned their offer. Why was that?"

"Ideological, I guess."

Sergei made a few notes. "Ideological. How so?"

"Political."

"I see. Your mother . . . Was she, by chance, influential on your thinking?"

Muller felt uncomfortable talking about his mother or his family. He just wanted to get through this and disappear off the face of the earth. "I guess."

"You studied political science and political theory before you switched to mathematics and science, then computers."

Muller sensed he was probing. "You're very thorough."

"We have our moments. And you wrote a quite brilliant dissertation on the data collection methods of the NSA."

"Have you read it?"

"Read it and loved it. 'A pervasive neo-Orwellian state within a state,' I believe you called it."

"I was a lot younger."

"You wrote that about a decade ago, not so long ago. I read somewhere that the NSA collects 700 million megabytes of information from phone surveillance, computer records, emails, texts, et cetera, each and every day. So, you weren't wrong."

"It's nearer 750 million the last I heard."

Sergei scribbled that down. "Three quarters of a billion. Every day. And you know that how, Hans?"

"A guy at NSA, where I was seconded—he gave me the figure. Actually, he showed me the figures from an internal report. Saying that it might be higher. But every government is at it."

"Including Switzerland, right?"

Muller smiled. "You know as well as I do, Sergei, that Switzerland is privy to intelligence sharing with Five Eyes, and a few others, as and when it suits them."

"That must be tough, knowing that."

Muller shook his head. "It's not tough. I can see why it's necessary."

"What happened to the idealism?"

"That got crushed out of me when I got a mortgage."

Sergei glanced at his colleague, who was staring at Muller, stone faced. "How much do you earn per annum, Hans?"

Muller sighed. "Not enough. Not what I give my country. Not near enough."

"I was studying the coding behind your biometric facial identification software. You more or less invented it."

Muller said nothing.

"Help me out here, Hans. I read somewhere that there was a patent on the software. A patent held by the NDB, is that right?"

Muller leaned back in his seat. "What's your point?"

"My point is, you are broke. But if you had been a freelance contractor, say at the NSA, you could have resigned and made hundreds of millions, perhaps billions. Am I right?"

Muller knew now they were fucking with him. It was a sore point with him. He had devoted thousands of hours to the project.

"Not to worry, you already have fifty million dollars in your accounts."

"I believe I'm due another fifty million still, right?"

Sergei smiled. He opened up the laptop and turned it to face Muller. "Face the screen."

Muller did as he was told.

Sergei handed him a cell phone. "Check for yourself."

Muller glanced down at the screen. The overall balance still showed only fifty million dollars spread over fifteen separate offshore accounts.

"That should hopefully make you feel better, right?" Sergei said.

"The fifty million outstanding?"

"That will be transferred the moment you leave here. Is that OK?"

Muller shrugged. "Why not now?"

"We just want to ask you some questions. It's just about jumping through a few hoops. We all have to jump through hoops every once in a while."

"Do I have any choice?"

"We all have choices. You can walk out of here. The only problem is that the Saudi intelligence people are not as nice as us, shall we say. They have some very medieval ideas of interrogation."

Muller absorbed the comment. "How long are you keeping me here?"

"I'm not keeping you here. The Russian government is not keeping you here. You're free to go."

"I mean, when will you be getting me to my final destination?"

"Your Brazilian island? It's very nice."

Muller nodded.

"You will be landing by seaplane in seventy-two hours, give or take."

"So, is that it? Is that all you want from me?"

Igor held up a black-and-white photo Muller knew only too well. It was taken in Zurich Old Town. "I believe you know who this is, right?"

"Anna Bruckmann. Founder of Verification Technology Information Corp."

"She's an American."

"I know. Her name and ID didn't register. But I got the real identity. She's CIA. It's part of the tranche of data in your possession. You probably know who she is."

Igor put down the photo as he exchanged a knowing smile with Sergei. "We have solid intel that says the American government is going to mount an operation to get her out of the country. At least that's what we've heard."

"She's been compromised?"

Sergei answered, "Not only that, Hans. By you reaching out to the NSA, Fort Meade has gone into a collective meltdown. CIA too. She was a long-term, multiyear operative. Collecting data from unwilling countries who signed up to her company's slick encrypted end-to-end bullshit marketing. But all the time the invaluable data and classified information on foreign clients is being sucked up and fed back to Uncle Sam, right?"

"Correct."

Sergei said, "Geneva seems to be an area of some interest to the United States."

"The US Mission to the United Nations houses a very capable listening station in Geneva."

"We know that. What about the range?"

"Some say sixty kilometers' range," Muller said. "My documents indicate nearer one hundred kilometers."

"And from there it would pass to . . . ?"

"Leuk satellite listening station."

Igor scribbled down the information. "Well known to us."

"And onward to the NSA on the East Coast. Utah Data Center will have access to that. But that's just the tip of the iceberg. As you know, Leuk was part of the Echelon satellite listening program, which was the forerunner to PRISM."

Igor smiled at Muller. "Before you began university, I didn't realize you were in the Army. I found that intriguing. I served my country too."

Muller remained silent.

Igor flicked through Muller's file. "I was wondering about that period in the Swiss Army. It's very sketchy. We're unsure of dates. Can you elaborate, Hans?"

"I can't remember much about that period. It didn't mean much to me."

Igor showed him a black-and-white photo of Muller in army fatigues, camouflage paint smeared on his face. "We think this is you."

Muller nodded.

"You were no ordinary soldier, were you?"

Muller said nothing.

Igor smiled. "We'll come back to that later. I want to talk a bit more about your motivation. You are passing on this information, highly classified information which purports to show all manner of top secret communications, documents, and lists and contacts of spies, throughout Western Europe."

Muller nodded. "What's your point?"

"You are betraying your country. Selling them out. For money, is that right?"

"Correct."

"Hans, I've handled agents for a long time. I know what motivates them, what drives them. Espionage is a dangerous business. You can wind up dead."

"I'm aware of that."

"This brings me to my next point. We will have to establish if you are who you say you are. Are you bona fide, so to speak."

"What are you talking about? I've passed on huge amounts of classified data already."

"We have several teams working through that. It's interesting. But, as you can imagine, we don't take things at face value. We need to verify. We need time to establish your true motivations."

"It's money, pure and simple."

"So you've said. In my experience, Hans, spies are not only dangerous people, but their loyalties shift. It's fluid. So, we have to be on guard against being fed false information by a double agent. All intelligence agencies know about traitors in their midst."

Muller was starting to feel deeply uncomfortable with the direction of the conversation. "I have reached out in good faith and have done everything I've been asked to do. And more."

"We'll be the judge of that."

"I appreciate your need to be one hundred percent certain of my motivations. I get it. But I've given you a treasure trove of Western intelligence. The finest hack of classified information ever, right?"

Igor and Sergei both took notes.

"What are you writing?"

Igor cleared his throat. "We're noting your mannerisms, your body language, your tone of voice, intonation. We can spot liars. We can spot traitors."

"I just want to pass on the rest of the data and get the hell out of here."

"All in good time."

"What does that mean?"

"It means we've got a lot more questions. We need time to dig deeper into the world of Hans Muller and find out definitively if you are a double agent or not."

Muller's eyes switched between the two men. "I want out of here."

Igor sighed. "Relax, Hans. A few more days, and I believe we'll have our answer."

Seventeen

Reznick rented a BMW in Arth and headed out of town. He connected his phone and called Trevelle.

"Going mobile, Jon?"

"Something like that. Wondering if you can do a bit more digging for me. This is personal."

"What do you need?"

"Anna Bruckmann has a housekeeper. Sophie Scheder." He spelled out the last name. "Her husband is Rudy, a handyman-slash-gardener."

"You want me to keep tabs on their cell phones?"

Reznick turned off the lakefront road as he saw a sign up ahead for the highway to Bern. He headed onto a ramp and was on the main route to the capital. "If they have them."

"Not a problem."

"Another thing. Franz Fein Removals of Geneva. They cleared everything out of the house in Arth. I'm looking to see if that company has a forwarding address to take the belongings to."

"Could be a storage facility."

"Could be."

"I'll take care of it."

"Appreciate that."

The traffic was surprisingly light, empty in stretches. He began to feel drowsy and stopped off in the quaint old town of Lucerne. He wolfed down a hearty steak and followed it up with a few cups of strong black coffee. He took a couple of Dexedrine. He felt better. More focused.

He strolled along the lake as the biting cold wind and amphetamines revived him. He sensed he was on the right track. He felt it in his bones.

Reznick could imagine sophisticated Elisabeth happy in such a fantastically picturesque town. It would attract other expats. It was only half an hour on the highway from Arth. He imagined her walking alongside the lake, visiting friends.

Reznick felt sharper now and headed back to his car. Mile after mile, headlights flashing in his face as he drove to Switzerland's capital city. He wondered if that was where she was, hiding out. Maybe protected by Agency operatives within the American Embassy. Bern made a lot of sense. Maybe she was living at the embassy. Protected. But perhaps Zurich—where she had been spotted on the surveillance video in Old Town—made more sense.

He drove on for another twenty kilometers. How would he react if he met her face-to-face? Would he demand answers? She had never reached out. But how could she? She was dead. At least officially.

Reznick glanced in his rearview mirror. Headlights flashing, fast approaching. He watched and waited. The car edged closer. It was the cops. Emblazoned on the car's hood was POLIZEI. He slowed down and pulled over, switching on his hazard lights as the car stopped behind his. A few moments later, a black SUV screeched up in front of him, blocking his exit. He knew this was no simple traffic stop.

Reznick's instincts were to speed away, smashing through the SUV. He sat and considered his options. One wrong move and he would be a wanted man. His trip to Switzerland would be over. Was this the NDB? Maybe the CIA? He wondered whether he could escape without killing anyone. Doubtful. Reznick decided to roll with it.

A tall Swiss uniformed cop got out of the vehicle, flashlight in hand. Jon instinctively reached into his jacket and unbuttoned his holster. He touched the familiar plastic grip of the Beretta for a fleeting moment.

The cop shone the flashlight at the rear of the vehicle as if checking the license plate. Then he walked around to Reznick's side. He leaned down and tapped on the window with the flashlight.

Reznick lowered the window. "Good evening, Officer."

"You English?"

"American."

"American, huh." The cop studied him for a few moments before he looked at the back seat. "Can I see your papers, sir?"

Reznick reached into the glove compartment and pulled out his ID along with the car rental papers and insurance.

The cop looked over the documents and shone the flashlight in his face. "So, American, huh?"

"I already said that."

The cop looked nonplussed.

Reznick glanced again in his rearview mirror and saw the cop's colleague in the driver's seat, cell phone pressed to his ear. He looked at the SUV blocking his exit. The two figures in the front just sat there. No, this was no ordinary traffic stop. "Who are the guys in the vehicle in front?"

"NDB."

"What seems to be the problem, Officer?"

The cop motioned for Reznick to get out of the car. He complied.

"Hands on head."

Reznick complied again. He felt the flashlight pressed against his neck. Then excruciating shockwaves through his body. He collapsed to the ground as electric shocks rippled and reverberated. He looked up, shaking uncontrollably.

The cop bent down as Reznick writhed on the ground.

The cop pressed the stun gun one more time against his neck. Waves of overwhelming pain and shocks spread through his body.

He heard himself scream out in pain.

Reznick tried to get back on his feet. He felt a hard kick to the head from the cop. Then another. An explosion of pain and lights flashing before his eyes. More repeated kicks to the head. More blows. He tasted warm blood. He looked up as if through a fish-eye lens.

The two men from the vehicle in front towered above him. Blows rained down as he lay prostrate.

He kicked out. But it was too late.

He looked up at the leering face of the cop. He felt himself drifting off.

Then it all went black.

Eighteen

Reznick squinted out of a swollen right eye. He took a few moments to try and get himself together. He seemed to be tied to a chair, harsh lights trained on him. He couldn't see anyone, but he sensed he was being watched.

He tried to move. He looked down.

He was strapped to a seat which was bolted to the floor. Handcuffs dug into the bones of his wrists. Leather restraints at his ankles.

Reznick's restricted gaze wandered around the windowless room. He saw a spectral figure standing in the shadows.

"Hello, Jon." A soft American voice. "Well, this is a pleasant surprise."

Reznick licked his lips as he squinted at the figure only a few yards from him.

"Sorry about those guys who brought you in. Very heavy-handed."

"Who are you?"

"We've got a few things we need to talk to you about."

"You're Agency."

"Very perceptive, Jon."

"What about the Swiss cop who stopped me?"

"He was one of us, Jon. Fluent in German. Bit of a sadist. But what do I know?"

Reznick rode out the waves of pain.

"Here's the thing, Jon. No one likes uninvited guests. And that goes for uninvited guests in a nice, orderly country like Switzerland. You don't strike me as part of the international jet set we all keep reading about. Davos and all that shit. And I certainly don't see you on the slopes."

Reznick's head was swimming, most of him wanting to fall asleep.

"You know how this thing works."

"How?"

"I need to lay out what you need to do."

"And what's that?"

"You need to go home, Jon, and forget everything. I heard you were down in the Keys before you came over here. It would be a good move to get back to the sun. Winter is the best time to be down there. Am I right?"

"I'm assuming you have a point."

The figure lit a cigarette and shook his head. "Jon, don't try and fuck with me. I'm the one who's fucking with you."

"What do you want?"

"You need to grab your passport and head on home. Nice and simple. And then we can all be happy again."

"Why would I want to do that?"

The man shook his head as he dragged hard on his cigarette. "Jon, you're killing me, man. We'll have a doctor look you over, get you showered and patched up, and you'll be good to go."

"And what if I don't?"

"That wouldn't be a good move. Not a good move at all."

"Go fuck yourself."

"Jon, I'm on your side."

100

The man dropped his cigarette and crushed it with his shoe. He began to pace the room. "Why are you here? I mean, why are you really here? The sooner you tell us, the sooner you can get back home to Florida, Maine, or wherever you want."

"I'm on vacation."

"That's not true, Jon. You were enjoying a short vacation down in the Keys not so long ago. That's more your speed, right? You're American. That's what we like."

"You seem to know a lot about me."

"That's my job, Jon. I look after American interests in this part of the world."

"Does that not include American citizens?"

The man laughed. "You have a point. Listen, there are forces at work which most people are never even aware of."

"Nice line."

"The great mass of people, as you know, go about their lives unencumbered by how our great nation protects not only itself, but its people and its interests, most specifically economic interests. Geopolitical interests. Anything which encroaches on that becomes a problem, doesn't it?"

Reznick peered out of his one good eye. "Where are you from?"

"That's no concern of yours."

"You miss your family?"

"I miss a lot of things."

"Maybe they're here enjoying the fresh air and skiing and fondues."

"We're getting off topic, Jon. I'm trying to cut you a break."

"Let me guess. School of Foreign Service, Georgetown? Bet they never taught you about getting your hands dirty."

"What's your point?"

"I know your type. I've met your type. They send people like me on missions. They might end their days lecturing at Harvard on

101

public service, and the merry-go-round continues. Nice platform to recruit the next generation too."

"You're an interesting man, Mr. Reznick."

"Go fuck yourself."

"I can make all this go away. Or what you are experiencing now will take a serious turn for the worse. I'm talking black site in sub-Saharan Africa. I myself have never been involved in such things. But I know people who were. I've read the classified reports. The briefings. Seen the videos. It's amazing how a man's spirit can be broken."

Reznick shot a look at the figure in the corner. His throat felt bone dry.

"So, here's the deal. And make no mistake, it is a very good deal. Nice and simple. You have forty-eight hours to clear out of Switzerland. What do you say?"

Reznick lifted his head as his vision blurred. "And if I don't?"

"Then, I'm afraid we'll have to fly you directly to a country of my choice, and you would be permanently disappeared. How does that sound?"

Nineteen

Gronski strode along Corridor 10, deep in the heart of the Pentagon, briefcase in hand, knowing he was already a couple of minutes late. It wasn't like him. He loathed tardiness. The meeting with the secretary of defense had run over by twenty long minutes. Now he was trying to get back on track.

He passed through a series of retina scans before getting to the ultra-secure conference room. It was a highly restricted inner sanctum for special access programs.

The door locked automatically behind him.

Gronski walked around the table and sat in his usual leather chair. He opened his briefcase, took out the notes and classified papers, and spread them out in front of him. He perused the papers for a few moments as he gathered his thoughts.

The huge screen on the wall flickered on. Staring back at Gronski was fresh-faced Deputy National Security Advisor to the President Philip Hudson.

"Nice to see you again, Charles," Hudson said.

Gronski smiled through gritted teeth at the sanctimonious little prick. Something about the guy irked Gronski like no one else. Maybe his first wife. "Apologies for being late. My last meeting went on forever."

"I thought you were a military man through and through, Charles."

Gronski sat and took it from his political master. He was thankful he wasn't line-managed by the little fucker. He didn't report to him. But he was still accountable to that scrawny fuck, so he had to hold it together.

"OK, Charles, I asked for an update on the situation in Switzerland. This is a heck of a mess."

"I concur."

"It's been brought to my attention that Hans Muller is almost certainly being handled by the Russians. The fucking Russians are running circles around us. Doesn't look good from my side of the fence."

Gronski looked at his briefing notes. "I just spoke to the secretary of defense, and we are on the same page."

"What are we doing about it? Everyone I ask about this passes me off to someone else, or they say to ask Gronski. So, Charles, what the fuck can you say?"

"The NSA are digging into any communications Muller had. We're still trying to piece together the chain of events."

"I'm aware of that. But what about those useless fuckers at the NDB? What do they have to say?"

Gronski didn't feel comfortable badmouthing a foreign intelligence service. "They're cooperating with us on this. They understand better than anyone how it must look."

"I've been given different figures as to how much the Russians are paying this sleazeball."

"The number I have is fifty million dollars. That's so far been transferred to more than a dozen new accounts opened in the name of a Zurich-based legal firm which has handled the accounts of well-known Russian oligarchs close to the Kremlin."

Hudson scribbled notes. "This is the first I'm hearing of this."

"NSA channels of communication need to be improved somewhat," Gronski said. "But I understand they are referring it all back to me."

"What a clusterfuck."

"We also have information from a crypto exchange in Zurich that an account had twenty million dollars' worth of Bitcoin appear one month ago, but then transferred to another exchange in Brazil. Maybe part of the same transactions. Part of the deal to get things underway."

"Fuck."

"He's a double agent, no question."

Hudson shook his head. "What are we doing about it? He's still out there somewhere."

"He might've been extracted and taken to Moscow."

"No evidence of that. Listen, Gronski, we need to find this fucker. American secrets have been compromised."

"I agree."

"Muller can't have vanished into thin air."

"Have you considered that he might've been spirited out of the country? Gone on the run like Snowden before the Russians got their hands on him."

Hudson nodded. "It's a distinct possibility. We have every intelligence agency in Western Europe looking for him. He has some incredibly valuable information we have shared with the NDB and major partners like Germany. But we can't get a fix on him. Why is that? What is the Pentagon doing about it?"

Gronski wondered when Hudson would cut to the chase. "We're all working hard to find Muller. Remember, he *is* one of the world's leading IT specialists. We taught him everything he knows."

Hudson went quiet for a few moments, then Gronski asked, "Is there anything else?"

"I want an update on special access programs that might be under the radar, operating in Switzerland. I'm assuming you can clarify what the position is."

Gronski had anticipated that Hudson would ask about that. He knew that Hudson and a few wonks in academia wanted a more open style of government, but with that came serious risks to national security. "You know this area is highly compartmentalized for a reason."

"Charles, don't put obstacles in my path. I need answers. What do you know? What can you tell me?"

Gronski could have told him everything he knew. Instead he decided to give him a few tidbits of information to try and buy some time. "We are working to establish the full extent of any special access programs."

"Why don't you have that information now?"

"We're waiting for clearance from Senate Defense and Intelligence Committees to release details."

"How long will that be?"

"A matter of days."

"Fine, tell me what you know."

"I can give nonspecific information which has been cleared for you, if that is of interest."

Hudson shook his head as he began to scribble notes. "Tell me what you can."

"It began . . . as an unacknowledged special access program instigated by the chairman of the Joint Chiefs of Staff in collaboration with the highest echelons of the CIA."

"Are we talking sleeper agent or cell?"

"Agent. I have been instructed that I can't identify the individual concerned. She is an American. And she has been working overseas, solely in Switzerland, for a company that was formed to capture electronic intelligence."

"The name of the company?"

"I'm not privy to that information," he lied. "This was all set up before I arrived. I'm waiting to find out when or if I can release that information."

Hudson scribbled more notes. "Was her identity or some part of it contained in this huge data theft in Switzerland?"

"I can reveal that her identity may have been compromised by Muller. We have fourteen separate secret operations running across Switzerland, tracking financial transactions for terrorist groups and individuals who may be funding them or supporting them. I'm talking everything from NGOs we support to tech startups. CIA fronts, some of them. They are heavily involved in our electronic data-gathering across Zurich and Geneva. But we also have eyes on Russia and China, both funneling large sums of hard cash, crypto, gold, and other payments to their assets across Europe."

"Let's assume this mystery woman in Switzerland . . . an American?"

"She may have entered the country as an American."

"Makes sense. But her identity is now known to a foreign power. Our enemies?"

"Correct."

"I'm assuming we have a contingency plan in place for extraction."

"We do."

Hudson shook his head as he scribbled more notes. "Charles, I'm at a loss to understand why she's still there. Get her the hell home."

"I'd like to be more forthcoming."

"So, why aren't you?"

"A delicate situation has become even more complicated."

"Charles, you're talking in fucking riddles. What do you mean?"

Gronski took a few seconds to compose himself. He wasn't used to being talked to like this. "Well, the situation has been somewhat complicated by a former ex-Delta 'ghost.' Jon Reznick has arrived on the scene."

"Reznick? Who the hell is he?"

"He is a badass. An assassin. A killer. Has done work for the CIA."

"How do you know?"

"He worked under my command once. Hell of a soldier. A warrior."

"So, this American . . . Reznick?"

"He's sniffing around Switzerland. And it very well might be related to our asset."

"Can't we grab him and get the Swiss to deport him? And why the hell is he there?"

"That is progressing as we speak. I'm hopeful we will get some good news on that front. I can't go into further detail until I get the latest update from some sources in Switzerland."

"I want to know more about this Jon Reznick and why the hell he's getting involved in this. But let's get back on point. What do we do to preserve the integrity of the special access program?"

"Plans are already underway to get the sleeper agent back to the United States. I believe a team is preparing to fly in to Berlin within the next twenty-four hours. And from there head to Switzerland for final extraction."

"What if that fails?"

"There are always contingency plans in place."

"So, what's the contingency?"

"I'm not at liberty to discuss that."

"Why not?"

"When I have been authorized to release the information, you'll be the first to know. As it stands, I think I've said enough."

Twenty

The whispered voices spoke in German.

Reznick could detect a few words. He lay on his back, eyes closed, a dull ache in his sides. He listened as someone spoke.

"Jon?" she said.

Reznick slowly opened his eyes and winced. He was lying in a bed, trying to get his bearings.

"Jon?" she repeated.

Reznick turned. A blonde nurse with ice-blue eyes smiled down at him.

"Guten Morgen."

Reznick used his elbows to try and sit up in bed. He felt a sudden stabbing pain in the side of his head. "Where am I?"

"You're in a hospital in Bern, Jon. You're in good hands. You're an American, yes?"

"American . . . correct." He cleared his throat. "How did I get here?"

"I don't exactly know. I started my shift this morning, and you were here. You were brought in here a couple of nights ago, according to the notes. Don't worry, you've been heavily sedated. It will take a few hours for you to shake off the effects."

Reznick felt a shooting pain behind his right eye. He touched where the pain was and felt stitches. It was tender, sore.

"You need to rest. Sleep."

Reznick turned toward the dresser at the side of his bed and saw his cell phone, ID, and wallet. "So, I've been here for two days?"

"That's right."

"I've been out of it for two days?"

"Heavily sedated. According to your medical notes, you were brought in unconscious. We cleaned you up. You were in a bit of a mess, I'm sorry to say. Were you involved in a fight?"

"A fight?" Reznick's mind flashed back to the attack by the cop when he got out of the car. The kicks, punches, and the excruciating pain of the stun gun. Then the interrogation room. "Something like that."

"You need to rest."

Reznick sat himself up and grimaced at the pain. He squinted at the Swiss nurse as he looked at her name tag. "Erika, thanks for the care. But I've got stuff to do."

"You're not fit to go anywhere."

Reznick looked around his private hospital room. His mind flashed back to the initial encounter with the fake Swiss cop. More flashbacks to the windowless room, restrained, listening to the CIA guy. He wondered if the Agency's Swiss crew had dumped him outside the hospital.

He remembered the dire warning the CIA guy had given him. He had to leave Switzerland in forty-eight hours. He had already been in here two full days and two nights. He considered the threats real. He knew mind games were standard CIA fare. But he took the threats to send him to a black site in Africa seriously.

Reznick pulled back the covers as he struggled unsteadily to his feet. The room swayed. His peripheral vision blurred for a few moments. The bastards had really worked him over.

The nurse helped him into the easy chair at the side of the bed. "Sit down for a little while. Your body needs to rest and repair itself."

Reznick closed his eyes for a few moments. She was probably right. But it just wasn't in his nature to sit around all day.

"Can I get you something to eat or drink?"

"A sandwich and coffee would be nice, thank you. And some Advil."

The nurse leaned in close, examining the stitches on his face. "These will dissolve in the next few days. But they are looking good. And clean."

"Clean is good."

"I'll get your sandwich and coffee. And some Advil. I won't be long."

Reznick reached to grab his cell phone, making a mental note to call Trevelle when he got out.

A few minutes later, there was a knock at the door.

Reznick slid the cell phone under a cushion. "Come in!"

The door slowly opened.

Lauren stood and smiled, tears in her eyes, holding a wooden tray of sandwiches and a mug of steaming-hot black coffee. "Hey, Dad."

Reznick felt his throat tighten. "What are you doing here?"

His daughter put down the tray on the bed and reached over to hug Reznick tight. "Dad," she sobbed, "I came as fast as I could."

"It's OK, honey, everything's fine. Don't worry."

"What happened to you?"

"You didn't need to come. It's nothing."

Lauren extricated herself from the hug and held his hand. "You look badly hurt. We need to get you home."

Reznick shook his head.

"Who did it, Dad?"

"Forget it. Besides, you should see the other guy."

Lauren gazed at him, eyes brimming with tears. "Why can't you do things like other guys your age? Play golf, go bowling."

"I don't want to play golf. I don't want to go bowling. I like doing what I do. Besides, I'll be fine."

"You don't look fine. One of these days you're going to get killed. I don't want to lose you."

"You'll never lose me. That's a promise."

Lauren wiped away the tears. "Dad, I don't know what to say."

"Why not *It's great to see you, Dad*?"

"Can you tell me what happened?"

"I don't want to talk about that."

"Why not?"

Reznick shrugged as he started eating the hospital ham sandwich. He ate greedily, famished. "This is nice."

Lauren sat down on the bed opposite his chair and smiled.

"Why on earth did you come out here? How did you find out?"

"I got a call."

"From who?"

"The clinical director, that's who. My details were in your wallet. She said you had been brought in at five in the morning two days ago. I caught the first available flight from New York to Zurich."

Reznick finished the sandwich and took a tentative gulp of the hot black coffee. It felt good to get some caffeine inside him. "You didn't have to. The FBI needs you."

"They'll manage without me for a few days."

"Work comes first. What have I always said?"

"Family comes first, Dad."

"Correct."

"So, that's why I'm putting you first. Besides, who looks after you?"

"I'm fine. And I've got things to do. Places to go. Truly, I'm fine."

"Dad, you're not going anywhere."

"Lauren, I've got work to do."

"In Switzerland?"

"Yes, in Switzerland. I can't go into detail. I'm doing a bit of consulting work, you know, here and there."

"For who?"

"Client confidentiality, sorry."

"Gimme a break. Was it your consulting work that got you beaten up?"

"Enough." Reznick finished his coffee and put the mug back down on the tray. "I want you to go home."

"But I came all this way."

"I know you did. And I appreciate it. But get yourself back home. You've seen for yourself that I'm fine."

"Not a chance. Besides, I talked to Martha about this."

Reznick took a few moments to take in what his daughter had said. "What?"

"I talked to Martha."

Reznick shook his head. "You talked to Martha about what happened to me?"

Lauren nodded.

"I would have appreciated if you had asked me first."

"I'm an adult, Dad. I can make grown-up choices about who I take into my confidence."

"This is my business."

"Dad, she's been very supportive. Always has been."

"What did she say when you told her?"

"She was worried sick. She wants to talk to you."

Reznick felt himself wince. It was the last thing he needed. He wondered what exactly Martha knew. Had she been in touch with the CIA and learned about Anna Bruckmann from them? Had she divulged anything about the true nature of his trip to Switzerland to Lauren? "I've got business to attend to. I need to get out of here.

You like being up-front. Well, I'm going to be up-front with you. It's not safe to hang around me."

"What?"

"There, I told you."

Lauren took out her cell phone and made a call. "Morning. Sorry to call so early, Martha. I've got my dad here."

Reznick couldn't believe his daughter was ordering him around. He wondered if the CIA or the NDB had monitored her movements from the airport. Had she been tailed to the hospital?

Lauren handed him the cell phone.

Reznick took the cell phone, pressed it to his ear. "Hey . . ."

"Jon?"

"You didn't have to get involved in this."

"What happened?"

"A few cuts and bruises, but I'm fine."

"How did that happen? Were you in an accident?"

"Long story."

"Is that right? Something tells me you were up to no good."

Reznick smiled. "Yeah, something like that."

"Are you feeling alright now?"

"Me? I'm great, never better."

"How did this happen, Jon?"

Reznick felt another stabbing pain in his head and winced. "Just a little scrape I got into. It's fine. A disagreement."

"I think you're holding out on me, Jon. I can't imagine anyone, one on one, getting the better of you."

"I'm not getting any younger, Martha, that's for sure."

"Are you in trouble, Jon? Can I help you in any way?"

"This is nothing I can't deal with."

"I can pull some strings to get you and Lauren back home tonight. How does that sound?"

"That won't be necessary. I'm staying a little while longer."

"I'd thought you'd want to get back home and recuperate."

"Don't worry, it's fine. I'm fine. It's all good."

A silence stretched between them for a few moments. "Do you mind telling me what exactly you're doing in Switzerland?"

Reznick wondered if she was holding back what she knew. He had to assume that she would have been tipped off about his run-in with the NDB and the Agency here in Switzerland. "I'll tell you when I get back. Martha, I appreciate your help, as always. Now, if it's alright with you, I'm going to hand you back to Lauren."

His daughter left the room, presumably to finish the conversation.

The nurse returned. "I hope you're not annoyed. It was important your next of kin was notified in some capacity."

"That's perfectly fine, thank you." Reznick slowly managed to get himself out of his chair and stand up straight. "I've overstayed my welcome. I'm checking out, ma'am. Right this moment."

Twenty-One

Muller paced a windowless room in the bowels of the Russian Embassy in Riyadh. He had eaten well, his every need catered to. But he felt sick. Not from the food. Not from poisoning. But from the thought that he had been played. Monumentally played.

He wondered how he could have been so naive. How could he have been so trusting? He had thought it would be straightforward. He would pass on the data. They would shelter him, then load up his secret bank accounts. It hadn't gone according to plan.

Muller had been duped. The Russians believed he might be a double agent. And he had to prove he wasn't.

It was so fucked up.

He had imagined they would want him to spend a few weeks dissecting the data with them. And that would have been fine. He had known there would be an intelligence debriefing. They would want to drill down through the intel. But it wasn't turning out like that. Not at all.

The sound of the door opening snapped him out of his dark thoughts.

A young, attractive, twentysomething Russian woman came in. She wore linen cargo pants and a gray Abercrombie & Fitch T-shirt. Toned, tanned arms. Very American. But she wasn't.

Muller straightened up and addressed the woman. "Where's Sergei and the other guy? I need to talk to them."

"Sit down."

"Why?"

"Sit down."

Muller did as he was told. "Who are you?"

The woman was standing there, hands on hips. "My name is Sasha. I work for the Russian Foreign Military Agency."

Muller felt sick again.

"You in the West refer to us as the GRU still. You may have heard of it."

Muller knew all about the GRU. It was now known as the Main Directorate of the General Staff of the Armed Forces of the Russian Federation. Fearsome reputation. The agency not only controlled the military intelligence service but also had its own special forces units. The agency was known for complex high-risk operations. Assassinations. Disappearances. It ran thousands of agents across Europe, many more around the world. But it also had tens of thousands of Spetsnaz troops under its command. They could be sent anywhere to track down dissenters. To be poisoned. Kidnapped. Never to be seen again. Was this really what they had in mind for him?

Sasha sat down opposite him. "Don't be afraid. I don't bite. Well, not much."

"I had a deal. An agreement."

"We don't see it like that. Contracts that are not written down are worth shit, are they not? Listen, Hans, you're the smartest guy in Switzerland. But we have a thousand other guys as smart as you in Russia. You might be indispensable in Switzerland. In Russia, you're just another brilliant mind. No big deal. And, here's the thing. You're expendable. We are all expendable."

Muller shook his head. "I've given you the crown fucking jewels. You'll have decrypted the contents of the SD card by now. Why aren't you happy with that?"

Sasha leaned back in her seat. "What can I tell you? We're Russians. We're never happy, right? At least that's what you in the West think."

"You think I'm a double agent. I'm not. There's nothing more to be said. I want to complete my side of the deal, then get the fuck out of here."

"I don't blame you. Not a great fan of Riyadh myself. But look, we are where we are. We need to establish where you're coming from. We can't take you at face value, can we?"

"How many times do I have to tell you? I stole the data and passed it to Russia. Not to anyone else. Not China. Not Iran. I gave it to you."

"And that is something we are very grateful for. We just want to make sure you are not an American spy. Our approach to the West and Westerners who help us has hardened somewhat since our special military operation in Ukraine."

"'Special military operation'? Is that what you call it?"

"We're at war. Make no mistake about it. We are at war with the West. Everyone is against us."

"And why do you think that is?"

Sasha smiled. "I'm not going to get into the semantics of NATO encroachment on our sphere of influence. I'm not going to get into a discussion about the installation of American missiles on Ukrainian soil before the invasion, aimed at obliterating strategic Russian facilities and infrastructure. I'm not even going to get into the Western encouragement of Ukraine to be a patsy to America and its interests on our doorstep, or the coup in 2014, which over-threw the Ukrainian government. No, I'm not going to get into anything like that. But what I will say is that we see you as more useful than Snowden. A way for us to let the world know about the nasty little secrets of the CIA and MI6 operations across Europe. The pervasive surveillance. No one's texts, calls, or messages are safe from prying, are they?"

Muller shook his head. He wondered how the hell he was going to extricate himself from not only Riyadh but Russian security agents. "How much more do you want?"

"We have conceived an idea which will give us definitive proof if you are a double agent or not. A way to prove to us that you are who you say you are."

"How many times do I have to tell you I'm not a double agent?"

"We have looked at your skill set. Thoroughly. And we're very impressed. Hans, we believe there is a way for you to convince us, definitively, that you are genuine."

"How?"

"We think you can do us a big favor . . ."

"How?"

"By neutralizing a CIA asset."

Muller took a few moments to let that sink in. He began to feel sick. "Have you lost your mind? I'm a cybersecurity expert. You want me to kill someone?"

"Deadly serious. You have other skills. And we believe this will allay any fears some of us have that you are a double agent. So, it's a win-win."

"It's not a win for me. I just want to get out of here and get on with my life."

"A decision has been made. You will have to return to Switzerland."

"I'm not returning to Switzerland."

"But you must." Sasha shook her head and leaned closer. "You will not be alone. I'm going to help you do what you've been tasked with doing. I will come with you. I will direct you. But you will neutralize the target, is that clear?"

"You're bluffing."

Sasha smiled. "Are you sure about that?"

Sasha picked up a remote control from the table and pointed it at the huge screen on the wall. "Watch! This is happening now. In real time."

Muller fixed his eyes on the screen. It showed his dear mother cleaning dishes in the kitchen.

"Gimmelwald. Way up in the Bernese Alps, right? A lovely old Swiss widow."

Muller felt tears fill his eyes. The mother who had doted on him. The mother who had sacrificed everything for him. The private schools. The private tutoring. The hiking. The outdoors. And the books, thousands and thousands of books. A quiet, respectable, brilliant woman.

"You love your mother, don't you? You loved your late father too. What would he want you to do?"

Muller composed himself and watched the real-time footage of his frail mother.

"We can get to her wherever or whenever we want. We know where she is twenty-four seven. The choice is yours."

Twenty-Two

The pain in Reznick's head subsided after a handful of Advil and some Dexedrine. He quickly got dressed, then left the hospital by a basement garage exit with Lauren, backpack slung over his shoulder.

Lauren tried to assist him as he grimaced and cursed under his breath.

"Dad, why are you being so stubborn?"

"I'm not stubborn. I'm independent minded. I don't want to be a sitting duck. Besides, I'm not going to die. At least not yet."

He checked them into a fancy hotel, Lauren in the adjoining room. "I'm starving," she admitted.

"Give me time to unpack. Then we'll eat."

Reznick dropped his backpack on a leather chair and opened the French doors to the balcony. He looked out over medieval Bern. In the far distance, the snow-covered Alps. A natural ancient protector against the elements for the city and its people. His instincts were and always had been to keep Lauren out of harm's way. He shielded her from things that she was too young to know or were too troubling. But she was a smart young woman. A special agent.

He wondered if this was the time to confide in Lauren. Was this the time to tell her the real reason he was in Switzerland? The fact remained that all he had were disparate pieces of a jigsaw puzzle. He thought he knew the big picture and how Anna Bruckmann fit into it. But he didn't know for sure. It was all just half-truths and educated guesswork.

But Lauren had a right to know. This was about her mother.

Reznick felt deeply conflicted about opening up to his daughter. He walked back inside, careful to lock the French doors. He went to the bathroom and checked himself in the mirror. He took off the dressings around his eye. It was swollen, black and blue from the savage beating. The abrasions and cuts were numerous. But they were clean.

He took a quick shower and put on some fresh clothes.

Reznick headed downstairs to the hotel restaurant for lunch, seeing a few glances in his direction as he walked over to where Lauren was already seated. His beautiful, confident daughter. He was so proud of her.

"How are you feeling, Dad?" she asked.

"Me? Hungry."

"Let's eat."

Reznick ordered a pizza and fries with a glass of red wine, while Lauren had grilled sea bass with a green salad and sparkling water.

"You're going to die with a diet like that, Dad," she said.

"We're all going to die."

"Yeah, but let's not rush it. You can't keep doing stuff like this."

"Don't lecture me, Lauren. It's not a good look. It's very puritanical. Besides, Europeans drink during the day. It's not frowned on."

"I know that."

"So, what's the problem?"

"I don't know. Find a hobby."

"Like what?"

"Tennis?"

Reznick winced. "Do I look like the kind of guy who plays tennis?"

Lauren laughed. "Fair point."

"Listen, I appreciate your interest in my health. It's very touching. But your old dad is fine. A bit beaten up, but fine. I just need you to get back home tomorrow morning while I get on with my work."

Lauren shook her head. "Not gonna happen, Dad."

"What do you mean?"

"It means I'm not going to the airport. I'm staying here, with you. I'm going to look after you."

"I don't need anyone to look after me."

Lauren pointed at his swollen eye. "You sure?"

"Are you following Martha's orders, is that what this is?"

Lauren blushed. "No, I'm not, as a matter of fact."

"Are you sure?"

"Positive."

Reznick leaned forward. "Here's the deal. I'll drive you to the airport tomorrow morning, first thing. And we can both get on with our lives."

"Nope. I know consultants. Management consultants. They worked for McKinsey, and they sure as hell don't end up looking like they've been hit by a truck."

"It's just cuts and bruises."

Lauren leaned in even closer. "Martha talked to my boss in New York."

"Why doesn't that surprise me?"

"He agreed to give me a couple weeks off. So, I'm here. And you need to get over it."

Reznick ate his food and wondered how much Martha knew about his investigation. "What else did she say?"

"She said . . ."

"What?"

Lauren spoke in a hushed whisper. "Dad, she mentioned that the CIA had taken an interest in you after you landed in

123

Switzerland. She said that your name had come up in recent high-level briefings."

Reznick said nothing.

"What's going on, Dad? Something is wrong. I need to know. Are you in some sort of trouble?"

Reznick stared off into the distance.

"Dad, you're miles away."

"Lauren, listen to me. You need to trust me. I can't explain right now. But I need some time alone."

Lauren rolled her eyes in disbelief. "Why is the CIA taking an interest in your trip?"

"That's what they do."

"Do you work for them? Did you used to work for them? Are you poking your nose into places it shouldn't be?"

"Let's not go there. Not now. Not here."

Lauren picked at her food, disinterested. "I'm here because I love you, Dad. You're all I've got. Just me and you. Mom's not here."

Reznick closed his eyes and bowed his head. He felt a sharp pain in his temple. He realized it was time to tell her what he knew. "Promise me that what I'm about to tell you, you won't share with anybody. I need you to give me your solemn word."

Lauren shrugged. "That goes without saying. Of course, I promise."

"There's no easy way to tell you what I learned. It's pretty devastating."

Reznick took out his cell phone and scrolled through his photos. He pulled up the grainy surveillance shot of Anna Bruckmann. He turned the phone.

"Who is she?"

"I think this woman might be your mother."

Twenty-Three

The hours that followed were a dark night of the soul.

Reznick and his daughter talked. He consoled her as she cried. He hugged her tight as they wrestled with the possibility that his wife and Lauren's mother might be alive.

Lauren sat in shocked silence, head in hands. She had been told that her mother died on 9/11. She had visited the memorial countless times. Inconsolable, each and every time.

"How is this possible, Dad? I want to know everything."

Reznick held her before he told her the full, terrible story.

"Let me get this straight. She joined the CIA before 9/11? Tell me how you connected the dots and ended up in Switzerland. This is unbelievable."

"My hacker friend, Trevelle. I've told you about him before."

"Sure."

"Trevelle put me in touch with a pal of his out in Colorado. Ex-NSA guy who had been sent a surveillance photograph from the Swiss IT expert who went on the run with classified information. Believed to be a Russian spy."

"That's insane."

"You can't even imagine. This Anna Bruckmann heads up a tech company in Geneva, apparently. The ex-NSA guy ran some advanced facial recognition tests using American intelligence databases, and it was a match for your mother. And I began to find out more about her. Whoever the hell she is."

Lauren listened intently as she eventually pulled herself together. Her face was pale, mascara smudged.

"It's shocking, I know," Reznick said.

"Is that why you got beaten up? For pursuing this?"

Reznick shrugged. "I was warned off by the NDB and a CIA crew. Told to go home, in no uncertain terms. I believe they were trying to shield Anna Bruckmann. I don't know why."

"So, you ignored the warning?"

"I want answers, Lauren! Yes, I ignored their warning. I believe Anna Bruckmann may very well be my wife."

Lauren dabbed her eyes with a handkerchief. "I seriously can't believe what I'm hearing, Dad. I feel like I've lost my mind."

"I went to a town called Arth, right on a lake, to what I believed was Anna's house. And it was."

"Oh my God. Did you speak to her?"

Reznick shook his head. "I spoke to her housekeeper. I learned that Anna had vanished a couple of days before I arrived. The whole house was cleared out."

"You think she was tipped off?"

"I believe she had been moved. No trace of her."

Lauren closed her eyes for a moment as if gathering her thoughts. "I don't want you to shut me out on this, Dad."

"I'm not going to shut you out. I will say that if you stay, your life could be on the line. These are serious people. That's why I want to get you back to the States."

"I'll take my chances. Besides, if it *is* my mother, I want to know why she left us. Why she left *me*. Why she disappeared. It's awful. And using 9/11 as a cover? That's sick!"

"Let's not get into supposition. This is very painful for both of us."

"I know."

Reznick's cell phone rang. The caller ID jumped from city to city across America. It could only be one person.

"I got something." The voice was tight. Tense.

"I'm listening."

"I've been looking around the computer files of the moving company. It's all online. The items were sent to a storage facility in Zurich."

Reznick grimaced. "I see."

"I'm not done. It took a lot longer than I thought, but I followed your advice and did some analysis of the cell phones of the housekeeper and her husband."

"She knew more than she was letting on?"

"Big-time. The housekeeper is more than just a housekeeper. She's a personal assistant. She sent messages via Telegram. Saying stuff like *Are you OK, Anna? Do you need anything? There was a guy looking for you.*"

"What was the response?"

"*Come to the chalet.*"

"'The chalet'?"

"This is where it gets interesting. The housekeeper's cell phone stays at her house in Arth. But the husband's cell phone I tracked remotely. GPS locations."

"Smart."

"I monitored his movements and tracked him to a chalet. It's located on the outskirts of Zermatt, right in the heart of the Swiss Alps."

Twenty-Four

The underground firing range was located in the soundproofed subbasement of the Russian Embassy in downtown Riyadh.

Muller felt goose bumps on his arms as he was escorted through the chilly corridor by Sasha.

"You'll be fine," she reassured him.

Sasha opened the door and nudged him gently into the range. She handed him a Glock and ear protectors. "American classic. Let's see what you've got." She pointed at the paper target. "Twenty meters, fifty meters, and then we'll try you with one hundred meters."

Muller felt as if he was living someone else's life. He put on the ear protectors. The cold steel of the Glock brought back memories of his short stint in the Swiss special forces. He had enjoyed the physical side of things. The running. The punishment. The days in the mountains. Survivalism. The guns. The boxing. But he had thought he left all that behind. His real skills were in computer security, cybersecurity, biometrics, mathematics.

Sasha put on her ear protectors. "Take aim! Twenty meters!"

Muller slowly raised the weapon. He took aim. He gripped the Glock tight. Then he squeezed off every last round. Fifteen shots. The paper target was shredded.

"Nice work! Let's see how you are at fifty and one hundred meters."

Muller surprised himself. He completed the tasks perfectly. His instincts were still strong.

"You know your shit. You sure you learned to shoot in Switzerland?"

Muller nodded.

"Let's do it a few more times."

"Fine."

Sasha ordered him to repeat the tasks five more times. Each time, Muller got the same results. He obliterated the target, no matter the distance.

"You're a natural."

Muller was already fast-forwarding to taking down the operative. He imagined catching a glimpse of the person's face. Then gunning them down.

"You got this, Hans," she said.

"Yes, I have."

Muller followed the svelte Russian operative to the elevator and headed up to the ground floor. He was escorted into what looked like a private cinema. Sasha indicated for him to take a seat.

Muller sat down on a large sofa as the screen lit up the darkened room. A few moments later a woman's face appeared on the screen. She looked immediately familiar. It looked like a surveillance photo of the American woman taken in Zurich.

"You have seen this face before," she reminded him.

"Yes, I have. She was originally identified as Anna Bruckmann. An American."

"But she's not, is she?"

"CIA asset?"

"Correct again. Look at her face. Memorize this face. You won't get a second chance with her. You need to kill or be killed."

"Wouldn't a sniper be better? Take her out from a distance."

"We want you to do it."

"But why me?"

"We want *you* to prove to us that you are on our side. We're testing your loyalty."

Muller took in the face of the man now on the screen.

"This is an American spy," Sasha said. "His name is Jon Reznick. He is a highly trained CIA killer. So, you might have your hands full."

"Who is he?"

"He's her husband."

Muller studied the images of Reznick. "You're sure this guy is in the country?"

"Correct. We have multiple intelligence sources giving us the same intel. And our files show that this is indeed Jon Reznick. A shadowy figure who has killed Jihadists in Berlin. Quds operatives in Africa. He is fearsome. I can't sugarcoat that."

"How can I get a gun into the country without being picked up at the Swiss border? How do I get through airport security?"

"Leave that to us."

"And you're confident I won't be searched?"

"Don't worry about specifics."

"I'm the fall guy. I'm the patsy. The Lee Harvey Oswald for you guys if it goes wrong."

"No, you aren't."

"How can you guarantee that I can get up close and kill this woman and get away from the situation?"

"We have a team working on multiple scenarios. The opportunity will present itself. You will be disguised, obviously."

Muller gazed into the cold eyes of the man on the screen.

"He is in Switzerland with one mission: he wants to get his wife. He is formidable. But you will take him out if required. Priority, Anna Bruckmann. You will blow her away. You will save your mother. And yourself."

Twenty-Five

It was nightfall as the train arrived in the car-free mountain resort of Zermatt.

Reznick stepped onto the icy platform with Lauren and surveyed the silhouetted Matterhorn in the distance.

They checked into a nearby hotel, not far from the chalet where Anna Bruckmann was believed to be staying.

"How are you feeling, Dad?" Lauren asked as she unpacked. "Your head, I mean."

Reznick felt like shit. Sharp headaches, pain in his ribs. "Nothing a couple of Advil and some Dexedrine won't fix."

"God, you need to cut out the speed habit, Dad. What is it with you and those pills? That is not healthy."

"Just a little amphetamine to keep me going. Only when I'm working."

"I think we need to talk about that."

Reznick held his daughter's weary glare. "I've got other things to worry about right now. I don't need lectures."

"Are we sure she's really here in Zermatt?"

Reznick hung up some polo shirts and a couple pairs of jeans. "She might be. The only problem with a direct approach is that the NDB might be hanging around. She might be under surveillance."

"Swiss intelligence?"

"Correct. A civilized crowd, most of the time."

"So, do we have a game plan?"

"I suggest we head over there, get a visual on the property. I need to know what I'm dealing with."

"You're not going to do anything without me, right? I thought we agreed that I'm not leaving."

"Relax. I just want to see the house up close."

Lauren frowned as if lost in her thoughts. "I'm worried you might get hurt. Really hurt."

"Get yourself settled in. I'll be back before you know it."

"And if you're not?"

"I will. Promise."

"What if she's not there?"

Reznick had wondered that himself. "Then we go to plan B."

"Which is?"

"We'll cross that bridge when we get to it."

Reznick trudged through the snow-covered streets, hands deep in his pockets. He had pulled on a gray beanie with a Swiss flag on the front, like so many tourists. The bars and shops were full, as were the sidewalks, mountain sports fanatics carrying skis and snowboards. The sound of pounding Euro dance music boomed out of one bar, then another. Part of him wished he was back down in the Lower Keys.

He brushed past a German family talking excitedly as he headed up a side road. He walked on the hard-packed snow for another couple hundred yards.

Reznick took out his cell phone and checked his GPS location. He was very close. He walked on for another fifty yards, past a couple of postal vans parked in the snowy road. His gaze was drawn to a modest wooden cabin cloaked in darkness. A number 2 was carved on a wooden plaque adjacent to the front door. He walked farther down the road toward a white police van. Was this surveillance of the property?

Reznick wondered if he could approach the house from the parallel road to check the rear. He headed past the police van and glanced inside. Front seats empty. But he noticed the rear windows were heavily tinted. Was there someone watching from the back of the vehicle, hidden from sight? He checked the license plate and made a mental note to run it past Trevelle.

He shuffled up a slippery incline and turned left, doubling back down a parallel road to the front of the house. He stopped at wrought iron gates with a number 2.

This was it.

Reznick was in luck. A pale light was on in an upstairs window. Was his wife in that house, behind that gate? Hiding in plain sight in a tourist town?

He was tempted to knock on the door. His instincts were telling him to walk up to the door and bang on it until someone answered. But he knew that would be foolish.

He returned to his top-floor hotel suite.

Lauren was waiting, expectantly. "So, what happened? Was she there?"

"No lights on at the front, but I headed around the back and saw a light on in an upstairs room."

"Maybe a preset security light?"

Reznick nodded. "Could be."

"Did you knock or ring the bell?"

"I decided to do nothing . . . for now. Let's watch and wait."

"I agree. We need to be careful. The last thing you need is to get picked up by the cops and handed over to the NDB or the American Embassy."

"A police van was parked a short distance away. One of the reasons I was reluctant to take the direct approach." Reznick took out his cell phone. "I think we should play this very carefully. The house might be key. It might not be. She might be in there. But if we knock or try and break in . . ."

"Who said anything about breaking in?"

"Let's just relax. Let me make a call."

Lauren shook her head, arms folded.

Reznick waited for three rings until a voice answered.

"Yo."

"I need some intel."

"Go!"

"The house where you believe Anna Bruckmann lives in Zermatt? Is there a landline?"

"I'm already ahead of you." Trevelle recited the number.

Reznick relayed the number to his daughter, who entered it into her cell phone.

"One final thing. I've got a Swiss police vehicle license plate."

"You're in Switzerland, Jon. You're going to get that."

"The police car was farther down the street. I'm curious. Can you run the plate through your system?"

"Not a problem."

"Just so I know what I'm dealing with."

Reznick gave the license plate. He heard Trevelle tapping on his keyboard. He waited for a few moments. "Anything?"

"That's interesting."

"What?"

"NDB."

"It's a police vehicle. I saw it clearly."

"Registered to the NDB in Bern."

Reznick ended the call.

"The NDB are the registered owners, despite the police insignia on the van," he explained to Lauren.

"That doesn't make sense."

"It's a way to blend in, locals thinking it's a police vehicle. It would arouse suspicion in the neighborhood if there was a big SUV no one had seen before."

"Maybe."

Reznick checked the street outside the hotel.

Lauren asked, "Swiss intelligence . . . You think they're in the house with her? Maybe a close protection team."

"It could be."

"That's problematic, to say the least."

"It's all supposition. Maybe the Swiss crew left the van there and checked into a hotel for the night."

Lauren began to pace the room. "We need to try to contact her, if she's there. We've come this far, right?"

"Slow is smooth. Let's get this right."

"Any ideas?"

"A few."

Twenty-Six

It was still dark.

Reznick had been awake for an hour and had showered and shaved. He brushed his teeth. Frayed stitches visible at the corner of his bloodshot, swollen right eye. He took a couple of Advil and a couple of Dexedrine. He knocked on his daughter's door to the adjoining room. "Time to get up, sleepyhead," he shouted.

A loud groan from next door. "Dad, are you kidding me? It's dark. What time is it?"

Reznick knocked hard again. "Get up!"

"Gimme a minute."

Reznick headed back into the living room. Lauren shuffled in, bleary eyed. She was wearing a Yankees sweatshirt, black jeans, and Timberland boots. She yawned. "What's the plan?"

"Breakfast. Then we move."

"You eat breakfast this early?"

"What the hell is wrong with you? Breakfast is first thing in the morning. When do you think breakfast is?"

"Dad, don't raise your voice."

Reznick smiled and hugged his daughter tight. "Sorry, honey, force of habit. What about some fancy Swiss croissants and coffee?"

"I'm starving. I'd love that."

They headed out into the icy darkness. They saw a few shops with their lights on, including a café. Reznick ordered a bag of warm croissants and two strong coffees to go. He and Lauren walked a couple hundred yards, eating their croissants and drinking their coffees. It wasn't long until they were close to the front of the chalet. He looked down the street. No police van.

"Surveillance vehicle is gone," she said.

"Maybe," Reznick said. "Maybe they just moved around the corner."

"Why don't we check?"

Reznick and Lauren walked along the road and up around the corner, then back down, which led to the rear of Anna Bruckmann's house. He pointed to the large iron gate. "This is it."

Lauren scanned the back of the house. "No lights on."

They found a bench fifty feet away, where they sat and ate the rest of their breakfast. When they finished, Lauren gathered the wrappers and cups and found a nearby trash can. Reznick stayed watching the dark house until a light went on in an upstairs room, behind the drapes.

Reznick saw a silhouetted figure behind the drapes, walking around. "You see that?"

"Got it."

"So, someone is definitely home. And they're an early riser."

"My stomach is in knots. What do you think we should do?"

"We don't know how many people are inside. It might be one, maybe two or three. But I think we should stay around here. I'd prefer our eyes on the front of the property."

"Agreed."

They got up from the bench and walked slowly around the corner.

Reznick and his daughter got less than a hundred yards away. Their position was partially concealed by other houses and some snow-covered fencing. He had a perfect sight line to the front door. "Still no white surveillance van."

"So, where are they?"

Reznick held his breath. His gaze was drawn to a hooded figure who emerged from the house. The figure wore a knee-length puffer jacket, a ski hat, dark glasses, thick gloves, and a scarf. He whispered, "We've got a visual."

Lauren bowed her head. "I don't want it to be true."

"Let's not get ahead of ourselves."

Reznick watched as the figure nearly slipped on the snow-packed road. He analyzed the gait of the figure. It was clearly a woman. Was that Anna Bruckmann?

"Is that her?" Lauren asked breathlessly.

"We don't know. Let's just wait and see. Take the other sidewalk. I'll tag along on the opposite side. Try and hang back as much as you can." He walked slowly through the dark streets in the wake of the figure.

The woman seemed to disappear for a few moments.

Reznick walked faster and caught sight of the figure again, near the edge of the center of Zermatt. She had a backpack over her shoulder. She headed down a snowy road flanked by big chalets. Then down another side street.

Reznick saw Lauren emerge in his peripheral vision. He stopped for a few moments. He took out his cell phone and called his daughter.

"Yeah?"

"I said hang back," he whispered. "No closer than fifty yards. You're way too close."

"You didn't have to call me."

"It looks better if she turns around, you'll be deep in conversation."

"Got it."

"Just try and hang back a bit more. Don't hang up. Stay on the line." He bent over as if tying his bootlaces as he watched the figure disappear down an alley. "You see where she went?"

"I see her."

Reznick hung back for a few agonizing seconds before going in the same direction.

He trudged on, head down. He got a visual once again, eyes trained on the figure a hundred yards or more up ahead.

The woman turned right into Zermatt's town center.

Reznick stopped as the woman took a call on the street.

"You see that?" Lauren asked.

"Don't panic. Cross over and walk with me."

Lauren shuffled up to him, shaking the snow from her boots. The figure kept going along the near-empty street until she arrived at a shop with its lights on. An Italian café, Frankies.

The woman went inside.

Reznick watched as she sat down alone at the window. He checked the location. The café was located on Kirchstrasse, beside Hotel Antika. Was she meeting someone there?

"Dad, I'm going in."

"What?"

"Think about it. If it is her, and you went in, she would recognize you immediately. She doesn't know what I look like."

"Do it. But be careful."

Twenty-Seven

Reznick positioned himself a bit farther down the street, diagonal from the café. He was cloaked in darkness, face swathed in a scarf, hood up against the cold. The woman continued to sit at a table and sip what looked like a cup of coffee. Lauren circled around behind her after ordering, trying to get a closer look without making herself obvious. The minutes dragged.

His cell phone vibrated in his pocket.

"Dad, it's not her," Lauren whispered.

"What?"

"I've got a visual. I managed to get a photo too. I just sent it to you as a secure message."

Reznick scrolled through his cell phone and opened the message. The woman looked Slavic. Beautiful. Definitely not his wife, though.

He forwarded the photo of the woman in the café to Trevelle with the simple message *Can you identify this woman?*

Reznick sighed. "Copy that, Lauren. Turn right when you leave. I'm farther down the street."

"What's the plan?"

"We drop back a bit and wait out of sight, until she leaves the coffee shop."

"But it's not Mom."

"I know."

"So, we follow her?"

"You got it."

"What's the point?"

"The point is to find out who this woman is or where she is going. Maybe both. Is she going to meet someone?"

"Dad, I'm starting to think this is all a waste of time. It could be a wild goose chase."

"Maybe it is. But we've come this far. Let's see how this plays out."

It was thirty-two long minutes later when the woman finally emerged from the café, backpack still slung over her shoulder. He began to track her as discreetly as he could. He could have been any winter tourist to the town.

She headed north along Bahnhofstrasse. Past Zermatt's upmarket bespoke jewelers, banks, restaurants, and bars, until she got to the railway station.

Reznick caught sight of Lauren on the sidewalk on the other side of the snowy road. She crossed over as he continued on his way. They worked in tandem as they followed the woman through the town.

Lauren got to the train station first. It was packed with skiers and tourists all bundled up. She waited until Reznick arrived a few moments later.

"Where is she?"

"I think she bought a ticket for the train that just arrived. She spoke German."

Reznick bought a couple of tickets. He handed one to Lauren. "Get on the train first. I'll join you in a minute."

They waited in line before they boarded separately.

Reznick got on near the back of the train and sat down. He had a clear line of sight to the woman. She had taken off her scarf and appeared to be speaking into her cell phone. He watched as Lauren slid into her seat farther forward, eight rows back from the woman.

He had no idea who the woman was. She might be a house-keeper. But she might lead them to Anna Bruckmann. At least that was the hope that had formed in Reznick's head.

A few minutes later, the train pulled away, the sound of metal grinding as it crawled from the station.

Reznick listened to a British couple talking excitedly about ski-ing off-piste. The train headed down from Zermatt into the winter wonderland below. He wondered where the woman was going. She didn't have skiing gear. But she must have spent the night in the chalet. So, that wouldn't point to a housekeeper.

The first stop came, and the train slowed down as it approached the village of Tasch. It looked bleak, nothing much there. He searched online. The village was five kilometers due north from Zermatt at a slightly lower altitude. He shifted in his seat. He watched the woman. But she didn't move from her seat, cell phone still pressed to her ear.

The train sat at the station. He didn't know what the delay was. A handful of snowboarders climbed on, laughing and high-fiving, as if excited about the day ahead on the lower slopes. Eventually, the train pulled away.

Reznick sat in silence. He remained alert. He glanced at Lauren, who was gazing at the back of the woman's head. The minutes dragged. A short while later, the train pulled up at Randa, a tiny mountain village.

A few tourists and winter sports people got off. The woman got to her feet.

Reznick didn't move for a few moments, swallowing the residue of the Dexedrine. He waited until everyone was off the train before he got off, Lauren following close behind.

He stood on the platform as Lauren brushed past him and set off after the woman. He waited a few moments as the train trundled away before he left the station. The woman dropped out of sight for a few moments. But he caught sight of her shortly after.

She headed into an alpine-style hotel, across from the tiny mountain railway station.

Lauren walked on past the hotel and stood at the far end of a snow-packed parking lot.

Reznick waited for a few moments. His cell phone vibrated.

"You there, Dad?"

"Yeah."

Lauren was a hundred and fifty yards or so up ahead, wrapped up, partially concealed by a delivery truck. "You got a visual?"

"Copy that. The hotel."

"How do you want to work this?"

Reznick saw a second exit farther down the street. "Cover the fire exit closest to you. You see it?"

Lauren turned and looked toward the emergency exit. "What now?"

"Watch and wait. She might be meeting up with a friend. Let's just stay focused."

"Dad, are we wasting our time here?"

"We'll see soon enough."

Twenty minutes later, the woman came back out and crossed the road back to the train station.

"The backpack is black, Dad," Lauren said. "She went in with a dark-brown leather backpack. I distinctly remember her looking inside the backpack at the café."

"Copy that." Reznick reflected on what that meant. "I'm going to hang around here. You see if she heads back to Zermatt."

"What are you going to do?"

"Don't worry about me. We'll rendezvous back in Zermatt."

Reznick watched as Lauren, cell phone pressed to her ear, walked back toward the train station.

"I'm going to see where she's going. She might be going back to the house in Zermatt."

"Maybe. Whatever you do, look after yourself."

"I got this, Dad."

"I'll see you back in Zermatt within the hour."

Twenty-Eight

He felt it in his bones that it was the location of a dead drop. Was the person Reznick and Lauren had followed a Swiss cutout? The woman spoke German. Was she in touch with Anna Bruckmann? Was the woman known as Bruckmann actually inside the hotel at that moment?

The more he thought about it, the more he realized how little he knew of his dead wife. How was it possible that he didn't know her at all? Was this deception because she was an unhappy wife? Was it a way to escape it all? Was it her way of coping with their fractured relationship? A relationship and marriage he had mistakenly thought was strong?

He had to take a slice of the blame. He remembered what he was like. A warrior locked into his private world of the Delta cadre. Months-long trips overseas. Training. Fighting. Killing. Then repeat. Desert warfare. Assassinations. Covert missions. Training. Deployments. The sheer madness of it all.

He had returned to his hometown a killing machine. A man who could only relate on a superficial level. Or so it seemed. Trapped with his thoughts about codes of honor. His Delta comrades. Blood brothers. Men he had fought with. Men who had died next to him.

The routine and dull everyday problems of bills, relationships, and small-town bullshit held no interest for him. So, he stayed out drinking. Elisabeth didn't like that.

His mind flashed back to the early days. The good times they had. Not only in the beginning, but after the birth of their daughter. Maybe that's when things had started to unravel. He stayed out later when he was home. Domestic life weighed on him. He struggled to adjust. To relate.

Now, he stole glances at the entrance of the hotel, occasionally checking his watch as if waiting for a friend. Skiers emerging from the hotel, hikers wrapped up, winter climbers carrying huge backpacks, climbing ropes and crampons attached.

Reznick turned and looked toward the station. He wondered if he should head back to Zermatt. But it was then, at that moment, he saw something.

Out of the corner of his eye, thirty yards or so away.

Reznick turned around. A woman wrapped up in a heavy black winter coat headed toward the hotel. She wore a plaid scarf wound around her neck and mouth, sunglasses on. Ski hat. The walk was familiar. Very controlled, arms tight to her sides.

It couldn't be, could it?

Reznick breathed hard, the cold air turning to vapor in the icy chill. His heart raced. It wasn't just the amphetamines and coffee. It had been more than twenty long years. There was something about the gait of the woman in the long black coat who was now heading into the hotel.

It couldn't be, could it?

She never strolled anywhere. She walked quickly. Striding as fast as she could as if late for a meeting.

Reznick took a few deep breaths, hands thrust deep into his overcoat pockets. He wondered whether he should call Lauren. She had a right to know about the woman's arrival. It could be her. But something within him, deep within the very fiber of his being, told him no. Not now. Not at this moment. This was his time. He had to know for sure. He had to know who that woman was for certain. He wanted it to be Elisabeth. But he needed to look into her eyes. Then he would know.

He gazed at the entrance of the alpine hotel, nestled high in the shadow of the Matterhorn. A world away from New York.

Reznick's cell phone vibrated.

"Jon, it's Trevelle."

"What you got on the photo I sent?"

"Name is Helena Gruber. She's senior NDB. Swiss intelligence. Do you copy?"

"Copy that."

"Anything else?"

"Good work, my friend."

"Take care, man."

Reznick ended the call. He had a clearer picture of what had gone down. He took a few deep breaths. He strode toward the hotel as crazy thoughts careened through his mind.

He pushed open the heavy outside door and went inside.

The log fire burned and crackled in the cozy lobby.

A young receptionist smiled warmly. *"Guten Morgen."*

Reznick took off his sunglasses and smiled. "Do you speak English?"

"A little. How can I help you?"

"I'm sorry to bother you. I'm supposed to be meeting a woman. Long black coat. She had a plaid scarf kind of thing. Sunglasses. I think I missed her when she came in just a few minutes ago."

The receptionist checked his computer screen. "Ah . . . let me see. Ms. Fischer. She'll be having morning coffee in the restaurant, sir. Just through there." The receptionist pointed in the direction of the restaurant.

Reznick saw a few rosy-cheeked people wearing thick sweaters.

"Go right through, sir."

"Thank you so much."

Reznick walked into the restaurant. A woman with short black hair sat at a booth by herself, checking her cell phone. Sunglasses still on, brown leather backpack by her side. The woman looked different from the wife he knew. It wasn't just the short hair. Her face seemed leaner, more angular. He wasn't sure.

He walked up to the table and looked down. It really was her.

She glanced up at him, and her gaze held.

"Hello, Elisabeth. Or should I call you Anna?"

The woman took her sunglasses off, blue eyes as icy as the snow outside. It was in that moment he knew it was her. *Elisabeth is alive.* But this woman was very different. Cheekbones slightly higher, more pronounced, as if she'd had Botox or maybe surgery. "Excuse me?" Her voice hadn't lost her New York accent. Highly educated, hard edge. "Do I know you?"

Reznick sat down. "A long time ago."

The woman stared at him.

"Well, this is awkward."

The woman said nothing.

"Look at me!"

The woman sat frozen, as if in shock. Her eyes gave her away. She had great eyes. You could disappear into them. At least that's what he had always felt.

Reznick leaned closer. "I know who you are."

"You are mistaken."

Reznick shook his head. "I don't think so. I can look into your eyes, Elisabeth, and see it all. It's you. Don't treat me like a fool."

A silence stretched between them. It seemed to go on for hours.

The woman cleared her throat as she looked deep into her coffee. "You shouldn't be here."

"I *am* here. I'm your husband. Remember me?"

The woman flushed a deep red.

The waiter came over with a coffee for him.

"What on earth are you doing here?"

"Are you serious? I was about to ask you the same thing. I'm looking for answers. I'm looking for my wife. The wife I thought was dead."

Elisabeth was quiet for a few moments as if gathering her thoughts. "This is not what I wanted."

Reznick took a few gulps of the coffee. "No kidding."

"How did you find me?"

"With some difficulty."

"I really, really don't know what to say."

Reznick leaned even closer. "Let me help you out. You go by the name *Anna Bruckmann*, but your real name is Elisabeth Reznick. You used to be married to this guy, couple of decades back. Bit of a crazy, wild guy. Military type. He was a lot younger then."

"I can't believe this is happening. This is not the right time."

"Bit of a mind fuck, right?" Elisabeth shut her eyes tightly, as if trying to block out Reznick's face. "Not the right time, huh? Really?"

"Please, this is not the right time to explain. You don't understand."

"What don't I understand?"

"You need to go."

Reznick shook his head.

"I said you need to go."

"Go where?"

"You need to go home. And forget everything. Forget you saw me. It's for the best."

"Why?"

"You can't be seen with me."

Reznick's gaze wandered around the near-empty restaurant. "It's only me and you, Elisabeth. Maybe an elderly diner or two by the door, reading their morning newspapers."

"I don't know what to say. You'll think I'm crazy."

Reznick shook his head. "That's where you're wrong. I think it's me who's crazy, Elisabeth. I've been under the assumption that you died more than two decades ago. Twenty fucking years. A lot of water under the bridge."

Elisabeth sipped some coffee, a slight tremor in her hand. "I know that."

"Do you? Do you really?"

"Listen to me, you need to forget you met me. Forget my face."

Reznick looked at her hand as it rested on the brown backpack beside her. "Neat little trick you guys pulled. The old dead drop routine, huh? That the cutout I saw?"

Elisabeth flushed.

"You want to tell me what's in the bag? Is that the same bag the woman from the NDB handed over? That's who she is, I know."

"You have no idea what you're talking about."

"Quite an elaborate deception you've got going, Elisabeth. I can't wait to hear the explanation."

"Why are you following me?"

"I'm asking the questions, Elisabeth. Or should I call you Anna? Is that your name in Europe?"

"You can't be seen with me."

"That's the second time you've said that."

"It's true."

"Why not?"

"I'm not going to get into it."

"Listen to me. I want answers, Elisabeth. Don't I deserve at least that?"

Elisabeth's gaze darted around the restaurant. "Keep your voice down. If they see you, you're in mortal danger."

"Who's *they*?"

Elisabeth shook her head.

"Talk to me! I deserve, if nothing else, an explanation."

Elisabeth nodded but said nothing. She kept her hand on the backpack.

Reznick set his coffee mug aside. "Now, I don't know if you had a breakdown, if you didn't want to live the life you were leading, or if you just wanted to get the hell out of New York, leaving behind your old life, your husband, and baby daughter. I don't know. Maybe it was me, fine. But what I want from you is a straight answer. You either tell me what's going on, what *has* gone on, or I will, so help me God, call the editor of the *New York Times* and tell him what I know. You want a media shitstorm? You know how that kind of thing plays out."

Elisabeth shook her head meekly.

"Think about it. Imagine the headlines. My wife, Ivy League lawyer and all that, dies on 9/11, or so we're all led to think. But all these years later she's found alive and well and living in Switzerland. Under an assumed name. You think that'll sell a few copies?"

"You have no idea what or who you're dealing with."

"Then tell me who I'm dealing with. And tell me the truth."

Twenty-Nine

The Eisenhower Executive Office Building, located next to the West Wing of the White House, hosted the offices of the National Security Council.

Charles Gronski passed yawning political interns who gazed at their cell phones as if in a trance. He abhorred the plethora of young academics masquerading as geopolitical military experts. Most of them didn't understand the first thing about the reality of warfare. The State Department was full of them. Graduates from Johns Hopkins, Tufts, Harvard. All the elite American schools. But none of the so-called advisors to his political masters would have fought. That was the thing. Very rarely did any of them have actual combat or military experience.

He preferred his own people. The men and women of the Department of Defense. The patriots. The folks who knew what war was all about. The dirty, messy, bloody reality which they all too rarely saw or understood.

Gronski had already been awake for more than three hours. He had already swum fifty lengths at the Pentagon pool and followed it up with a workout at the gym. Then he followed that with a light breakfast of muesli, fresh-squeezed orange juice, and a double espresso.

He walked into the open conference room and sat down opposite Philip Hudson. The little brat smirked as if he had devised some *fiendishly difficult* question or hypothetical scenario, as Hudson was fond of calling them. The guy liked the sound of his own voice. He was a candy-ass.

"Morning, Philip," Gronski said. He sat down and took out the briefing papers from his briefcase, laying them neatly in front of him.

"I was talking to a friend of mine in Qatar about our situation," Hudson said. "He mentioned you, interestingly."

"In what context?"

"In the context of seeming to be part of a delegation three months ago lobbying for America to supply Qatar's military with our finest surface-to-air missiles, as well as a whole bunch of other hardware."

Gronski shifted in his seat. "Small potatoes, nothing more."

"Is it?"

"You know very well that it is."

"I don't want any distractions now. I want your full attention, Charles, on this issue in Switzerland. Are we clear?"

"You got it."

"So, Charles," Hudson said, "I just got off a secure line to the CIA station chief in Switzerland."

Gronski had an inkling of what lay in store. "Glad someone is up early."

"Here's the thing. The President seems to be out of the loop here. And it annoys him. Why is that?"

"I don't accept that, Philip. I can assure you he has all the relevant information."

Hudson gave a patronizing smile. "Let's set that point aside if we can. Thing is, we're still no closer to knowing the whereabouts of the missing IT expert. That sounds to me quite incredible with all the resources of the CIA and the State Department at our disposal."

Gronski leaned forward, checking his notes. "You're asking the wrong person. I have oversight of special access programs."

"But the hunt for this guy encroaches on covert operations the CIA and the Pentagon are running."

Gronski eyed Hudson. He knew the advisor was probing. "What's your point?"

"The update I received this morning is that Jon Reznick and now also his daughter, an FBI special agent, no less, are looking for Anna Bruckmann. I mean, what the fuck is going on?"

"I believe I know what this concerns."

"Well, good. So, what's the Pentagon saying? What's the line?"

"To your first point, the Pentagon is leveraging all our resources and assets in Western Europe to find the whereabouts of Hans Muller. Latest intel reports he was doing some online Russian classes over the last six months."

Hudson flushed like an errant schoolboy. "I didn't know that."

"CIA back channel informed me that Muller's computer was checked. The search history, the cache, a deep clean, the full code. However, we have identified another secure login he was using."

"So, he's using other computers?"

Gronski nodded. "Wrapped up in a virtual private network based in Iceland, but the NSA has cracked the code. So, it's pointing to Russian espionage."

"A Swiss Edward Snowden, is that what you're saying?"

"Potentially as damaging."

"So, this guy is on the run, maybe hiding out in a safe house, with Russian operatives protecting him, and with the potential for all our American secret communications shared with Switzerland to be in Russian hands?"

"One hundred percent correct."

Hudson scribbled some notes. "What a clusterfuck."

"I don't disagree."

Hudson frowned at Gronski, looking like some spoiled trust fund kid who thought he knew everything. "Let's talk about Anna Bruckmann. Have you ever met her?"

Gronski checked his notes. He knew this was where things were going to get testy. He couldn't allow Hudson to know all the details on this operative. He wouldn't put it past Hudson to gossip to his pals who hung out at the nearby Union Pub, close to Capitol Hill. "She's safe, for now."

Hudson scribbled some notes. "So, I've written here verbatim, *She's safe, for now.* OK?"

"Correct."

"Tell me more. Lay it out for me."

"A Swiss intelligence official is being used as the cutout to communicate. That's about as much as I can say. But Anna is safe."

"Anna is safe . . . for now . . ."

Gronski sat in silence as Hudson bit his lip and studied his notes.

"The CIA is saying," Hudson conveyed, "that the Pentagon has sent a specialist extraction team to Switzerland. Have they arrived?"

"They have been sent, that's correct. But they've encountered a few logistical problems."

"What?"

"I won't go into detail. But they are expected to arrive within the next few hours in Bern. We're liaising with German intelligence too. It's under control."

"So, we should get her back on American soil tomorrow or the day after?"

"We're taking this hour by hour. But yes, that's the plan."

Hudson leafed through his notes for a few moments. "Let's get back to Jon Reznick. I'm a bit thrown by this guy."

"Why?"

"Correct me if I'm wrong, but I believe you've worked with him in the past. Tell me more about this wild card."

"I'm not going to go there."

"Why not?"

Gronski steepled his fingers. "Some stuff is classified, you know that."

"Don't fucking patronize me, Charles."

"I wasn't patronizing you. I was just telling you a fact."

"Has Reznick ever worked on highly classified operations?"

"I can't discuss that or even acknowledge such operations, if they existed. That's just a simple statement of fact."

"Charles, tell me what you can about Reznick. I'm curious."

"I can't elaborate on any operations or intelligence aspects."

"Can't or won't?"

Gronski said nothing.

"I'm not asking you to talk about operations. I want to know more about Reznick, the man. I've talked to quite a few people in the intelligence community."

"And?"

Hudson was quiet for a few moments. "A few have said he's a rogue soldier."

"Not the man I knew. At least not when I knew him."

"A few mentioned that he was a psychopathic killer. Their words, not mine."

"Not true. Categorically not true."

"How can you be so sure?"

"I've seen his file. Have you?"

Hudson shook his head. "Can I have access to that?"

"Not a chance."

"You say he's not a psychopathic killer. What evidence do you base that on?"

"CIA psychology reports. Very extensive."

"And what was the conclusion? Give me a broad insight."

"He had a very, very rare skill set, psychologically speaking."

"Meaning?"

"Meaning he could compartmentalize his job, namely killing people, but still continue to function, to empathize, to sympathize, the way an ordinary man, like you or I, would."

"And that's definitive?"

"Absolutely. He's not crazy. He is, let's say, attuned to his environment. Like he's got a sixth sense. But he has fearlessness, courage and toughness, relentlessness, combined with high intelligence. It made him one of our very best."

Hudson smiled an empty smile. "Here's the thing, Charles. He's getting in the way."

"Reznick?"

"Precisely. He's inserting himself into a highly sensitive special access program. That is what this is all about, right? The special access program. Anna Bruckmann."

Gronski cleared his throat. "Philip, my main focus and concern is protecting the integrity of special access programs."

Hudson adroitly changed the subject. "What's the very latest on the extraction team you've sent?"

"As I said, a few logistical holdups."

"What else?"

"Well, our intelligence partners in Europe are on the same page. We know the importance and potential consequences if we don't bring this Swiss traitor to justice."

"MI6 in London and the Bundesnachrichtendienst in Berlin— they're kept fully abreast? I'm not going to get any unusual surprises when I speak to London in an hour's time?"

"Correct. But I have something you might find interesting ahead of your chat. But also worrying. I'm trying to be as forthcoming as I can."

"What've you got?"

"The head of British intelligence gave the Pentagon a briefing late yesterday. It highlights the latest British intelligence on Russian penetration of European institutions and telecommunications networks."

Hudson took more notes. "Why don't I know about this?"

"My office is couriering a memo outlining the main points to you within the hour."

Hudson scribbled some more notes. "What did the British say?"

"Hans Muller is not the only Swiss intelligence operative working for the Russians."

"You're fucking kidding me."

"According to the Brits, the NDB has been penetrated at a high level by another operative."

"You got a name?"

"Yes."

"Can you divulge that name?"

"Her name is Helena Gruber."

Hudson wrote down the name. "Gruber?"

"Right."

"I met her at a NATO summit in Madrid last year. This is concerning."

"To say the least. What is most concerning from the Pentagon's point of view is that Gruber has not only gone undetected for so long, but she is also an influential member of Club de Bern, the intelligence-sharing forum between the intelligence services of the twenty-seven European Union countries, as well as Norway and Switzerland."

"Are we sure Gruber is working for the Russians?"

"The British are quite clear on that. They have photographs of her talking with the daughter of a Russian émigré who lives in Milan, in a private dining room at a restaurant in Rome. They believe the daughter is a back channel. It threw up all kinds of red flags."

Muller scribbled more notes. "I can imagine."

"What's more, Gruber has access to a ton of intelligence which could compromise American operations and intelligence-gathering networks in Switzerland and beyond."

"We need Anna Bruckmann out of there."

"I know we do. But this is a very delicate matter. We need to consider Reznick and his daughter. How we deal with that side of things."

"I don't care about Reznick. He's expendable."

Gronski tried to stay level-headed. "It's not as simple as that."

"Fuck Reznick and his FBI daughter. I want our asset out of there now!"

"This will happen in an orderly manner. You can't rush these things. That in itself can cause alarm. Moscow will notice sudden arrivals in Switzerland. We don't want to show our hand. Not yet."

Thirty

Reznick was struggling to take it all in. Here he was sitting in a hotel in Randa, high up in the Swiss Alps, next to a roaring fire. And staring back at him was his dead wife.

But it wasn't how he remembered her at all.

Elisabeth shifted in her seat. "Stop looking at me like that, will you?"

"You had some work done?"

"Is that a problem?"

"Change of face, change of identity, right?"

"Why does that concern you?"

Reznick shrugged.

"Yes, I did, now that you mention it."

"Part of the new you?"

"Yes, the new me. A surgeon in Zurich, if you're interested."

"'A surgeon in Zurich,'" he parroted. "Fabulous."

"Don't be so sarcastic."

"I've heard about stuff like this. Was this a requirement speci-fied by the Agency?"

Elisabeth closed her eyes as if tired of all the questions. "It was easier. Made sense."

"Who paid for it? The CIA?"

Elisabeth nodded.

"That was nice of them. Looks expensive too."

"I didn't want this to happen. I didn't want any of this. I didn't want you to see me again."

"But it did happen, didn't it? I can't unsee you."

Elisabeth nodded.

"And I still haven't gotten any answers."

"I can't talk about what I know."

"Why not?"

"It's classified. You know how it works."

"You've changed. You're colder than the woman I knew."

"Why do you think that is?"

"I don't know . . . Guilt? Maybe what you did has eaten away at you. I don't know."

"I just want to get on with my life."

"What about our daughter? Lauren? Have you forgotten about her?"

"No, of course not."

"Are you interested in her?"

"Yes, of course. What do you think I am?"

"Do you understand the impact you leaving had on her? Not then, she was just a baby. But growing up. She asked me all the time about you. She had a scrapbook of photos of you."

Elisabeth stared back at him, almost defiantly.

"Do you know that your daughter, our daughter, is here?"

Elisabeth gasped in shock. "Lauren? Here in Switzerland?"

"She's all grown up now. Real smart. Like her mom."

"I can't face her, Jon. I just can't. I can't do this. This is what I feared would happen. That it would all unravel one day."

"Will you, for the love of God, stop being so self-absorbed? What about your daughter? Aren't you worried about what this will do to her?"

"I'm sorry, this is hard for me too. I'm struggling to find the words. I'm trying to process all of this."

"How do you think she feels? How do you think *your daughter* feels?"

"Who does she look like?"

"You. How you used to look. She's beautiful. She really is."

Elisabeth put her head in her hands.

"I don't know what the hell you were thinking," Reznick said. "I don't think I'll ever understand. I don't know if I want to. But you need to see your daughter."

"Where is she exactly?"

"She's tracking the woman who gave you the backpack."

"Oh my God. She needs to be careful."

"Why? Who is she?"

"Swiss intelligence."

"Gruber?"

Elisabeth nodded. "How did you know?"

"You don't need to know. Your daughter is tailing her back to Zermatt."

"She's at risk. You're both at risk."

"Don't you think I know that? You need to talk to your daughter."

"I can't face her. I want to try and explain." Elisabeth took a deep breath. "One day. But not now."

"Why not? Don't I deserve an answer? Doesn't Lauren deserve to know why her mother abandoned her? She was a baby. You abandoned your baby. Did you ever consider what that would do to her? You know, she asks about you. She wanted to know what sort of person you were."

Elisabeth's gaze wandered around the restaurant. "You're getting loud."

"What do you suggest?"

"Can we talk somewhere else?"

"Where?"

Elisabeth whispered, "My cabin."

"You live in this village?"

"No. I live about half an hour away. It's a short hike. Isolated. Can't approach by car."

"Why not?"

"It's on the other side of the suspension bridge."

"What?"

"Hope you're not afraid of heights."

"Why?"

"It's closed in the winter. And it's a long, long way down."

The skies darkened as the snow fell.

Reznick walked in silence with Elisabeth to the far end of the village of Randa. Past a small church, then up a snowy path. He wondered if he should contact Lauren to let her know. He figured he could get in touch once he and Elisabeth sat down to talk. But it had to be alone.

Elisabeth pulled her hat down low and flipped up the collar of her thick coat as they hiked through heavily wooded forest above the village. "Tell me about Lauren."

"Are you serious?"

"Tell me more about Lauren. You said she's smart."

"She's smart, no question. And tough. She's an FBI special agent in New York."

"Are you kidding me?"

"No, I'm not."

"I have to meet her, don't I?"

"Most certainly."

"I'm scared."

"Let's take this one step at a time, Elisabeth."

Elisabeth quickened her pace. "It's been twenty years. I haven't seen her in over twenty years. She was a baby when I left. Does she even want to meet me?"

"She will."

"She won't judge me?"

"Maybe. Try and imagine things from her perspective. She's spent the last twenty years thinking you were dead."

The pair of them trudged along the snowy incline for a few hundred yards more.

Elisabeth turned to Reznick. "She has every right to judge me."

"She absolutely does."

"I'm worried, Jon."

"We'll figure things out. First things first."

"I don't mean on a personal level. You have to understand, things are dangerous in Switzerland."

"You think you're being watched?"

Elisabeth shook her head. "I don't know. But you're at risk."

"I know all about risk."

"And Lauren?"

"She's not naive."

"Jon, you must hate me."

Reznick shook his head. "I don't hate you. I just want to understand. That's all I want."

"It's a lot to talk about."

He walked on, climbing up the icy path as they headed through a heavily wooded section. "How far to go?"

Elisabeth pointed to a clearing up ahead in the woods. "It's on the other side."

They continued on and approached a breathtaking sight: a high suspension bridge across the snowy ravine.

"Like I said, hope you're not afraid of heights."

"You live on the other side?"

"I just moved in last week. This is the Charles Kuonen Suspension Bridge."

Reznick took a tentative step onto the icy bridge and looked down at the sheer drop. "You weren't kidding."

"It's closed in the winter. No one comes up here. I'm safe, at least for now."

Elisabeth led the way across the bridge, partially covered by snow.

The bridge wobbled, fresh snow falling down into the ravine below.

Reznick followed her across as the bridge swayed and creaked. The icy high-altitude wind buffeted them as they made their way across. It took about ten minutes to reach the other side. His heart beat fast the entire time.

"Almost there," she said.

Reznick stepped off and looked back.

Elisabeth trudged on.

Reznick followed close behind through another heavily wooded section and down a winding, icy path. He wondered if she was as safe as she assumed. He thought it was too isolated. She would be trapped if she needed to escape or call for help.

"Here we are!"

The log cabin was covered in snow, nestled deep in a mountainous Swiss forest.

Elisabeth unlocked the door of her alpine safe house and invited Reznick inside. He thought she was a sitting duck. No one would be able to hear her scream if she was tracked down. But he didn't share his thoughts with her. She carefully triple-locked the door behind them.

"Well tucked away, that's for sure."

"That was the point. Helena Gruber and I meet up occasionally at the hotel. The Agency thought the cabin was the perfect place for me. Can I get you a drink?"

"Coffee's good. Strong black."

Elisabeth fixed them each a mug of steaming hot coffee. She sat down on the sofa opposite him. "This is weird," she said. "I feel like I'm going to be sick."

Reznick drank some coffee and set down the mug on a coffee table on the fireside rug. "Please don't."

"You have every right to be angry. Your world was destroyed. The life you had was gone."

Reznick averted his gaze.

"I want to tell you. Actually, I need to tell you. You already know my true identity."

"How did this start for you?"

"Switzerland?"

"The disappearance. Everything."

"What do you know? And how do you know?"

"A set of circumstances. A freak occurrence."

"What do you mean?"

"It was only a week or two ago that I learned you worked in World Trade Center Building 7."

Elisabeth scrunched up her face.

"So, you want to know how I know? It started when I visited an ex-Delta guy, Brad Jameson. You remember him?"

Elisabeth shook her head.

"He was dying. He's gone now."

"I'm sorry . . ."

"Literally dying in a hospital bed as I was visiting. What he said was so different from what I knew about you that I attributed it to him being high on painkillers."

"What did he say?"

"He said that you worked for the CIA. A friend of his had told him that. And when I met up with his friend, he confirmed it. He actually met you at the New York office, WTC 7."

Elisabeth's face was ashen. "That's a terrible way for you to hear about it."

"As far as I knew, you died on 9/11. That's what I'd been told. That was the story. The official story. The cover story."

"I'm so, so sorry. No one was supposed to know. Where do you want me to start?"

"Wherever you want."

Elisabeth sighed long and hard. "It started in early 2001. I was deeply unhappy with my job as a tax lawyer, my life . . . I was unhappy being a new mother. Suicidal. I wasn't well. You were away."

"And that was it? What about me?"

"What about you?"

"Were you unhappy with me?"

Elisabeth closed her eyes as if trying to block out the memory, tears spilling down her cheeks. "I was angry with you. Angry with myself. You were away eleven months out of every twelve. I grew to resent you. I grew to hate you. Your freedom."

"My freedom?"

"Being away, that's what I mean. I was working fourteen hours a day in the office, perpetually exhausted, picking up Lauren from my mother, then back to the apartment. Up to Rockland once a month if I was lucky. You weren't in our lives."

"That's true. But I was working. Africa, Norway, joint exercises in Europe, the Middle East. And that was before 9/11."

"I was in despair, Jon. I was struggling with depression."

"Why didn't you tell me? Why didn't you talk to me?"

"You were never there. I wasn't going to tell you when you called home."

"Did you talk to anyone about it?"

"I spoke to a psychologist. They said I was clinically depressed, on the verge of a nervous breakdown. Maybe I had one, I don't know. But I struggled on. Alone with my thoughts and fears. My mood swings."

Reznick began to feel a twinge of guilt. "I'm so sorry. I wish I'd known."

"I was so lonely. I hated myself. I wanted someone to talk to. But I had no one. I had all the trappings of success. Senior position in a law firm, beautiful child, handsome, decorated Delta operator as a husband—it looked good on paper. But it didn't feel good. I felt empty. I was unfulfilled emotionally. I took a couple of months off to recuperate. You were away for a six-month overseas posting to Jordan or someplace. I took medical leave from the firm. Then in the spring, I got a call from a woman."

"A woman . . ."

"She seemed to know an awful lot about me. She said she wondered if we'd like to meet up. An interview."

"What kind of interview?"

"I'll get to that in a minute. I thought she was a headhunter. A recruiter. She said she worked for a company who did work for the government in and around DC. But I said I wasn't interested."

"What changed?"

"I began to feel better a little while later. But I was curious about the job. I wondered if I should reach out to the woman who had called me. I spoke to my father and told him about the call. He said, *Why not go and find out what it's all about? A change might be good.*"

"But this was the Agency, right? You hadn't approached them? You had no idea it was them?"

"Correct. So, I was invited to a nondescript office in DC. I was introduced to a guy from the Pentagon. He was ex-CIA, and he mentioned that my name had come up in conversation."

"In conversation with who?"

"My father."

Reznick took a few moments to wrap his head around what he was being told. "Your father?"

"My father initiated this. He thought it would do me good. He thought I'd be a good fit."

"Working for the CIA? Not exactly a known cure for clinical depression."

"My father worked for the Agency way back in the '70s. He was a middle-ranking geopolitical analyst before he became a consultant."

Reznick sat in stunned amazement. "I had no idea."

"Neither did I. Weird, huh?"

"I'm shocked."

Elisabeth winced as if embarrassed at the tangled web of secrets and lies. "I told them about my condition, and they asked me to get checked over by a couple of their psychologists. A psychiatric evaluation. They both said that my mental health was fine, serotonin levels had been boosted by the medication I had been prescribed. You see, by that stage I really was feeling better. A lot stronger. But they wanted to check. They did a series of further psychological tests. Apparently, I fit the profile for a new permanent posting overseas in Europe. Erudite, cultured, that kind of thing. The catch? I would have to assume a different name and backstory."

"And this was in May 2001?"

"How do you know?"

"I did a bit of digging."

Elisabeth gave a rueful smile. "Why doesn't that surprise me?"

"Go on. I need to know how it changed."

"Events overtook the timetable. Here's the thing. The job was supposed to take me to Switzerland before the end of 2001. December, I think. That was the plan. The job would have had me as an American boss of a startup company, seed funding, technology. Cutting edge."

"You don't know the first thing about computers."

"I was a figurehead."

"When were you going to tell me?"

"When you came back in October, just before your next over-seas assignment. I was going to tell you I was leaving then."

"And you were going to take our daughter?"

"No."

Reznick held up his hands as he tried to get his head around the whole outrageous idea. "Hang on, you were going to leave her in New York?"

"I knew she would be cared for by my mother and father."

"I don't think I know you."

"I didn't know myself, Jon. I didn't know who I'd become. You have to believe me: I felt like a different person."

"That's as cold as it gets."

"I'm trying to explain."

"So, explain!"

"I wanted this job, Jon. I wanted to get away. Forever."

"You abandoned your daughter?"

"This isn't easy for me, Jon."

"How do you think it is for me?"

"People leave their families all the time. It happens every day, Jon. Hate me if you want. You've got every right to. But how do you think it felt for me, you being away most of the time?"

"A lot of people put up with stuff like that. They don't disappear forever."

"You weren't blameless, Jon."

"Are you serious? You're blaming me?"

"I only saw you a few weeks every year. Then you were off again."

"It wasn't a nine-to-five job. I can't believe what you're saying. My job didn't have regular hours."

"Neither did mine. I made the decision to turn my back on you and Lauren. The job was important to me. It was my escape. I was going out of my mind. I had postpartum depression. It's a form of major depression. I associated my old job, my baby, my old life with all my problems."

Reznick nodded.

"The new job offered me a way out."

"The job? Are you sure?"

"Yes, the job. The job was important for national security intelligence-gathering. But in the hours following 9/11, I was given a choice. I had to make a choice there and then."

"Slow down . . . What are you talking about? Tell me what happened to move the date up from December."

"The world changed that day, Jon."

"I'm aware of what happened."

"It changed forever. You should know that better than anyone. As the world collapsed around me, literally, the windows blowing out of my offices in WTC 7, we had to flee downstairs. It collapsed much later in the day."

"And you made that decision in the building at that moment?"

Elisabeth shook her head. "I never made the call on that day. I was given an ultimatum."

"An ultimatum? Who made the call? Who asked you?"

"Why is that important to you, Jon?"

"I want to know. I deserve to know."

Elisabeth took a deep breath. "As I was making my way out of WTC 7, after the first plane hit the adjoining tower, we were in full evacuation mode. It was horrendous. I had a lot of friends in the tower that was hit. Colleagues at the law firm. But my evacuation out of WTC 7 was not with everyone else, all the other tenants."

"Why not?"

"We were escorted down to the basement levels. I thought they were security guards. But in hindsight, I think they might've been Agency. So, we took another route. The basement. Suddenly it was all surreal, and it was happening like a nightmare in real time. We

171

got out of WTC 7, and we had to make our way through the small fires that had broken out, through dust and chaos, and we escaped through a basement tunnel, I think."

"You think?"

"That's what happened. We walked for what seemed like miles. Eventually we emerged somewhere in the East Village."

"My God."

"We were picked up and driven to a safe house in North Bergen. We hunkered down there until nightfall. Then we were picked up by a CIA crew and driven out of town, toward northwest New Jersey. The day after the planes hit."

Reznick sat in silence.

Elisabeth wiped away tears.

"Go on."

"I'm alive. And from the bottom of my heart, I'm sorry. I was going to tell you in October and leave in December. But 9/11 changed everything. I was told to disappear."

"Told? Who told you to disappear?"

"The decision was made by my boss, and my new handler at the Pentagon."

"What are their names?"

"I'm not going there, Jon."

"What did they say?"

"A decision had been made, they said. If I wanted the overseas posting, I had to rip up my old life. I would be smuggled out of America as soon as planes were allowed to fly, and make my way to Switzerland on a false passport, false identity. The timetable brought forward."

Reznick shook his head. "And you were OK with this?"

"I agreed to this. No one forced me. They suggested it. But it was spur of the moment. And I complied. Have you heard enough?"

Reznick got to his feet and began to pace the cabin, shaking his head.

"I know it doesn't look good, Jon."

"I want to know the whole story. Your work here in Switzerland. I want to know how this whole false identity seems to have become compromised."

Thirty-One

The Gulfstream touched down in the dead of night in Switzerland. It had made the flight direct from Riyadh and landed at Lausanne at 02:33. The plane was registered to a company in the Caymans whose majority shareholder was a reclusive member of the Saudi royal family. The airstair unfolded. Three men in suits got off and waited at the bottom of the stairs. Eventually, the two passengers emerged.

Muller wore a surgical mask and sunglasses, a baseball cap, and woolen gloves as he climbed into the back of a waiting SUV. Sasha followed. A driver and a thickset man with dead eyes sat up front. The vehicle pulled away and headed through an airport security gate and sped away into the night.

"Keep your mask on until we arrive at the house," Sasha said.

"What house?"

"The safe house. We will await instructions."

Muller was often taken to Lausanne as a child. His parents had owned a little cottage on the lake. It was idyllic. Hiking up along the blazing mountain trails in summer. Ice-climbing in the winter months. His mind replayed the images. Freezing lake-swimming in the summer. The heart-stopping cold. The wholesomeness. It was a time he was truly happy. He was the center of his parents' world. And they were the center of his. It felt like a million years ago. God, how he wished his father was alive today. Not only for his mother but for himself. A man with sound judgment.

The car turned off the road and headed up a gravel driveway to a beautiful, sprawling, neoclassical mansion, nestled among the snow-covered spruce and fir trees. The car wound its way around the mansion and pulled up to the rear of the building. It parked outside a modern extension.

He was ushered inside, Sasha right next to him, then down a series of corridors to a set of elevators. Cameras watched their every move.

"Nice place, huh?" Sasha said.

Muller said nothing as they waited for the elevator door to open.

"You OK?" Sasha asked.

"I'm fine," he lied.

The elevator opened, and he and Sasha stepped in.

"Who owns this place?" he inquired.

Sasha pressed the elevator button marked -3. It had to be the lowest basement of the house. "I believe a woman from Jeddah. A princess. Her brother's company owns the plane."

"Why are they helping you guys out?"

The elevator started its descent. One level. Two levels. "I assume by *you guys* you mean the Russian government?"

"Right. I thought the Saudis were tight with the American government. Isn't the Fifth Fleet based in Bahrain, patrolling all across the Persian Gulf?"

The elevator door opened, and they stepped out. "This is all true," she said.

Muller walked with Sasha down a long, featureless corridor. "So, what's changed?"

"Don't you watch the news? Don't you read magazines?"

"Not much."

"Let me tell you, my Swiss friend, there are a lot of influential people who want the Saudis to pivot away from America."

"Why?"

"Realignment with China and Russia and India."

"But why?"

"The tectonic plates of the world are shifting, Hans. Saudi Arabia is not perfect. They can see it's all in flux. They're getting on board in whatever way they can."

"This is insane."

Sasha smiled as she approached a steel door and positioned her face in front of the retina scanner. "Follow me."

The door clicked open, and they walked inside.

A man wearing desert military fatigues stood in front of a whiteboard and glared at them as they entered the room. It appeared to be a classroom, chairs against the wall. He wore black boots. His sleeves were rolled up to show he meant business. Arms like lamb shanks. He pointed to two seats. "Let us get started," he said gruffly in a chain-smoker's Russian accent.

Muller and Sasha pulled up a couple of chairs and sat down.

The man cleared his throat and stared long and hard at Muller. "Here is what you need to know. You have been tasked with neutralizing Anna Bruckmann, also known as Elisabeth Reznick. My job is to ensure you complete that task. Do you understand?"

"Yes."

"Failure to comply will result in your death. Understood?"

Muller meekly nodded. "Yes, sir."

"Let's get down to business. A woman—Anna Bruckmann is her cover name—is still here in Switzerland. Her real name is

Elisabeth Reznick. And she is CIA. You've seen a photograph of her in Zurich, right?"

Muller nodded.

"To complicate things, we believe her husband, Jon Reznick, has arrived. He is ex-CIA. This is unfortunate. But we will deal with him when we locate him."

"And you're sure that the woman is American and her husband is in Switzerland? Do I have to kill them both?"

"Killing Elisabeth is the mission. If you kill him too, that is a bonus."

Muller saw a slight tremor in his hand, resting on his thigh.

"We have the added complication that his daughter, Lauren, is here as well. She is FBI. We could look at it as a double bonus if you get her and the husband."

"Hang on," Hans said. "Jon Reznick, Lauren Reznick, and a woman called Anna Bruckmann, who is a longtime sleeper agent of the CIA, real name Elisabeth Reznick? You want them all dead?"

The Russian sneered at him, "Have you got a problem with that?"

"Yes, I have a big problem with that."

"We can send you back to the embassy compound in Riyadh. That can be arranged. But there will be consequences. Do you want to go back there?"

"Don't bother."

"Killing Anna will count as completing the mission."

"I kill Bruckmann and I'm free to go, and my mother will not be harmed?"

"Not only that: you and your mother will be protected for life at your retreat on the Brazilian island."

"What guarantees are you offering?"

"The Russian government doesn't offer guarantees. You either take it or leave it."

Muller turned and looked at Sasha. "You're going to be with me during this operation? Even though this could be a suicide mission?"

"We will get them. We will be heroes."

"Or we'll wind up dead," Hans said.

Sasha smirked at him. "We will neutralize the target. Or we die trying."

Thirty-Two

Reznick paced the isolated log cabin near Randa. "I still don't understand. You've explained how this happened. The sequences of events. But you're reciting an itinerary. The lack of real remorse or self-awareness of what you've done is staggering."

"What more do you want from me?"

"I don't want anything from you. But you don't seem to appreciate the magnitude of your decision. You're just brushing it off as if it never happened, and now we should just move on."

"I'm saying nothing of the sort."

"You don't seem to get it. And I still don't understand why you did this."

Elisabeth sat with her head in her hands. "Don't judge me. I've already judged myself harshly. The last thing I need is for you to bring all of this back to the surface."

"I'm not going to judge you. I'm just trying to understand how you thought this was rational. I can't think of a more sickening betrayal. Clearly I never knew you, really knew you. That's what you're saying, isn't it?"

"Who knows anyone, truly?"

"What the hell are you talking about?"

"The only person we really know is ourselves."

"Sounds like therapist talk to me."

"Sometimes our judgment at a point in time is clouded, or a set of circumstances comes into play. A chemical imbalance, maybe. I don't know."

"Are you fucking serious? Did a doctor tell you that? Or are you just making shit up?"

Elisabeth closed her eyes. "There you go again. Acting aggressive."

"Gimme a break."

"I just wanted to forget. I don't know if you realize what you were like then."

Reznick stood, hands on hips. "What do you mean?"

"Jon, you scared me. You're scaring me now."

"I scared you?"

"Not initially. But over time, the more I got to know you. I saw a coldness, a detachment about you. It unsettled me. The Agency was my way out. But 9/11 accelerated the process."

"Accelerated the process. I . . . What were you? A sleeper agent? A long-term deep-cover sleeper agent? Is that the term?"

Elisabeth shrugged "I still am, in a sense. This is all classified."

"There you go, hiding behind security classifications. Gimme the truth."

"You want the truth?"

"After they evacuated you. What was the name of the town you were taken to?"

"I can't remember."

"Why?"

"I don't know. I just know it was isolated. A place small enough to have no cameras around for miles."

Reznick was trying to build a mental picture.

"We stayed there for a few hours. Watched the nightmare unfold on TV. And a decision was made for me to disappear. It was clear America was under terrorist attack. The Pentagon wanted me in place ahead of the October 7 US and British attacks on Afghanistan."

"I was told that you were in a State Department plane that touched down in Switzerland on September 23rd, 2001."

Elisabeth blushed. "I can't believe you know that."

"It aligns with what you're telling me. They rushed operatives like you into position ahead of the attacks in October. That's how it happened?"

"Exactly. It was viewed as Day Zero, 9/11. It was a race against time. And it was imperative that intelligence operatives and special forces were moved into position. The schedule got moved forward."

"You went along with this?"

Elisabeth nodded, eyes closed. "I wanted to disappear. I also wanted to serve. This is where the government wanted me to be."

Reznick began to feel the first twinge of sympathy for Elisabeth.

"Didn't you always talk about a chain of command?" she asked. "Following orders. Carrying out orders, no questions asked?"

Reznick sighed. "What happened after the decision was made? What did you do?"

"I lived alone in that isolated house in rural New Jersey. Supplies were dropped off. It was only a few days I lived in that house, not going out, curtains drawn. No visitors. Then there was a knock at the door. A car arrived with heavily tinted windows; I remember that. I was driven all the way down to Camp Peary."

"I know it well. They call it the Farm."

"That's right. I spent a few days training, getting briefed, then being given a whole new identity. My hair was cut and dyed."

"I noticed."

Elisabeth blushed.

"Then what?"

"I was flown by a CIA pilot first to Rome and then on to Switzerland in the early hours of September 23, as you said. From that moment on, I was Anna Bruckmann. I swear to God, that's the sequence of events."

Reznick stood in disbelief.

"It's a lot to take in, I know. I'm sorry. I'm so very sorry."

Thirty-Three

Elisabeth sat on the sofa, wiping away tears. "I'm a terrible person. I can't imagine how you must feel."

"I feel like I didn't know you. I feel hollowed out. I'm beginning to think that our whole marriage was a sham. You were a sham. Our relationship was a sham. Frankly, I feel like shit. A worthless piece of shit."

Elisabeth closed her eyes tight, as if she didn't want to hear any more.

Reznick said, "You know, in the days after 9/11, I lost my mind. I fell apart. And your mother and father had to look after Lauren for a while."

"I didn't know that."

"And then, more than twenty years later, I found out you weren't even who I thought you were."

Elisabeth sighed, hands clasped, tears streaming down her face.

Reznick continued to process everything he'd just been told. "So, the CIA office in WTC 7—what was the purpose of that?"

"Jon, I don't want to talk about it."

"It doesn't matter now! Your cover has been blown."

"The New York station, at the time, was, among other things, a base of operations to spy on and recruit foreign diplomats stationed at the United Nations."

"I was always under the impression it was just Langley and the Farm doing that in this country."

"There are quite a few other satellite offices, houses, buildings that are used from time to time. That was a pretty steep learning curve, coming from my legal background."

"Some interesting people work for the Agency. I was one of them for a while."

Elisabeth scoffed, dumbstruck. "You worked for the CIA?"

"I was recruited after I left Delta. A few years after 9/11. I was interviewed. CIA selection panel. Well, that's my story. So, when you were here in Switzerland working for the Agency, I was working as a contractor on various jobs around the world."

"Contractor. What kind of contractor?"

"You don't want to know."

"Why not?"

"None of it was good. It's the dirty work that no one wants to talk about."

"But someone has to do it, right?"

"Precisely."

Elisabeth buried her head in her hands. "It's been a long time, Jon. A long, long time. I couldn't go back even if I wanted to."

"Did you ever want to come home?"

"Sometimes . . . but it passed. I knew I couldn't. It wasn't possible. I'm dead, remember?"

Reznick nodded.

"I can't believe you don't hate me."

"I don't hate you."

"Maybe you should." She looked at Jon then, fondness in her eyes. He wanted to hug her. And forgive her. "What are you thinking?"

"Just trying to work it all out, fit the pieces together. I grieved. And I went to a dark place."

"What do you mean?"

"I drank until I blacked out. I disappeared for days. I couldn't remember where I'd been. Then I snapped out of it. I got back to doing the only thing I was trained to do."

"I was grief stricken too. At what I'd done."

"You don't know the first thing about grief. Part of me died that day. Ironically, it meant I could do my job better than anyone."

"Jon, don't."

Reznick looked across at this short-haired woman he barely recognized. His wife. The woman who now went by another name. "The other part of me, still left intact, wanted to die. I went on missions. I enjoyed it. I had to kill to feel alive. I was dead inside. Nothing bothered me."

Elisabeth scrunched up her face. "Oh dear God, Jon."

"I'd never have believed that you were CIA. Never in a million years."

"My old identity was wiped."

"I'm curious," Reznick said. "What else did the CIA's undercover New York station do? Specifically, what did you do in the first few months before 9/11 and your disappearance?"

"This and that." Elisabeth sighed. "I was tasked, if you must know, with debriefing American business executives and others willing to talk to the CIA after returning from overseas. We posed as diplomats or business executives, depending on the nature of the intelligence operation. Also, we used honey traps for UN officials in New York."

"Not you, I'm assuming."

Elisabeth's face turned to stone. "Correct."

"That's a big departure from tax law, that's for sure. I heard you worked in Geneva when you came here?"

"Who told you that?"

"A hacker friend. He said you were involved in a tech firm. Two-stage text message verification or something or other."

Elisabeth's pale skin flushed pink again. "The company I founded was a CIA front. My company allowed backdoor access for the NSA and CIA to spy on Middle Eastern governments, companies, surveillance targets. That's it in a nutshell."

"And the information would be relayed in real time back to the States?"

"Exactly. Invaluable, raw, human intelligence of foreign nationals. Emails from politicians. Military figures. Terrorists too, many posing as students. Text messages of prominent media moguls in Africa, the Middle East, the Far East. And across Europe. It was a slow-burn operation. But the results were spectacular."

"So, countries like Iran, Egypt—we were spying on their activities and people in Europe?"

"Twenty years ago, everyone used specifically licensed or modified versions of our original technology. And that included our allies."

"Son of a bitch. That's ingenious."

"Indeed."

"Your work is done now, right?"

"It's evolving. It's changed over the years. It's still technology. But as it stands, at this moment, yeah, my work is done. I've been told to get out of Switzerland. My cover has been blown, it's true. They want me out of the way. But it will be difficult getting me back. My true identity can never be known."

"So, you're going back?"

Elisabeth was quiet for a few moments. "Maybe."

"What does that mean?"

"It means I've been instructed to go home."

"'Instructed'? The CIA is working on this?"

"Supposed to be. But my cover op is hopelessly compromised, at least in certain intelligence circles."

Reznick sat down again. "Who knows you're here at this precise location?"

"In this country? At this location? Well, apart from the CIA in Bern, the Pentagon in Washington, I believe only two people. My handler in the NDB—the woman you followed, Gruber—and her boss, the head of Swiss intelligence."

"The Swiss IT operative who dropped off the grid, what about him?"

Elisabeth stared him. "How do you know about that?"

"I know a few things."

"Alright, I've been forthcoming. Do you mind if I ask a few questions?"

"Fire away."

"How did you find me?"

"Remember I told you about the CIA guy who worked in WTC 7, who got the ball rolling."

"Right."

"The real breakthrough happened when a hacker friend of mine, ex-NSA, told me about a guy he knows in Colorado. And he put me in touch. Turns out this guy worked with the Swiss IT guy at the NSA. Then Muller, the Swiss guy, sends him a still photo taken in Zurich Old Town in the dead of night. Sound familiar?"

"That's incredible."

"It was a break, I guess. Anyway, Muller, the Swiss guy, couldn't establish who the woman was in the photo. So, he reached out to his ex-NSA pal in Colorado. All he knew was that the name that came up was *Anna Bruckmann*. But there was some irregularity in the photo, something like that. The guy ran the image through a lot of American databases, and it brought up a match with someone he couldn't identify."

"What was it?"

"It was a match for you. Your CIA image was still stored in some NSA servers somewhere."

Elisabeth covered her face.

"So, the Swiss guy, Hans Muller, was trying to establish who this was right before unearthing this database cache of intelligence. He was given the information. The Colorado NSA guy was unaware that guy was stealing the crown jewels of Swiss intelligence. Then the Swiss guy disappeared suddenly. I'm assuming from the photo that you were meeting up with a handler from the US Embassy, maybe a contact."

"Dead drop."

Reznick nodded. "I see. So, Swiss guy is still AWOL, with a ton of top secret classified information that the CIA, the State Department, and MI6 had shared with the NDB."

"He's a Russian spy. That's what I've been told by the Agency."

"Money?"

"And ideology. We've learned that his mother flirted with the Communist Party during her student days in Geneva."

"How was he given security clearance?"

"There's nothing on her file indicating her political beliefs. Let me get this straight. It started with that surveillance photo sent by Muller to the guy in Colorado?"

"Precisely. And Muller would have shared all that with his handlers." Reznick looked at her and saw the sadness etched on her face. "You had a house by a lake in Arth. I met your housekeeper."

"So I heard. That how you found me?"

"Eventually, in a roundabout way. I got a fix on the house in Zermatt. But the NDB lady was visiting or staying there."

Elisabeth smiled. "Interesting."

"The problem is, if I, not a countersurveillance expert by any means, can find you, so can a highly trained crew."

Elisabeth picked at the cuticles on her fingers.

"You said so yourself: the Russians are behind this. You need to be worried. They don't fuck around. Never have. It's not in their DNA. If they can identity and neutralize a valued CIA intelligence asset, a deep-cover sleeper, they will do it. No compunction about deleting you. I want to get you someplace safe."

Elisabeth looked at Jon, held his gaze while the fire roared next to them. "Do you love me?"

Reznick looked away, not wanting to be drawn into that emotional minefield. He didn't want to talk about anything like that. He had moved on. He had met Martha. Thank God he had. But Elisabeth didn't need to know about that. Maybe later. Someday.

"What happened to us, Jon?"

"Who the hell knows? What does anyone know?"

"You didn't deserve what happened to you. What I did to you."

"Maybe. Maybe not."

"I'd like to meet Lauren."

"You sure?"

"Is that going to be a problem?"

"Maybe. Problem is, I don't know how she'll respond to you."

"I understand. But I still want to meet her. I'm assuming she'll want to meet me."

"She'll want to meet you." Reznick's cell phone rang. He grimaced. "Sorry." He checked the caller ID.

"Who is it?" Elisabeth asked.

"Speak of the devil. It's Lauren."

Elisabeth began to sob.

Thirty-Four

Reznick took the call as Elisabeth dabbed her eyes with a handkerchief. "Talk to me, honey."

Lauren's voice was tight. "Dad, I have a problem."

"What is it?"

"I seem to have lost the woman I tailed. She went into a ski shop in Zermatt, and I waited and waited. I held back. And then a few minutes later I went in and she was gone. Through the back entrance, they said."

"Classic tradecraft. She's trained well. Listen, are you OK?"

"Yeah, pissed that I lost her. How did you do in Randa?"

Reznick wondered what he should say or reveal. He looked at his wife, who had folded her arms, facing the fire. "I'm sitting with your mother."

Elisabeth turned and smiled at him.

"Seriously, Dad?"

"Seriously."

"Can I talk to her?"

Reznick put the call on speaker and handed the phone to Elisabeth. "It's encrypted. Best in class. Don't worry."

Elisabeth closed her eyes for a moment before she spoke. "Hello, Lauren."

"Mom?"

"That's right, honey. It's Mom."

"It's nice to hear your voice."

"Yours too."

"I want to meet up."

"Where are you?"

"I'm in Zermatt."

"Your dad found me."

"I knew he would," Lauren said.

"Lauren, things are kinda tricky right now. I don't want to put you in any danger."

"I want to see you, Mom."

"I know you do."

Reznick signaled for Elisabeth that he wanted to talk.

"Lauren, we'll meet up with you soon, I promise. Here's your father."

Reznick cleared his throat. "I'm worried that the Swiss intelligence woman might have been spooked by someone following her. She might have triggered a backup group to meet up with her. We need to be cautious."

"What do you suggest? What should I do?"

"You need to get our things at the hotel, check out, and move to a different hotel in Zermatt."

"Copy that, Dad. I'll be in touch as soon as I can."

"Got it."

Reznick reached over for the cell phone and ended the call. "A lot to take in, right?"

"No kidding."

"Elisabeth . . . you don't mind me calling you Elisabeth, do you?"

"That is my name, Jon."

"I'm worried."

"What about?"

"Your situation . . . but I'm thinking also of your handler, Gruber. She's Swiss intelligence, right?"

"Very senior. I like her. She's very understanding. Superdiscreet."

"Tell me more about her."

Elisabeth was quiet for a few moments. "I don't know much about her."

"How were you introduced?"

"She approached me after Hans Muller disappeared. She was the reason I moved up to the Randa area. She uses the cabin down in Zermatt. I've met her there once. And in the village of Randa. That's the setup. At least for now."

"This place here, she picked it?"

"No. CIA suggested this place."

Reznick looked around as he wondered why the Agency had picked such an isolated place for Elisabeth. It was way too isolated. No one to hear or see a thing. Literally cut off from the outside world in winter. He understood the logic of being out of sight in a safe house up in the mountains. But he had always thought living in a city, more anonymous, in spite of the cameras, was the way to go.

"You think there's something wrong, don't you?"

"I don't know."

"What do you mean you don't know?"

"I'm confused why the Agency has allowed Swiss intelligence to lead on this. I would have thought extraction would be done without delay, especially with the Russian connections to the Swiss guy. What have you been told?"

Elisabeth shrugged. "That I'm to wait here for further instructions until it's safe to go. The dead drop was the second stall in the bathroom at the hotel."

Reznick looked over at the backpack on the ground. "What's in it?"

Elisabeth reached over and opened the bag. She pulled out a laptop, Ziploc bags stuffed with euros, and a cell phone. "Cash is for emergencies so as not to use credit cards."

"The laptop and cell phone to communicate securely?"

"Exactly."

"Or if they want to know where you are at all times."

Elisabeth shook her head. "What do you mean? Do you mean I can't trust Gruber?"

"Trust no one. That's my motto."

"Should I trust you instead?"

"That's your call, Elisabeth."

She stayed silent.

"I'm not an expert at tradecraft—far from it—but I know a few fundamentals. What I'm saying, Elisabeth, is that Swiss intelligence has a fix on your approximate location."

"And that's a problem?"

"Consider this . . . If the Russians have penetrated the Swiss intelligence agency, NDB, and they got hold of Hans Muller and this huge haul of classified files, then the cell phone number of your female handler will be able to be tracked all the way to Zermatt. Then Randa. You will be in grave danger."

"I think that's a stretch."

"Think about it. The Swiss have been compromised. Western intelligence and all the contacts in Western Europe have been compromised. A CIA spy, an American woman—you see where I'm going with this?"

Elisabeth sat impassive.

"What if Gruber has led the Russians right to you?"

"I've only been here a few days."

"Today was the first day that the dead drop got used, right?"

Elisabeth nodded.

"You have the electronic equipment sitting right here, in this cabin. Not activated, so far."

"I think I can trust her."

"You need to be smart, Elisabeth. You trust no one."

"And you're sure I can trust you?"

"Yes. You could always have trusted me, Elisabeth. That won't ever change. It all comes down to who you trust. So, do you trust me?"

"I do, Jon."

"How much?"

"I trust you with my life. With my daughter's life."

Reznick felt his throat tighten. "Thank you."

"OK, let's assume what you're saying is right. What should we do?"

Reznick cocked his head and pointed to the door. He got up and headed outside as Elisabeth followed, shutting the door behind them. They stood outside in the freezing cold.

"You think they might've bugged the cabin?"

"I would have."

"How do I get in contact with Helena without sending a message or calling on the cell phone she provided?"

"We take the cash and get rid of the electronic devices. But we don't say a word until they're out of earshot."

"That's pretty drastic."

"Better safe than sorry."

"I have an idea."

"Shoot."

Elisabeth went back inside. He followed her and watched as she carefully lifted out the Ziploc bags of cash. She placed them on the coffee table. Then she picked up the backpack containing the laptop and cell phone and cocked her head, and he followed her outside again.

She trudged through the snow to the rear of the cabin, where he spotted a snow-covered well.

"What do you think?" she said.

Reznick nodded. "Go right ahead."

Elisabeth dropped the bag down the well. A dull splash and then a thud as it hit the bottom.

"Better safe than sorry. Can you make sure there aren't tracking devices in the bag or attached to the bills?"

"Sure thing."

They headed back inside, and she opened up the wads of cash. She flicked through every pile. She gave the thumbs-up sign.

Reznick pointed again to the front door, and they went outside for the third time, shutting the door behind them.

"Clean," she said. "So, what now?"

"I need to understand. Do you want to go back to the States, knowing what we know now?"

"Yes, I do. Definitely."

"What are your instructions?"

"To sit tight; I told you."

Reznick's gaze wandered around the isolated alpine setting. "How do you communicate with the CIA? There must be someone else apart from Helena."

Elisabeth nodded. "In Ramstein. Germany."

"How exactly do you get in touch?"

"Shortwave radio supplied by the CIA."

"Where is it?"

"The attic."

"Let's get up there and make contact. We need you and Lauren out of here now."

Thirty-Five

The windows of the attic had frosted over.

Reznick looked around the wood-paneled space. One entire wall was lined with empty bookshelves. In the far corner, a small TV sat on a wooden cabinet. Adjacent to that was a small wooden desk and an old chair. "Quite a place you have here. Very cozy."

Elisabeth gave a rueful look. "Yeah, right."

"So, how does this work?"

Elisabeth carefully unlocked the cabinet. She reached in and pulled out a shortwave radio, a compact antenna, and headphones and placed them on the table. She pulled up the chair and sat down at the desk.

"Interesting."

"This is equipment to receive coded messages from the Agency."

"CIA-issue?"

"Pentagon."

"Are you sure?"

"Definitely. This has nothing to do with the Swiss. The Department of Defense is overseeing this." Elisabeth checked her watch. "It's two minutes to the hour."

"What does that mean?"

"There's something you don't know?"

Reznick shrugged. "I'm assuming you're listening for instructions from an American handler?"

"Exactly. I can tune in and receive up-to-date coded messages on the hour. It's for agents operating in foreign countries."

Reznick realized exactly what she was doing. It was a shortwave radio station where numeric and radio-alphabetic coded messages were sent at a specific time to agents in the field by, in this case, the CIA, GCHQ—the British signals intelligence agency—or the Pentagon. "They're running a numbers station?"

Elisabeth looked impressed. "You're more than a pretty face, Jon."

"Gimme a break. That's an old-school technique, if I'm not mistaken."

"It works. Allows us to bypass more traditional tradecraft channels. Popular before the digital age."

"So, let's get going."

Elisabeth shifted in her seat behind the desk. She switched on the shortwave radio, and it crackled to life. She put her headphones on in case the transmission was hard to hear and checked her watch again.

Reznick watched, amazed and struggling to get his head around the turn of events. He was watching his dead wife operate the same sort of radio that specialists embedded with Delta operators used behind enemy lines.

The radio crackled into life. "Tango Delta 55, Tango Delta 83521, Six-Niner-Zero-Oblique-Five-Four, Foxtrot 7." Elisabeth turned up the volume on the small speakers of the radio. "Tango Delta 55, Tango Delta 83521, Six-Niner-Zero-Oblique-Five-Four, Foxtrot 7."

The voice repeated the phrase again and again in a monotonous manner for three more minutes. Then it was just static.

Elisabeth scribbled the details down. She turned off the radio and took off her headphones.

"Numbers station. Very cool."

Elisabeth checked the codes she had written down.

"What are they saying?"

"The code is clear. *Stay in place.* Help will be here at 0430 hours. Eight operatives are en route."

"Chopper?"

Elisabeth shook her head.

"Why not?"

Elisabeth folded her arms as if exasperated. "Jon, with all due respect, this is not your particular area of expertise."

"Extraction? Are you kidding me? I've done dozens of them over the years. All over the world. We figure out the fastest and safest way to get the target securely to safety."

"These guys are good."

"I'm sure they are. Here's my concern. I don't understand why they haven't done it already. That doesn't make any sense. Secondly, this should be a simple chopper extraction. In and out, wham bam. It's over."

"I don't know the full story. Maybe there are logistical problems."

"That doesn't add up. You need to be choppered out, or a SEAL or Delta team needs to be sent in to take you to an American military base."

"That's not the plan. The Pentagon is running this. It's their game. Their rules."

"A high-value intel target like yourself would be gold dust for the enemy. They will have you out of the country and back to a dungeon in Moscow so quick your head will spin. Then they will go to work on you."

"Jon, you're scaring me. I've lived for twenty years without your voice and intensity in my ear, and I've managed just fine."

Reznick paced the attic floor for a few moments. "I can't stress enough how concerned I am that your handler has deemed this extraction method and timetable acceptable. You're on your goddamn own. A sitting target. You should have been out of the country days ago."

Elisabeth said nothing.

"That's my honest appraisal of the situation."

Elisabeth was quiet for a few more moments. "The aim is extraction. And every day is crucial, right?"

"Every hour. And now they're saying to sit tight until four thirty in the morning. And we'll come and get you?"

"I agree, it doesn't make sense."

"It does to me."

"Jon, what the hell are you talking about?"

"You took down the coded message. And you said it was 0430 hours. Right?"

"Right."

"Break it down."

"There were three aspects they conveyed. The first part identified my radio code name, the second identified the time, and the third identified it was manual extraction."

"Fine, but what if your assumptions that they're going to come for you are wrong?"

"I don't follow."

"What I mean is that you're a sitting duck."

"I am not."

"Think about it. You've outlived your usefulness."

"Do you believe the Pentagon wants me dead?"

Reznick held her eyes.

"What do you suggest?" She rolled her eyes. "We cut and run?"

"Exactly! We need to get you out of here now. Let's not sit around and wait and see what happens."

"I play by the rules. Always have. What's so difficult about following orders?"

"Sometimes when things smell wrong it means something has gone rotten. And you'll end up dead. I say we get on the move. Elisabeth, do you have an emergency number to call?"

"I've got a CIA desk officer's number in Bern."

"Call him. Right now."

"And say what?"

Reznick handed her his cell phone. "This is a military encryption cell phone modified by my hacker friend I told you about. So, it's fine."

"I don't know if that's secure."

"I'm telling you it's secure. It's cutting edge. Might even be ahead of the CIA on the encryption front."

"What should I say?"

"Ask why the delay. And let's see where the conversation takes you. We might be in a better position to try and ascertain the true position."

"OK."

"Turn on the speaker so I can hear."

Elisabeth switched on the speaker and dialed the secure CIA number in Bern. It rang five times before it was answered. Elisabeth said, "Clarence, is this line secure on your end?"

"This number is not coming up as verified. So, I can't authenticate."

"It's secure."

"Is this . . . ?"

"It's Anna."

"Sure . . . shit, Anna. OK, I'm worried that you're not coming through on a secure line."

"Listen to me. This is secure. I'll give you my blood type, maiden name, hospital I was born in. Do the voice analysis."

"It's just that . . . this is irregular, you know that."

"Damn right, it's irregular. Listen, Clarence, if you don't believe me, I'll hang up right now. Is that what you want?"

"Don't do that. Relax. I believe you."

"You want to do a voice comparison?"

"You're fine on that. So, talk to me . . . You got the message?"

"I got the message, copy that."

"And?"

"What is taking so long?"

"Things are complicated."

"How so?"

"I'm going to level with you. I'm running into all sorts of shit to get you out of the country."

"What exactly is the problem?"

"Washington. Pentagon, to be precise. They decided against a chopper team."

"Clarence, who made the call? Was it you?"

"Negative."

"So, who the hell was it?"

"Orders direct from the Pentagon. I was told to shut the fuck up and follow orders."

"So," Elisabeth asked, "what am I supposed to do? Just sit and wait?"

"It's not ideal, I know."

Reznick felt a tickle in his throat and cleared it as quietly as he could.

"Who the hell is there with you?"

"Jon Reznick is with me at this moment." A silence filled the line. "Did you hear what I said?"

"Can you say that again?"

"Jon Reznick. Do you understand? Do you know him?"

Silence in response. The line had gone dead.

Thirty-Six

The hours dragged for Hans Muller. He was in a secret location, somewhere in Switzerland. But he was taking orders and sweating his guts out for Russians in a brutal boot camp.

Muller knew what lay in store. He was being put through his paces ahead of the assassination. A team of tattooed Spetsnaz maniacs screamed in his face. A schedule of runs, boxing in the gym, hand-to-hand combat, and shooting practice at the outdoor range in a nearby private forest. Medics checking his vital signs—his resting heart rate, reflexes, blood pressure.

Muller was mentally and physically exhausted. He had spent years behind a fancy desk, staring at computer screens, working out real-time problems in cyberspace. His life was mostly sedentary. He didn't have an ounce of fat on him. But he had gone soft.

The Russians shouted some more. He was put in the ring and fought savage, sweat-drenched fighters. He was pounded and battered. Then he was made to do it again.

Sasha watched from the sidelines, monitoring his progress. He was being toughened up ahead of the mission.

"Go on, Hans, fight back!" Sasha screamed. "That's it! Fight! Kill him!"

Muller felt the fire inside him ignite. He summoned a hidden rage he thought he had extinguished years ago. He lashed out. He jabbed hard, then hooked his opponent. He smashed the guy right in the guts. He was in a fight for his life. His mother's too.

A red mist descended.

Muller ducked and dived and punched, blood pouring from a cut lip. He thought of his mother at home high up in the Swiss Alps, unaware she was being watched. Unaware her life was at risk if he didn't succeed. The more he thought about his predicament, the angrier he got. He counterattacked. Jabbed hard. Again and again. Then wild hooks. He floored the guy.

Sasha cheered him on. "Yeah, motherfucker! Go, Hans!"

Muller had endured. He won that battle. But would he win the war?

He showered. He changed into fresh boxing gear. He got a break for a couple of hours. He immersed himself in the relentless psychological tests. Then it was back to the hard stuff. Running, fitness, and fighting.

He had only been there twenty-four hours. His body ached like it had never ached before. He bled from his mouth and nose and ears. He got patched up. Then he fought again. He felt his sense of self gradually being eroded. In its place, a machine. A killer.

Muller was sent back to his bedroom and given headphones. He was told they were playing meditation tracks. But it was really brainwashing.

He lay back on his single bed and peered up at the ceiling. He adjusted the headphones. Then he closed his eyes. He heard the words *töten oder getötet werden* in German. Again and again.

Kill or be killed. Kill or be killed.

Muller felt himself floating over darkness on a black lake. He was losing himself. The voice became harder, as if it spoke with a renewed urgency. *Kill or be killed. Kill or be killed.* Over and over again.

He listened as he dropped in and out of sleep. Then he felt himself slipping into the abyss, disappearing into the waves.

Muller was shaken awake. He opened his eyes.

Sasha chucked his chin. "Hans, we've got a briefing in two minutes!"

"How long have I been sleeping?"

"Long enough. Now get ready."

Muller got to his feet, ribs aching still. He went to the bathroom and splashed cold water on his face. He winced as the water doused the cuts and abrasions on his skin. He studied his reflection. Wounds still raw, eyes bloodshot, lower lip cut. He had been roughed up. They had really done a number on him. But he needed to focus.

He followed Sasha down a corridor and back to the biometrically secure room.

The burly Russian guy was wearing jeans and a T-shirt, displaying both tattooed biceps. "How you feeling, Hans? You enjoy kicking ass?"

Muller sat in silence.

"What's wrong?"

"Nothing. I just want to know when and how this is going to go down. I want this over with."

"We're good, Hans?"

"We're good."

"It is important that you understand this. In life, rules change. Instead of being a cool hacker enjoying his fortune, you're staring at a new reality, right?"

"I want to know when this will go down."

"Good attitude. Here's what I know. Reznick, his wife, and his daughter are in the Zermatt area. We have a small reconnaissance team nearby. They have orders to kill too."

"So, where do I come into this?"

The Russian grinned. "You never heard of a plan B? Even plan C?"

Muller nodded.

"You're primed. And you've got this. It will be a backup operation in case we can't take the target out."

"Where and how?"

"I can't divulge the full details yet. But it will be close up. You'll see the whites of the eyes of the target before you kill her. Can you cope with that?"

"I'm ready. Let's do it."

Thirty-Seven

The sky was darkening as the last remnants of the winter sun disappeared behind the mountains.

Reznick paced the attic room of the cabin near Randa as Elisabeth scanned the world outside her frosted window. "What is it?" he asked her.

"It's nothing."

"What do you mean?"

"I don't know, it must be a trick of the light. Thought I saw something, a flicker, but it must've just been branches by the bridge. Changing light, maybe."

"Where?"

"Over the bridge, on the other side."

Reznick snapped. "Get out of sight. Away from the window."

Elisabeth ducked down and lay flat on the floor. "Jon, you're scaring me. What is it? Can you see something?"

"I don't know. Sit tight." Reznick went downstairs, picked up his backpack, and climbed back upstairs.

"Jon, talk to me."

Reznick crouched down beside Elisabeth and pulled out his powerful military binoculars. He edged closer to the window and scanned the area on the other side of the bridge. Back and forth, across the bridge, around the bridge.

"Nothing, right?"

Reznick scanned for another few moments. He fixed on an area deep within the dark woods, maybe forty yards away from the far side of the bridge.

"Jon, it was probably nothing."

He was beginning to wonder if Elisabeth had a vivid imagination. The darkening sky was turning inky black. He kept the binoculars trained on a small, wooded section across the bridge. He peered harder. A flicker of movement. Then he saw something.

A spectral figure, crouched facedown, in winter camouflage gear, face smeared with dirt, edging closer, inch by inch. Rifle in hand, headed toward the bridge.

"I don't want you to freak out, but we have a problem."

"What is it?"

"I got a visual. Camouflaged guy in the woods, just across the bridge. And he appears to be armed."

Reznick signaled her over, and she crawled head down toward him. He handed her the binoculars. "Just over the bridge."

Elisabeth scanned the area for a few moments.

"You see him?"

"I see him. Maybe he's part of the extraction team getting into position?"

"Negative. Why would he be in place twelve hours before? What's the point?"

"No point at all."

Reznick whispered, "Exactly."

Elisabeth handed the binoculars back. "A hunter, maybe?"

"A hunter, hiding just over the bridge from your cabin, only hours ahead of a scheduled extraction of a CIA agent? Long shot. A very long shot."

"Maybe someone is scouting out the area. Maybe recon. Maybe they've decided to move things up by a few hours."

Reznick shook his head again. He crouched beside the window and scanned the woods again. He brought the view into sharp focus. The figure was motionless, prostrate on the snowy ground. A military headset, as if he was communicating in real time with a handler or others nearby. "It might be extraction . . . but not by the United States."

"We need to figure this out. No one followed us to the cabin."

"Not true."

"What do you mean?"

"Think about it. The backpack. The cell phone and the computer. Classic devices for GPS location."

"Helena?"

"I can't think of anyone else. I'm assuming you have a gun."

"Glock 9mm."

"I've got a Beretta 9mm. Have you got anything else stored here?"

"I think you're in luck. You want to see the basement?"

The concrete basement was a windowless room. It had been built two levels underground and could be accessed only by a retina scanner attached to a concrete pillar.

"What the hell is this? James Bond?"

"Pretty much. The Agency built this ten years ago. Only two people have stayed here before. A Bulgarian double agent who worked for a Swiss bank and her CIA handler."

Reznick looked around. "Pretty bare."

Elisabeth opened a wooden door.

Reznick went into the room and looked around. Gun racks all over, shelves with countless boxes of ammo. Tens of thousands of rounds. A selection of hunting knives hung from the wall. "You are certainly full of surprises, I'll give you that."

Elisabeth walked into the tiny bespoke armory and shrugged. "What do you want?"

Reznick carefully examined the myriad rifles and handguns on the racks. He picked a compact Belgian submachine gun, an FN P90, preloaded with a fifty-round magazine. He checked out the knives and grabbed a Remington eight-inch drop point. And he took a silenced 9mm handgun and tucked it into his waistband. "This should do the job."

"Jon, I'm not sure you should engage. We don't know who he is."

"That's my concern."

Reznick and Elisabeth headed back up to the attic room with their weapons. He picked up the binoculars and scanned the woods again. The man lay spread-eagled in the snow, hunkered down, covered by tree branches. "Fucker is digging in."

"Jon, what if I call the Pentagon number again?"

Reznick handed her his cell phone. He took a few moments to consider this option. "Explain that you have a visual on a guy in the woods. Is he part of the extraction team? Yes or no."

Elisabeth made the call. He listened as she went through security questions before she asked the question. "Copy that. What about NDB?" She nodded. "Affirmative, copy that." She handed the cell phone back to Reznick.

"What did they say?"

"Definitely not our guys. Not NDB, not their MO. They told me to sit tight."

"Not an option now."

Reznick stared at the figure in the distance. "Fucker is still there, talking away on his headset."

"What's the plan?"

"We can't wait until the middle of the night. I have no idea who that guy is. He's not one of our guys. He's not NDB."

"So, who is he?"

"I'm not about to wait and find out."

"So, we kill him?"

"Not if we don't have to. Take up position here. You can keep an eye on him. If he or anyone else puts a foot on the bridge, pull the trigger. Kill them. You got that?"

Elisabeth lay down on the floor and got into position with the submachine gun. She looked like she had done it before. "Copy that. Where are you going?"

"I'm going to head up the path and cut back higher up the track, before I head over there."

"You're not going to leave me here, are you?"

"Just for a little bit. Keep an eye on him, and if he sets foot on the bridge, take him down."

Thirty-Eight

Reznick headed out the back door and traversed up the rough, snowy incline, through the woods, knife in hand. He had endured countless Arctic training episodes in the far north of Norway during myriad NATO training exercises. This was routine for him.

The snow was getting deeper as he headed higher, through the woods, before he doubled back down a treacherous path. He picked his way through the pines as he crunched on the snowy ground amid conifers, down into a steep ravine.

He crouched behind a tree, getting his bearings. Running water gurgled farther down beyond the woods.

Reznick's eyesight adjusted to the darkness. He scanned his surroundings. Wind rustling in the trees. He listened. And watched.

His breath turned to vapor in the icy cold.

Reznick slowly got to his feet and made his way to the fringe of the woods. He saw the black water. He crossed the rocky shallow tributary. He turned and looked up and saw the silhouetted suspension bridge, about one hundred yards downstream.

He took a few more moments to get his bearings, turned, and saw the tree line he was looking for. He was getting close. He scrambled up the steep bank and crouched down.

He didn't move for a minute or two. The smell of cigarette smoke drifted his way.

Reznick was working on instinct. He had no night vision goggles to help him navigate. He began to crawl over the cold, snowy ground, facedown, limbs spread out, the powder muffling his movements.

A man talking low, the acrid smell of cigarette smoke. The voice went quiet for a few moments as Reznick lay still, face pressed into the snow, ferns, and dirt.

The man coughed.

Reznick peered over an icy fallen branch. A man in snow camouflage, leaning against a tree, dragged hard on a cigarette. Cell phone pressed to his ear. A whisper. *"Spasibo."* The guy was Russian.

Reznick held his breath as the man coughed and muttered. He watched and waited until the man ended the call. The man adjusted his position and spread-eagled in the snow, binoculars trained on the suspension bridge.

Reznick was only five yards away at most. He slowly got to his feet. He took a couple of steps forward and kicked the man hard in the side of the head. The man rolled.

He smashed his fist repeatedly into the man's jaw. Four, five, six, seven times. Blood spilled out, and the man moaned.

The guy swung around.

Reznick grabbed the man by the throat and squeezed tight on the carotid artery, knife pressed against the man's neck. "Not a fucking word!"

The man was shaking his head, teeth clenched.

Reznick pressed the knife into the man's white flesh, carving a small incision. "Who are you? Talk or you die."

"I am a hunter." The thick accent was unmistakably Russian.

Reznick rabbit-punched the man, who quickly blacked out. He unzipped the pocket of the man's snow jacket and rummaged inside. He pulled out a map of Switzerland. A Nikon camera. And a laminated Russian ID for the embassy in Bern. The guy's name was Alexei Garabov, his occupation listed as plumber.

He put the ID in his back pocket and the knife back in the sheath, and he pressed the silenced gun to the man's head. He slapped him hard until he awoke.

The man's eyes rolled back in his head for a few moments.

"Alexei," Reznick hissed, "what are you doing here?"

"I'm a hunter."

Reznick was losing patience. "No, you're not, you piece of shit." He pressed the gun tight up to the guy's temple. "Why is a Russian plumber with credentials from the Russian Embassy in Bern hanging out in the woods at night? Doing a bit of nocturnal bird-watching?"

"Don't kill me. I can answer your question. It's just a mix-up."

Reznick pressed the gun even harder against the Russian's jaw. "Bullshit. What are you doing here?"

"I'm watching . . ."

"Watching what? Answer me or I swear to God you get a bullet in the head!"

"The woman! I was watching the American woman."

"Give me her name and you'll live."

"Bruckmann. That is her name!"

Reznick seethed as he rummaged in the man's backpack. He pulled out bottles of pills, duct tape, wire cutters. "What's all this for?"

"I was told to cross the bridge at midnight . . ."

"What were you going to do?"

"Drug her."

"What else?"

The Russian closed his eyes tight. "Throw her off the bridge."

"Who else is involved?"

"No one else. Please, I am nobody. I am just a working man, trying to earn a living."

Reznick squeezed the guy's neck. The whites of his eyes widened, teeth clenched. "Last warning. Give me a name."

"Go fuck yourself, American!"

Reznick stared down into the Russian's cold gray eyes. He pressed the gun to his head. Looked away. Then calmly squeezed the trigger. A dull *phut* sound. Blood poured from the head wound. Brain splatter on his jacket. He rummaged in the Russian's trouser pockets and pulled out a cell phone. He placed it in his back pocket. He got to his feet, backpack slung over his shoulder.

He grabbed the boots of the dead Russian and dragged the body deeper into the woods. He wanted to be as far away from the snowy mountain path as possible.

Reznick stopped after he was maybe a couple hundred yards into the snowy woods. He kneeled down beside the body, and, using his bare hands, he dug into the snow and earth. Within fifteen minutes he had created a rudimentary shallow grave. He stood up and kicked the dead Russian in. He quickly covered it up. He shoved in mounds of earth and snow and pine and larch branches, along with frozen twigs.

He knew that more snowfalls would cover it further, freezing and entombing the body until the spring.

Reznick retraced his steps as he headed through the dark forest. A few minutes later he saw the bridge. He walked halfway across, the deep ravine below, and stopped. He took the Russian's cell phone out of his pocket and prized out the SIM card. He dropped the phone down into the water below, SIM card in his pocket, in the hope that texts or phone numbers could be retrieved at a later date.

Reznick scrambled up the snowy path toward the cabin in the woods where his wife was waiting.

Thirty-Nine

He climbed up to the attic where Elisabeth was, submachine gun in hand. She looked up. "What the hell happened?" she asked.

Reznick shook his head. "You don't want to know. All you need to know is that we need to get out of here very soon."

Elisabeth furrowed her brow and paced as he took off his filthy, blood-soaked outer clothes.

"Burn them!"

"Jon, what happened?"

"A Russian was five hundred yards from this cabin, watching and waiting."

"Who was he?"

"A Russian spy, operative, whatever."

"Did you kill him?"

"Yes, I did."

Elisabeth closed her eyes tight.

"You work for the CIA. You know how this works."

"I understand."

Reznick showered as Elisabeth burned the bloodied clothes on the log fire. He changed into a pair of jeans and a T-shirt and wrapped up warm. He headed downstairs and took a couple of Dexedrine.

Elisabeth handed him a tray with a ham sandwich and a mug of hot coffee.

"Thanks."

"Was there anyone with the Russian?"

"It was only him that I saw. But he was talking to a handler, perhaps. The whole thing is fucked up."

"What now?"

Reznick wolfed down the sandwich and gulped down the hot coffee. "Now, we move." He checked his watch. "2000 hours. OK?"

"Where exactly are we going? What if there are others waiting?"

"Listen, this watch-and-wait shit would have gotten you killed if the Russian hadn't been neutralized. There will be more."

Elisabeth went quiet.

"You're not safe here. Are we clear on that?"

Elisabeth nodded as she pulled on a thick Canada Goose coat, hat, thermal gloves, and heavy boots.

Reznick pulled on his boots and zipped up a spare coat against the biting high-altitude cold. He pulled on his backpack with weapons and supplies as Elisabeth did the same. "You OK?"

"I thought I had turned my back on the world."

"Life's like that. Comes at you when you least expect it."

Elisabeth looked around the cabin as if she had forgotten something.

"Ready?" he said.

"Let's go."

Reznick led the way. He left by the back door and headed up over the snowy ridge again. The same path he had taken an hour earlier. Then a fork over the ridge and onto another winding snowy trail. They hiked up and along a twisty icy ridge, deep in the forest, which snaked its way back down into the village of Randa.

"What's the plan?"

Reznick checked his cell phone and pulled up the map. "We keep on moving." He figured they still had time to catch the last train to the nearby town of St. Niklaus, which was farther down the mountain. They trudged through the deserted village. The lights of the railway station were up ahead. "Get a pair of tickets for St. Niklaus."

Elisabeth bought the tickets, and they walked out onto the floodlit, deserted platform. The last train. Her warm breath hit the cold air.

"Relax, it'll be fine."

"Easier said than done. My nerves are shredded."

The sound of a train approaching. A few minutes later it screeched to a halt in the snowy darkness.

Reznick waited until Elisabeth was on the train before he boarded. She sat down at the back of the rear carriage beside the window. He sat down next to her.

The train idled for a few minutes.

"Never a dull moment, huh?"

Elisabeth nodded as she sat in silent contemplation.

Reznick took out his cell phone and texted Lauren. *Take the train to St. Niklaus. I'll meet you there.* He and Elisabeth sat tight together, legs touching. It felt strange after all this time.

An elderly couple in heavy coats, hats, and thick wooly gloves suddenly boarded the train and sat near the front.

Reznick's senses switched on. He wondered if they were tourists or locals. Or people following them.

A whistle from a guard on the platform. The train pulled slowly away into the darkness.

"What exactly happened back there?" Elisabeth said. "I want to know the details."

"Trust me, you don't."

"Did you kill him with your bare hands?"

"It's over! We need to move on. Things are happening. And we need to be on our toes."

"We're on the run like fugitives. This is crazy. They have an extraction team on the way."

"So they say."

"What does that mean?"

"People lie."

"You think my handler is misleading me?"

"Human nature. Besides, the Russki who was hiding out in the woods, near the bridge—not a good sign. Almost certainly got a support team on the way."

"Jon, what did you do to the guy in the woods? Please tell me."

"Elisabeth, he had been sent to kill you. OK?"

"You don't know that."

Reznick nodded. "Yes, I do."

"How do you know?"

"He told me."

"And you killed him for that?"

"That's what I do. It's not nice."

"No, it's not." Elisabeth regarded him coldly. "This might be normal for you, but it's not for me."

"I'll give you that. Point taken."

The minutes dragged as an icy silence opened up between them. A short while later, the train slowed down, pulling up sharply, grinding to a shuddering halt in the small mountain town of Tasch.

Reznick watched as the old couple farther down the train car got off. But no one got on. Two minutes later a whistle blew, the doors closed, and the train pulled away again into the night. "Look, I'm sorry. This isn't your world, I know that."

"I shouldn't have snapped."

"Forget it. We're like an old married couple, right?"

Elisabeth smiled and nodded as she looked back out the window. "Are we going to make it out of here alive?"

"That's the plan."

Reznick's cell phone vibrated in his pocket. He checked. A text message from Lauren. *Got the last train. See you in 38 mins.* He looked at Elisabeth. "You OK?"

"Who was that?"

"Lauren. We're going to see her."

"Now?"

"How do you feel about that?"

"Scared. Numb, actually. I feel like it's not actually happening."

Reznick patted the back of her hand. "It'll be fine."

The train headed through the snowy darkness at speed. A few miles later, the train slowed and stopped at the deserted St. Niklaus railway station.

Reznick adjusted his backpack as he and Elisabeth disembarked. He got off the train and headed toward signs leading to the parking lot. He strode to the far end, keeping an '80s-style Volkswagen RV in sight. It was perfect. He turned to Elisabeth, who was lagging behind. "Keep a lookout," he said.

"Why?"

"Just do as I say!"

Reznick got to work.

He took out his Swiss Army knife from his back pocket. He opened it up and worked the blade into the lock. A few seconds later, it clicked open. Reznick opened the door and crouched down. A micro-screwdriver on the knife quickly removed the plastic cover of the steering wheel. He shone his cell phone light inside. He saw the loose wire he was looking for. He pulled out his knife and cut off a couple of inches of the insulation around the wires and twisted them together. Suddenly, the engine spluttered into life. "Get in the back!"

Elisabeth slid into the back seat. "This is way out of my comfort zone."

"All part of the fun." Reznick checked his watch. "Not much longer. Assuming it's on time."

"It's Switzerland. Everything is on time."

Reznick watched the train tracks. The red lights turned to green. A few minutes later, right on schedule, a train pulled into the St. Niklaus station. A few people carrying skis, crampons, and huge backpacks stepped off the train.

The last person to emerge was Lauren. He wound down the window and flashed his headlights as he signaled her over. He turned and smiled at Elisabeth. "Don't be nervous."

"I am."

Lauren was stone faced as she approached the vehicle. She stopped and stared through the back window at her mother.

Elisabeth leaned over and opened the door. "Hi."

Lauren climbed in the back without saying a word.

Reznick felt the tension between them. He glanced in his rearview mirror and smiled. But neither of them smiled back. He eased the RV into first gear, pulled away, and disappeared down the mountain road.

"It's nice to finally see you again, Lauren," Elisabeth said.

"Yeah." A monosyllabic reply from Lauren.

Reznick drove on. The headlights of the RV pierced the icy darkness ahead.

"This is really awkward, I know, Lauren."

"Yeah, you could say that."

"I'm so very sorry, Lauren."

Lauren said nothing.

"I just wanted to say that I hope that someday, somehow, you can find it in your heart to forgive me."

"I hope so too."

Elisabeth bowed her head and began to cry. "I never meant for any of this to happen. You have to believe me."

"But it did happen. You left me. You left us."

"And for that I am truly, truly sorry. I wish I could turn back the clock and do things differently. I don't know what happened to me. I got lost. Lost in myself. Lost in my world. This world. It was selfish. I was selfish. I just didn't want to deal with my life. I wasn't well."

"You never came looking for me."

"I never stopped thinking about you. I missed you. I missed you both. But I just wanted out. And it was a way out. A way to escape. But I . . . I didn't realize what I had done until it was too late."

Reznick drove on and glanced in the rearview mirror. He watched Lauren touch Elisabeth's cheek.

"I want to start again, Lauren," Elisabeth said.

"I thought you died on 9/11. So did Dad. That was what we were told. But it was a lie, Mom."

"It was a terrible, terrible thing to do. I know that now."

"I tormented myself for years thinking of you, trapped high up in the towers, being engulfed in smoke, terrified and screaming for your life. I thought about that a lot."

Elisabeth sobbed. "Oh, Lauren, please, I can't bear it."

"I only have the photos of us when I was a baby, back in Rockland, or New York. That's all I have of you. Glimpses of you."

Reznick felt his throat tighten as he listened. It was almost too much to handle.

"How could you do that? How could you abandon us?"

"Selfishness. Pure selfishness. A need to escape my state of mind. I was hanging on by a thread. I thought I was losing my mind. I couldn't see a way out."

Lauren sighed and bowed her head.

Elisabeth wrapped an arm around Lauren and held her tight, as if afraid to let her go. "I'm here now, honey. Please forgive me. Just know that I love you. And I love your dad. But I don't love myself. And that's the honest-to-God truth."

"What does that even mean?"

"It means I missed you desperately. I wanted to come home after a couple of years. But I was told that wasn't an option."

"Is that true, Mom?"

"Yes, it's the truth. I did want to come home. I asked to come home. But it was too late. My old life was gone. For good. And I had to deal with that."

"That must've been hard," Lauren said, a tinge of sympathy beginning to creep through in her tone.

"It was my own fault, Lauren. I'm to blame for whatever happened to me, you, and your dad."

Lauren sighed. "Why didn't you at least try to call?"

"That wasn't possible. I wanted to. But they said absolutely not. No emails, no messages. It was then and only then I saw the full extent of the mistake I'd made. A monumental mistake."

"I had no idea, Mom. I missed you so, so much."

"And I missed *you*. I'm so sorry. I love you."

The two women embraced, both weeping.

Reznick glanced in his rearview mirror as he headed down an alpine road.

Forty

Reznick sped past isolated little hamlets and remote mountain farms. He glanced in the rearview mirror for the umpteenth time. In the back seat, Elisabeth and Lauren were talking things out.

"I tried to look you up, online," Elisabeth said. "I wanted to know you were OK. And that's what I did over the last ten years or so. But the people who oversaw what I was doing, people in the government, warned me not to leave any digital links back to you or your father. And that was that."

"That must have been difficult."

"Nothing like what you've been through. Or your dad. Nothing at all."

Reznick glanced in the mirror and smiled back at Elisabeth.

"I'm racked by guilt. And I will be to my dying day."

"But you lived here."

"I had to. Elisabeth Reznick didn't exist anymore, remember. I couldn't go back even though I wanted to. I was told I could never return to America. No matter what."

"Shit."

"I must've been naive, stupid, dumb, or maybe just plain crazy to do what I did."

Reznick cleared his throat. "What's done is done. I don't think this is the time for recrimination and pointing fingers."

Lauren hugged Elisabeth tight. "I want to be friends."

"I'm more than your friend. I'm your mother. And I love you."

The pair of them began reacquainting themselves like long-lost friends. It was a sight he thought he'd never see. And it was the one saving grace of the whole sorry saga. A reconciliation. Not the most conventional of reconciliations, that was for sure. But a reconciliation all the same.

His heart swelled with joy. Despite everything, and after all this time, he did care for Elisabeth.

Reznick tried to change radio channels. It was stuck, set to a Zurich classical radio station. It played piano music. Soft, moving. He didn't know much about classical music. But he knew Elisabeth loved it, having played the piano as a child.

He drove on, listening to the whispered conversation in the back seat. The talk was of careers, a deep longing to connect with the other after all these years, and expressing how much they had missed each other.

Elisabeth apologized again and again, sobbing as Lauren comforted her.

He pressed his foot down, wanting to make haste. He had no idea what the specific plan was. But his main focus was on getting them out of the country. Alive.

"Sorry to interrupt, Elisabeth," he said. "I'm assuming there was a place, a fallback position you could go to. In emergencies."

"Meiringen Air Base, one hundred kilometers away."

Reznick made a mental note. "Directions from here?"

"Due north on this road. Takes you to Lake Thun. Then head east on the A8. The air base is a few miles beyond the most easterly point of Lake Brienz."

"And the air base was your fallback position if the shit hit the fan?"

"Absolutely."

Reznick sped on into the darkness. He drove hard. The full moon illuminated the alpine winter villages.

He glanced one more time in his rearview mirror. Lauren's head rested on Elisabeth's shoulder. They were fast asleep.

Forty-One

Reznick drove on, restless.

He contemplated the merits of Elisabeth being told to head to Meiringen if all else failed. It made perfect sense for an extraction. Was an American extraction team—a backup—waiting for his wife and daughter? Maybe a CIA-registered private jet to whisk them off into the night? All of that made sense. But he could not shake the nagging doubts that bothered him. The loose ends. The lack of real planning. It gnawed away at him. Why was that? What exactly was bugging him so much?

His mind flashed back to his killing of the Russian. He wondered if the Russians had assumed his wife would be alone and easy to deal with. How exactly had they tracked her down? Was Gruber the weak link? Maybe she was simply a Russian agent who had led them to his wife.

He kept glancing in the rearview at Elisabeth and Lauren. Reznick was glad he was here. He had to be here. He reveled in such situations. He was used to adversity. The trick was to stay focused and work the problem. Never panic. Cold detachment.

The lights of a car coming up behind him snapped Reznick out of his reverie. He checked his rearview mirror. From what he saw in flashes of street lighting, it looked like an SUV, a BMW X5, an infinitely more powerful vehicle than the beaten-up old RV. The vehicle edged closer. He saw a silhouetted figure driving in the front, maybe someone else in the back.

Reznick drove on, his wife and daughter quiet and peaceful, sleeping, entwined in each other's arms. He wondered why the SUV wasn't overtaking them. It was a four-liter V-8 monster of a car. It could easily hit more than 150 mph in seconds. He checked his speedometer. He was doing a steady sixty miles per hour, probably the limit of the ancient VW's engine.

He checked his rearview mirror again. The vehicle was maybe seventy or eighty yards back, headlights on. The driver seemed content just to sit at that speed, trailing Reznick.

Reznick saw the neon lights of a gas station up ahead. He pulled off the main road and drove up next to one of the gas pumps. He watched as the BMW cruised by. He waited until it was out of sight.

Lauren stirred in the back seat. "Why are we stopping, Dad?" she said.

"Getting gas."

Elisabeth leaned forward and peered, bleary eyed, at the dashboard. "It's three-quarters full, Jon."

"Listen, it might be nothing, just a BMW that was on my tail. Just hung in there behind us for a few miles. I thought it wise to pull over, just as a precaution. I don't know . . . It might be nothing."

Elisabeth nodded.

Reznick got out of the RV and quickly filled up the tank. It didn't take long. He went inside, picked up some chocolate bars and bottles of water, and paid the kid in the kiosk. He got back in the RV and handed over the bag of goodies. "In case you're hungry."

Elisabeth touched the back of his head. "Thank you, that was nice."

Reznick glanced in the rearview mirror and smiled. "You're welcome. Do you want to take the wheel?"

"Sure. Do you need some shut-eye?"

Reznick shook his head. He had his reasons. "Nope." He turned and faced Lauren. "You OK?"

"I'm fine, Dad. What's in your head? I know what you're like."

"There was no reason for that BMW to tail us on an empty road. None at all."

"So, what are you saying?"

"I'm saying we need to be ready. For anything."

Reznick got out, picking up his backpack, and got in the back seat with Lauren.

Elisabeth slid into the driver's seat.

Reznick buckled up and unzipped the backpack. He pulled out the compact Belgian submachine gun, the FN P90, loaded with a fifty-round magazine.

"Jon, seriously?" Elisabeth said.

"Be prepared. Always."

"Jon, if the Swiss police stop us, we are all going to jail."

"If anyone else stops us, jail will be the least of our worries. Let's go, Elisabeth."

"Dad, we're in Switzerland, not Texas."

Reznick rested the weapon on his lap, locked and loaded. "Just as a precaution."

Elisabeth turned around. "You want to continue to the air base?"

"Drive. The vehicle we need to look out for is a dark-blue BMW SUV, an X5."

Elisabeth pulled away from the gas station and got back on the road.

"I think you dozed off for a while," he said.

"I did. Thank you."

Reznick touched the back of her head. "You OK?"

"I'm fine. Scared. But glad you're here."

"Me too."

Elisabeth accelerated. She drove mile after mile down the near-deserted Swiss road, headed for the air base. No sign of the BMW.

Reznick looked farther up the road. A sign for Lake Thun, only eight kilometers away. "You drive this way before?" he asked.

"Quite a few times."

"You like it?"

"The road or the location?"

"The place."

"It's lovely. I like it a lot."

"Not missing New York?"

"Not so much."

"What about Rockland? You remember the house we had there?"

Elisabeth forced a smile.

"Did you ever think of us?"

"More than you'd think."

Reznick stared straight ahead. "You ready to go home now?"

"I think I have to, don't I?"

"Pretty much."

The three of them sat in a companionable silence for a few minutes. Then it all changed. Headlights dazzled in the rearview mirror.

"Where the hell did they come from?" Elisabeth said.

Reznick spun around as the powerful SUV approached. He was sure it was the same license plate. "Fuck! It's them!"

Lauren took out her handgun and pulled back the slide. "You sure?"

"Billion percent sure."

Elisabeth said, "You want me to floor it?"

"This thing is doing sixty. The thing behind us is a monster by comparison. Just lower yourself down and keep driving."

The SUV edged closer. Thirty yards. Twenty yards. It accelerated and rammed the rear of the RV.

The collision jerked them violently.

Reznick looked back. The passenger in the back was leaning out of the window, gun drawn. A shot rang out. The rear window glass shattered, showering Reznick and Lauren with fragments.

Elisabeth screamed.

"Stay down!" Reznick pressed the submachine gun through the VW's missing rear window. He took careful aim. He had the passenger in the crosshairs. He fired off a volley of shots. As if in slow motion, the bullets tore through the BMW's windshield, shattering the glass.

The rear passenger slumped in his seat.

The SUV swerved as the driver struggled to control it.

Elisabeth shouted, "Did you get him?"

Reznick took careful aim again. He stared down the sights. He focused on the front left tire. He squeezed the trigger. The tire exploded. He watched as the SUV lurched wildly back across the road.

Lauren took aim. She fired two shots as the BMW careered onto the shoulder. "Got him! Driver—shoulder and chest, I think."

Reznick kept the submachine gun trained on the out-of-control SUV, which swerved as the injured driver lost control. He had the driver's silhouetted head in full view. He fired a volley of shots.

The driver slumped over the wheel.

The SUV veered wildly across the road, flipping over multiple times, before it exploded into a deafening ball of flames, lighting up the night sky.

Forty-Two

Elisabeth drove on for a few hundred yards before she spoke. "What do we do now, Jon?"

"Get off the road."

Elisabeth shook her head as she gripped the steering wheel. "What?"

"Get to the nearest town! Dump this goddamn RV! You understand?"

"Please don't shout, Jon."

"Just do it."

"Who were those guys?"

"We can let someone else figure that out. Who the hell knows. Get off the road, Elisabeth!"

Elisabeth took a sharp turn off the dark highway and drove through a tiny Swiss hamlet.

Reznick turned and looked at his daughter. "You OK, honey?"

"I'm OK, Dad. That was nuts back there."

"You did great. Proud of you."

Lauren smiled, tears in her eyes. "Mom, you OK?"

"I'm fine . . . Really, I got this."

Reznick grinned. "Excellent. Working as a team."

"Sorry for freaking out. It's just that . . ."

"You don't have to explain. It's fine. You're fine."

Elisabeth drove on past a dozen chalets.

"Find a quiet spot."

She got to the outskirts of the village and headed up a near-deserted side street where she parked the vehicle.

Reznick slung the backpack over his shoulder as he got out of the RV. He walked over to a small Mazda and took out his knife. Within two minutes he had gained entry to the car and hot-wired the vehicle. The engine purred into life.

He got in the driver's seat, as Elisabeth and Lauren got in the back. He pulled away quickly, up a snowy incline, engine revving hard, before he made it back onto the main road.

"We all OK back there?" he asked.

Elisabeth and Lauren were holding hands. "Who was that, Dad?" Lauren said.

"No idea. We have to assume they were from the embassy. Russians. I caught one hiding out in the woods near your mother's cabin."

"What happened?"

"He was neutralized."

"You killed a diplomat?"

"That's what happened. You need to deal with that. This is not a game. I suspect the guy I ran into had accomplices who were targeting your mom too. They must've gotten a fix on us. It's either kill or be killed. Time to get up to speed."

Elisabeth leaned forward. "Jon, let's just get to the air base in one piece."

"I don't know."

"What don't you know?"

"I don't know if the air base is a good idea now. I don't know if your plans have been compromised."

"I'm sorry, I don't understand."

Reznick's mind was switched on. He sensed that they weren't safe and sound. He wondered if this might be a trap.

"Jon, the air base is where I have been told to go. That's my off-ramp. It's a place of safety."

"Maybe it is. Elisabeth, you need to level with me."

"About what?"

"I need the full picture. I need the ins and outs of what you know."

"I've told you everything."

"You haven't told me who your handler is. The person at the Pentagon you talk to. There must be one person. One point of contact. Who is it?"

"Why do you want to know that?"

"Something isn't right. Something's off, and I don't like it!"

"What don't you like?"

"Everything. It's all fucked up. The extraction in the middle of the night, waiting around for days and days after your cover was blown. You were a sitting duck. No chopper extraction. The Russian in the woods. The BMW chasing us. It's a mess, every step of the way."

"I don't disagree. But it's the best plan we have."

"Someone wants you dead, Elisabeth. They want you dead at any cost. They want no trace of you. Again."

"Dad, can we just get to the air base?" Lauren asked.

"You're both not seeing what I see. I believe what we've encountered so far isn't the end of it."

"Are you saying I wouldn't be safe at the air base?" Elisabeth asked.

"Swiss intelligence has been compromised. Their plans, their people, their codes, their agents, Western spy agencies in the country—you name it. The Russians will not stop just because you're on an air base."

Elisabeth nodded. "Fair enough. All it would take is one maintenance guy who works there, a pilot, the head of the base, anyone, to be compromised."

"But also, the security measures in and around the base. Those would be compromised. You have to assume the worst. Prepare for the worst."

"I think I would prefer to take my chances at the air base."

"Elisabeth, listen to me. We've been shot at. You were being watched. There was a Russian waiting in the woods to kill you. Do you know what he told me?"

"What?"

"He was going to drug you and throw you off the bridge. That was his mission."

"Please don't shout at me, Jon."

"I'm not shouting."

Reznick sped on as Elisabeth kept her face pointed straight ahead.

"I'm just trying to make you understand. I need to know more."

"What else? And why?"

"I need to know, before we go to this air base, that we have all the angles covered."

"The Russians are out of the way for now. We can get back to America and talk about it all then. I need to be debriefed first."

"This is a shitshow. Your guy at the Pentagon or State Department is already furious, probably, that the decades-long deep-cover act of yours has blown up. The operation has been compromised. You're compromised. You know too much."

Elisabeth snapped, "Shut up!"

"You know everything. Can you imagine if this information leaks out in America? A woman who supposedly died on 9/11 was actually living a double life in Switzerland as part of a covert spying operation? The Agency, the Pentagon, everyone, would look ridiculous. But it would also expose this classified operation of yours to the wider public."

Elisabeth sat stolidly beside Lauren. "What's really bothering you about this, Jon? It's not just the Russian threat, is it?"

Reznick sighed. "Correct. I'm worried about driving you up to the military air base in a couple of hours and simply handing you over. I want to talk about your handler. So, are you going to talk to me?"

"What exactly are you getting at?"

"While you are alive, you could reveal so much about the operation. You could be kidnapped by foreign agents, either at home or abroad. The Pentagon doesn't give up secrets easily. The mission is everything. The person is expendable. I know that better than anyone."

"So, what are you saying?"

"I'm saying you're expendable. Like the rest of us. Like me. The blowback from this operation becoming public would be incalculable."

"That's not going to happen!"

"Not if you're dead! Don't you understand?"

Elisabeth shook her head. "You're crazy. So, not only the Russians, but my own side, the United States government, wants me dead?"

"America was spying not only on its enemies through two-stage verification technology and all the rest, but also its friends. The furor would be insane. And that's why I need to know the name of your handler! Who is it? Gimme a name!"

"General Charles Gronski."

The name crashed through Reznick's brain like a truck. "Gronski? Chuck Gronski?"

"You know him?"

"Damn right, I do. He was a former commander of Delta, back in the day. And yes, he knew me."

"Are you kidding me? You know him?"

"He's a double-crossing bastard. Cold as they come."

"Are you serious?"

"Gronski, I know. And he's definitely your point man? The handler?"

"He's the only one I talk to. Direct line. No one else."

Reznick took out his cell phone, one hand on the wheel. He brought up Trevelle's number.

"Hey, Jon, what the hell? I thought I wasn't going to hear from you again."

"Trevelle, listen to me. I want everything on a General Charles Gronski. Personal details. Whatever. I need them within the hour."

"Copy that."

Reznick ended the call and drove on.

"Dad, are you sure this is the right play?" Lauren said.

"While we are on foreign soil, you are at severe risk of being disappeared. That's my judgment. That's my call. The way I see it. Nothing more, nothing less."

A silence filled the car.

"What do you suggest? Can you guarantee I'll be safe with your plan? Do you even have a plan?"

"No guarantees in this game. Your best hope to get back to US soil is if you fly commercial. In plain sight. With your Anna Bruckmann documentation."

Elisabeth said, "What do you think, Lauren?"

"I trust Dad. I think you should trust him too."

"I do trust him."

"So," Lauren said, "let's go with Dad's plan. What do you say?"

"What if it all goes wrong?"

Lauren cleared her throat. "Mom, Dad's right. We can't guarantee, here on foreign soil, that a Swiss military base is the safest. Their intelligence has been compromised. And as for the Pentagon, who's to say that you, as a CIA operator, won't be taken to a secret base and never seen or heard from again? You don't exist, after all."

Forty-Three

The fast helicopter took off with Hans Muller and Sasha buckled up tight in the back. Muller looked down on the familiar picturesque snowscape of Lausanne, the pristine lake glittering like a mirror ball in the sun.

Muller adjusted his headset. "You hear me, Sasha?"

Sasha shifted in her seat. "Copy that, Hans. It's plan B. And you're on. Next stop, Zurich."

"I got this."

"This is a fluid situation. The intel we have has just come through."

"Source?"

"Swiss police radio intercept. They have a fix on a stolen Mazda. Reznick and his wife and daughter are en route to the international airport in Zurich. So, we will arrive before them. We have plenty of time to get in place."

"Copy that. What about facial recognition at the airport?"

"We've got you covered. We've remotely modified your fake identity to match another person."

"Sergei putting this together?"

Sasha gave the thumbs-up sign. "Copy that. He spotted a vulnerability in the servers used by the airport. And he saw a way in."

"Done it myself."

"The ID will show you as Felix Lumberg, a security operative who covers the terminals and who matches your description. It's all been taken care of. We will wait in the international departures lounge. And we will await instructions. Sergei and his team will be monitoring on the airport's surveillance system. We will both be wearing AirPods. We will be able to communicate with each other, but most importantly, receive instructions in real time."

Muller leaned his head on the window. Flying low, dipping, then veering upward as the pilot got on his assigned flight path to Zurich. His heart raced fast. He closed his eyes. A Russian voice in his head-phones. *Kill or be killed. Kill or be killed.* He had been activated. He had a mission. He had a purpose: kill Elisabeth Reznick. The element of surprise was crucial. He had that. He would be waiting.

"You've gone quiet on me," Sasha said. "Everything alright?"

"Affirmative."

"Just got an update. A drone we're using has a fix on the vehicle Reznick is driving."

"Copy that. So, how do we get up close?"

"The airside security pass will give you access to go wherever you want. Access to all areas."

Muller felt a frisson of excitement pass through him.

"Plainclothes security. Sergei just sent me the details."

"Where do we pick them up?"

"We already have it. It's an electronic key fob."

"If it's airside, they'll be using the biometric photo surveillance system they installed only two years ago."

"We know. But trust us on this. Sergei has just deactivated any retina scan or photo scan of Hans Muller. For the next three hours, your face will come back as the face of Felix Lumberg, Zurich Airport security. Sound OK?"

"Let's do it."

Forty-Four

Reznick drove hard until he reached the outskirts of Zurich. He pulled up and looked down Josefstrasse.

"Where are we stopping, Dad?" Lauren asked.

Reznick turned around. "Everyone out. We'll get a cab to the airport from here."

"Why?" Lauren said. "We've still got a few miles to go."

"More anonymous. This vehicle might already be reported stolen. I don't want any last-minute problems."

Lauren called a local taxi company. She gave the pickup address and ended the call. "He spoke perfect English. They'll be here in ten minutes."

"Good, it gives us time."

"Time for what?" Lauren said.

"We need to dump all of Elisabeth's weapons so we can get through airport security without any hitches. Everything that's hers. Keep what's yours." Reznick saw a dumpster across the street and threw the bag in there. He walked back to his wife and daughter. "You guys OK?"

Elisabeth wrapped her arm around Lauren. "We're fine."

A short while later, the cab pulled up.

Reznick sat up front alongside the driver, and Elisabeth and Lauren sat in the back. "You speak English?" he said, turning to the thickset driver.

"Yes, sir."

"International departures terminal. And let's get a move on. We're late."

"You'll want Terminal E."

"Terminal E. Sounds good."

The cab screeched away as the driver turned on some bass-heavy German hip-hop. The driver smiled. "Great stuff, right?"

Reznick forced a smile. He wanted to rip the radio out of the dashboard.

"You from England?" the driver asked.

"Me? No."

"America?"

"Yeah, that's right."

The driver nodded. "Have you had a nice holiday?"

"Very nice, thank you."

"Will you return to Switzerland?"

"Maybe one day."

The driver nodded as the music pounded out. "Just about finished my shift."

"Good for you."

"I think I'll go for a drink and relax."

Reznick ignored the chat. He was tempted to turn off the music. But he decided to try and block it out. He watched the road ahead and endured the mind-crushing awfulness of the beats.

Twenty minutes later, the cab pulled up at the terminal.

Reznick paid the driver in cash, handing over a fifty-euro bill.

"Too much," the driver said.

"Keep it."

The driver shrugged. "Thanks."

Reznick was relieved to escape. He got out of the cab with Elisabeth and Lauren and headed straight into the airport terminal. All glass and modernistic forms. The shops were upscale. Boutiques, chocolate shops, fancy bars, restaurants.

He checked the departure times on a board. The next flight to New York wasn't for three hours. It was good timing.

Reznick headed over to the ticket counter and bought three SWISS airline tickets for the nonstop flight to JFK. They went through security and showed their passports. Then they went into the plush Alpenblick Bar and enjoyed a selection of ham and cheese baguettes, coffee, and a couple of bottles of mineral water. He patted Elisabeth on the back of the hand. "You OK?"

"I'm fine. Thanks for everything."

Reznick checked his caller ID as Elisabeth and Lauren dug into their food. He saw a familiar number on his phone. "Yeah?"

"It's Trevelle. Got some information on Gronski."

"Where is he at this moment?"

"At home."

"Where's that?"

"A palatial house in a nice gated community in McLean. He also has a ranch in Big Sky, Montana, and an oceanfront house in Palm Beach, not to mention a penthouse condo in Grand Cayman."

Reznick smiled as he watched Elisabeth and Lauren enjoying their baguettes and coffee. "He works for the fucking government. How can he afford that?"

"Exactly. I figure, conservatively speaking, all that would cost a cool thirty-five million, give or take."

"Does he have any other jobs or income? Directorships? Consultancies?"

"None. Just his salary from the DoD. His wife is a homemaker. Has been for twenty-five years. He has been in the military all his life. His wife was a cook at a local diner before he met her."

"So, where does he get all the money? Good investments? Bitcoin?"

"Maybe. But more likely, military procurement, spending, dipping into that over the years."

"Kickbacks, huh?"

"The oldest game in town. Has to be. Offshore companies set up by lawyers who work for US defense manufacturers sending him money in Swiss and Panamanian bank accounts in his cousin's name, or his wife, under her maiden name, with dual access."

"And you know that for a fact?"

"I got it right here in front of me."

"Son of a bitch."

"That's not all. Listen, I see you're at the airport."

"Correct."

"I assume there's a reason you're flying commercial with your wife."

Reznick got up and walked out of the restaurant and onto the terminal concourse, next to a chocolate shop. He wanted to be out of Elisabeth's earshot. "My instincts told me that the extraction delay and the method of extraction were putting my wife in mortal danger."

"How so?"

"The Russians were on to her. I had to neutralize a few. But I suspect it served the Pentagon's purpose if she was never heard from again."

"Your instincts served you well. There's more on Gronski. Something even more damning."

"What?"

"I got access to the Defense Information Systems Agency. They're based at Fort Meade, where I used to work when I was at the NSA. I know a couple of contractors there."

"Is that how you did it?"

"Can't possibly comment. What I can say is that those guys deal with secure military communications. Messaging, email, voice messages, calls. I checked on Gronski's voice messages. He spoke to the CIA station chief in Bern forty-eight hours ago, telling them to stand down with regards to extraction of A. B."

"That has to be Anna Bruckmann."

"One hundred percent. Second call made by Gronski to his superior at the Pentagon, saying he has reason to believe the Russians might be close to locating their agent. Gronski was told to stand down too."

Reznick stood in the terminal, churning up inside, mind racing. "Are you one hundred percent sure? The Pentagon top brass are hanging her out to dry?"

"Pretty much. Do you want me to send the transcripts, Jon? It's not a problem."

"Negative. I'll deal with this."

"Jon, there's a fair chance the Russians already know this. They've hacked the shit out of Fort Meade for as long as I can remember. You heard of APT29?"

"Russian military hackers?"

"Correct. They're associated with and controlled by Russia's foreign intelligence agency, the SVR. They gained access via the servers of a company that supplies software for a lot of the Pentagon."

"What a mess."

"You're telling me."

Reznick turned around and saw Elisabeth calling him back over. "Listen, got to go. I owe you one, Trevelle."

Reznick ended the call and went back to finish his coffee. He relayed what Trevelle had told him to Elisabeth and Lauren.

Elisabeth said, "I don't believe that. Not for one minute."

"It's all true. I don't trust Gronski. I never did. No one who has ever run into him does."

"But how does that help us?"

"Leverage. Safe passage."

"He's not going to kill us?" Elisabeth asked, incredulous.

"Are you listening to what I'm telling you? He's corrupt. He will want to neutralize you. Your reappearance, even with a new identity, would expose the whole operation."

"Are you going to blackmail him?"

"I wouldn't call it that."

"What would you call it?"

"It's like an agreement, quid pro quo. I speak his language."

Elisabeth sighed. "You want me to call him?"

"I'll deal with this, if that's OK."

"What are you going to say?"

"Let me worry about that."

Reznick took out his cell phone as Elisabeth recited the secure number for Gronski. He tapped in the number. It rang four times before it was answered.

"Who's this?" growled Gronski.

Reznick turned his back on his wife and daughter for a moment. "Hey, Charles, I wake you up?"

Silence.

"Remember me? Way, way back."

"I think you've got the wrong number."

"I don't think so, Charlie. Delta, you remember? A long time ago, I know, but thought I'd give you a call. Old times' sake, and all that. What a shitshow in Somalia, right?"

"Reznick?"

"Correct."

"Where are you calling from?"

"None of your business."

"Listen to me, Reznick. You don't understand what you're getting yourself into. This has nothing to do with you."

"That's where you're wrong, Charlie."

"Don't call me that, you hear?"

"Why not, Charlie? Does that bother you?"

Gronski sighed. "Don't do anything rash, Jon."

"First-name terms. I'm flattered."

"Are you with Anna?"

Reznick said nothing.

"I asked you a question. Is Anna with you?"

"Yes, she is."

"Listen to me, son . . ."

"I'm calling the shots now, Gronski. I want to know why she wasn't extracted on the first day this all went to shit."

"I can't talk about classified stuff. You know that full well. Now you need to—"

"Shut the fuck up. I thought it was strange. The whole thing is a fucking shitshow. But when I realized there wasn't a quick extraction, and the extraction that was planned wasn't via chopper, and then the fucking Russians had located Anna and targeted her, I realized what had happened. She was expendable. And now I have confirmation. You messaged the CIA station chief and told him to stand down. And you relayed this to your boss, that the Russians were on her tail. I've got it all. You guys were going to let her get neutralized, weren't you?"

Gronski said nothing.

"I know how this works. You would allow the Russians the time to get her. Was that through the Swiss intermediary? She's compromised. Swiss intelligence is compromised. And you're compromised."

"You're crazy, Reznick. You always have been. I'm going to see to it that we make your life hell."

"Listen to me, you corrupt piece of filth. You're a disgrace."

"Is that why you called?"

"No."

"So, why are you calling?"

"I'm calling to tell you there's been a change of plan. Anna has her own extraction plan. I don't trust you."

"When you finally make it back home, Reznick—*if* you make it back home—you're going to wish you were never born. You're a dead man."

"Charlie, you've always been a piece of shit. I know that. You know that. So, I'm giving you a heads-up so we both understand each other. We're flying commercial. That includes Anna. In plain sight. If anything happens to Anna, whatever you want to call her, at any time, I will hold you personally responsible."

"Listen to me, Reznick—"

"No, you listen. I'm with my wife. And my daughter. And we're flying home."

"That's not possible. I'll arrange transport. Where are you?"

"Negative. I want to talk business. Big Sky, Palm Beach, and McLean—that's an excellent property portfolio. I nearly forgot the Caymans penthouse. Great part of the world. Very tax efficient. Do your superiors at the Pentagon know about this? Does the *New York Times* know about this?"

"Now you listen to me—"

"No, you listen to me, you piece of shit. Here's the deal: I have a friend who has compiled the details of all your property holdings. And he has the secure communications you sent. If anything happens to Anna or my daughter, even an accident, I will hold you responsible. Now do you want me to visit you at your home to talk this over, or are we good?"

Silence. Reznick let the threat sink in for a little while longer, then asked again. "Do you want me to come to your home and talk this over, or are we good?"

"We're good."

"You will resign in the next twenty-four hours. That's the deal. Take it or leave it."

Gronski stayed silent.

"Take it or leave it. Your choice."

"I'll take it."

"Good call. Now don't disappoint me, Charlie. Get the resignation letter written. And do the country a favor. You piece of shit."

The line went dead.

Forty-Five

Hans Muller's chopper touched down on the helipad, two miles from Zurich Airport. His stomach churned. Maybe this would be his last day on earth. Only time would tell.

He took off his headset. "What now?"

"Walk with me," Sasha said. "Stay close."

Muller followed her through a door by the helipad and down a flight of stairs. She entered a four-digit code, and they headed into a locked suite of offices. A brown leather suitcase lay on a desk.

Sasha pointed to the bag. "You're going to work. Get changed. It's all in the case."

"You want me to get changed here?"

"Do you want me to turn away, protect your modesty?"

Muller shook his head. He unzipped the case, stripped off his clothes as Sasha watched, arms folded. Five minutes later, he was ready. He checked his reflection in the mirror.

"Very smart," Sasha said.

Muller wore a navy Zurich Airport–issue single-breasted suit, black Oxford shoes, white shirt, and navy tie. He hung a lanyard around his neck with a photo ID. His name was Felix Lumberg. He had a fake photographic, fingerprint, and biometric identity set remotely by Sergei. His mind raced with thoughts of his mother. *Kill or be killed.* Maybe it would be both.

"Let's go, handsome."

Muller followed the Russian operative out of the office to a parking garage.

Sasha pointed to a waiting Honda SUV. "That's our ride. I'll drive. You sit up front in the passenger seat."

Sasha pressed a key fob, and the car doors unlocked. She slid into the driver's seat and started up the engine.

Muller sat up front as she requested, buckling up tight.

She looked at him, her cold blue eyes steady. "We good?"

"We're good. So, this is it?"

"Nearly there."

The closer they got to the airport, the more he felt a strange sense of calm wash over him. He began to zone out, as he had been trained to. He had imagined a dream life on a private Brazilian island. Maybe he would still have that. But he knew that his mother came first. The sacrifices she had made. His parents had scrimped and saved. They hadn't taken foreign holidays. One car, a beaten-up twenty-year-old Volvo.

The face of Anna Bruckmann captured in Zurich Old Town. It had brought him to this point. It had activated the Russian intelligence networks. He wondered what she was doing at this moment. Was she in the terminal, drinking a glass of wine, waiting for her flight home?

Doubts still gnawed at him. He wondered if he was being played again. Maybe the Russians were doing this as a favor for America. A problematic CIA operative would be neutralized. Dead men tell no tales. Neither did dead women. The woman known as Anna Bruckmann would be caught up in a terrorist shooting at the airport. The world of espionage was smoke and mirrors. What if Muller himself died in the process? How would that be reported?

A Swiss spy on the run gunned down by brave armed police? Had someone been sent to kill him? Was he the patsy in this whole operation?

It was a monumental mindfuck.

"You've gone all quiet on me, Felix," Sasha said.

Muller smiled. "Felix, of course. Right." The vehicle approached the staff parking zone on the south side of Zurich Airport.

Sasha pulled up and turned off the ignition. "You got your earpiece in?"

Muller touched the plastic earpiece with his index finger. "Copy that."

"Are you hearing me OK, Sergei?" Muller said.

The voice of Sergei in the earpiece. "Copy that. So, nice and easy, no smiling, serious. You are a security official, Felix, do you copy?"

"Copy that."

"Good, Felix. So, part one: calmly and quietly, get out of your vehicle and approach Gate 140."

Muller nodded to the voice in his ear. "Copy that."

"Then you will swipe the card on your lanyard, Felix, where security will see that new hire, Felix Lumberg, is turning up with Petra Gottman."

Hans turned to Sasha. This was new information, delivered inconveniently late. Another thing to keep track of. "You're Petra?"

"I am. Copy that, Sergei." She turned to Muller. "We good?"

"Let's do it."

Forty-Six

The lines for the secondary level of security were long as Reznick and his wife and daughter waited to get to their gate for the New York flight.

Reznick and Lauren were both pulled aside. Swiss police and security interrogated them about their weapons. Despite protestations, they were forced to place the weapons and ammunition in the checked luggage.

"Sir," Reznick said, "my daughter and I both have full FBI authorization to carry weapons."

The security official shook his head. "Not today you don't."

"What do you mean not today?"

"I have a note that you and your daughter cannot carry any firearms onto a plane. Sorry."

"You have a note. From who?"

"It is of no concern to you, sir. You either agree to this or you'll have to get yourself home some other way. Sorry."

Reznick argued for several minutes. The official and his supervisor weren't interested.

"Rules are rules. This is Switzerland, not America."

Reznick handed the supervisor the business card of FBI Assistant Director Martha Meyerstein. The official scanned the card. "Please call this number. I passed through the first security screening without a problem. Please call the number. She will vouch for us. She will answer any questions."

"No, sir. It's a no go if you insist that you must have the firearms."

Reznick took Lauren aside for a few minutes and talked it over. He agreed with her that it was futile and that they needed to get her mother home as soon as possible. They reluctantly complied with the Swiss security officials. Under their watchful eyes, he and Lauren placed their firearms and ammo in a special container, which was taken away.

"I'm sorry, these are security precautions we are putting into place for the next twenty-four hours." Despite their protestations, they would not be allowed to bring their weapons and ammunition.

Reznick felt naked without his trusty 9mm Beretta. They were interviewed by police again and again. It took nearly an hour to emerge from the security screening.

Elisabeth waited beyond the security screening, arms folded. Reznick explained the problem they had encountered.

"Jon, let's just get home."

Reznick wondered who had notified the Swiss. It was strange that the restriction would be in place for twenty-four hours. He smelled a rat, a rat named Gronski.

Forty-Seven

Muller strode through the terminal building, hands behind his back, looking officious. Surveillance cameras watched his every move.

A voice in his earpiece. "OK . . . so, Felix, we are watching you. Do you copy?"

"Copy that."

"Good. You're headed through the terminal, nice and easy. You're doing great. Pay attention. Fifty meters up ahead, on the right, there is a set of security lockers."

He saw the lockers up ahead. "Copy that."

"Locker 32, do you see it? Clear your throat to confirm."

Muller scanned the lockers and spotted the number. He cleared his throat.

"The four-digit code is 5-7-9-1 . . . Key in that number. Inside is a large backpack."

Muller entered the number, opened the locker, and pulled out the navy Adidas backpack. He slung it over his shoulder.

"Now proceed to the escalators farther along the terminal, then head down one level. When you get to the floor below, directly opposite the escalator, head to the men's restroom."

"Copy that." Muller went down the escalator and walked toward the restroom. He spotted a yellow *Staff Cleaning* sign outside. "Don't worry about the sign. We put it there to keep people out. It's empty. Go inside and go into the stall farthest from the door."

Muller again did as he was told. He went into the bathroom then into the stall at the far end of the room, away from the urinals. He locked the door. "Copy that."

"Open the backpack."

Muller opened it up. Inside was a black military gas mask, night vision goggles attached to a helmet, black coveralls, and a Glock 9mm, locked and loaded.

"Put on the gear and wait there for final instructions."

Muller pulled on the coveralls over his navy suit. He then put on the mask and the helmet with night vision goggles attached. He held the loaded gun in his hand. His breath came fast behind the mask. "Copy that."

"Just relax. You're doing great."

Muller did some breathing exercises to get control of himself. He needed to focus.

"You're doing just great, Felix. Excellent."

"What now?"

"Five minutes, thirty-four seconds. Sit tight. And then you're on."

Forty-Eight

Reznick sat with Lauren and Elisabeth in a quiet corner of a small airport bar, nursing a cold beer as Lauren and her mother drank coffee.

"Sure you don't want something stronger?" Reznick asked.

Elisabeth shook her head. "I'm fine. I'll have a drink when we're on the flight home. Can't really relax until I'm on the plane and in the air."

"It'll be fine."

"Will it?"

Reznick reached over and touched the back of his wife's hand. Her skin was warm. "It will be."

"What about us? What's going to happen to us?"

"We'll figure it out. Let's get home first."

"Why did you come looking for me, Jon? Anyone else would've just turned their back and tried to forget the betrayal."

"I don't do walking away. You should know that by now."

It could have all been so different if he hadn't come to find her. He didn't know if they would be able to piece together their old life again. Maybe she didn't want that. Then again, there was Martha. He wondered if he should tell Elisabeth about her. But he realized there was no point. It wasn't the right time.

He wondered if his relationship with Elisabeth could or would be rekindled. Maybe just as a friend. A woman he had once known well. That made more sense. But his main focus was on returning Elisabeth safely home, with Lauren as a part of her life. He would settle for that. Then again, maybe, just maybe, the fragments of their relationship could be pieced together once more. A new start.

Reznick's cell phone vibrated in his pocket. He took out his phone and pressed it tight to his ear. "Yeah?"

The voice of Trevelle: "Jon, you've got a problem."

"It's fine, I spoke with Gronski. I think we're good."

"Forget about that. You got another problem."

"What is it?"

"I was watching you guys arrive at the airport. I think you've got company."

"Who?"

"I think Hans Muller is in an adjacent terminal at Zurich Airport."

"How is that possible? Wouldn't that have been picked up by facial recognition as he went through security?"

"You would think so. I'm telling you, my facial recognition system is pinging like crazy."

"So, why aren't the IT systems pinging at Zurich Airport?"

Trevelle could be heard typing in the background. "Jon, I ran what we call a penetration test of the systems at the airport. Multiple vulnerabilities, that kind of stuff. It has been compromised for the last twelve hours, minimum."

Reznick glanced at Elisabeth and Lauren, who both looked anxious. "What are you saying? Wouldn't he need to be out of the country?"

"Consider this. What if Hans Muller, who is a traitor to Switzerland working for the Russians, is doing them one final favor?"

Reznick peered around the lounge, then stuck his head back into the terminal. "And that might explain why someone has remotely accessed the systems? So he could walk back in, in plain sight, without anyone noticing?"

"I tried to get through to Meyerstein to see if she could contact Swiss police to grab Muller. But no luck, her number was going straight to voicemail."

"Stay on the line."

"Copy that."

Reznick covered the cell phone and leaned in close to Elisabeth and Lauren. "Don't freak out. But I think Hans Muller is here at the airport. The next terminal. And I think he's coming for us."

Lauren turned to her mother. "You need to contact your handler in Bern. They need to take care of this."

Reznick shook his head. "Too late for that."

Elisabeth looked long and hard at Reznick. "Who gave you this information? Is it a reliable source?"

"The best there is. Trevelle has penetrated the systems here at the airport. But the Russians, or someone working for them, got there first."

Suddenly, the lights went out, plunging the terminal into pitch-darkness.

Forty-Nine

Muller sat still in the darkness of the airport restroom. A few moments later his night vision goggles kicked in. Suddenly his view was algae green. He moved his head from side to side. He could see in the dark.

A voice in his earpiece. "Kill or be killed."

"Copy that."

"Kill or be killed, Felix. Time to move. Time to kill."

Muller opened the stall door and strode out of the restroom. He stood still as crowds walked past, some with their cell phones illuminating the terminal's darkness.

"Turn right, up the escalator, then left."

"Copy that."

Muller turned right and walked toward the escalator, pushing past people. He sensed a growing panic. He saw people picking their way through the darkness. A blinding flash of light and the sound of an explosion. Smoke fogged up his vision.

The voice said, "Don't panic. Stun grenades and smoke grenades. One of our team."

Muller knew the grenades were used to temporarily disorient a person's senses. He turned left and saw a cop up ahead, submachine gun pointed at him.

The cop, covering his mouth with a handkerchief, approached him. "Halt!"

Muller instinctively dropped to the ground and fired at the helpless cop. The shots rang out. The cop lay motionless, algae-green blood pooling around his head.

"Move forward."

Muller strode forward. The screaming echoed across the chaotic, smoky terminal as passengers swarmed past him like locusts in a dust storm. He moved on with purpose. He had killed a cop.

The voice in his earpiece. "One hundred yards, straight through the terminal."

Muller felt alive. Wildly alive. And crazed. "Copy that."

"You're nearly there. Reznick and his family are just around the next corner."

Fifty

Reznick lay with his family on the floor of the bar, arms wrapped around Elisabeth and Lauren to keep them close. The sounds of multiple explosions, gunshots, and screams echoed through the terminal. Then smoke choked everyone, engulfing them all. Chaos spread as people ran in all directions. More shots.

"Keep your head down. Don't move until I say so."

Reznick crawled toward the entrance, keeping low. He peered through the smoke and coughed as the gas hit his lungs. A woman had tripped and was writhing on the ground in agony.

He wanted to pull her away from the chaos. But he had to think of Elisabeth and Lauren.

Reznick crawled back inside, grabbed Elisabeth with one hand and Lauren with the other. "We go out of here and turn right. Run!"

"Let's go!" Elisabeth shouted.

Reznick gripped their hands tight as they ran from the restaurant and sprinted down the terminal. "Keep moving!"

They ran past people crying and wandering around. Some huddled in corners on their cell phones, which illuminated their ghostly faces.

A shriek as Lauren tripped over an abandoned stroller. She stumbled again as she tried to get to her feet.

Lauren screamed out in pain. "My ankle! I can't move it!"

"I'll carry you on my back," Reznick shouted back.

Elisabeth pointed behind them. "Jon!"

Reznick spun around. Through the fleeing crowds in the darkness, a figure emerged. The figure was no more than seventy yards away. A silhouetted man wearing night vision goggles, handgun trained on them.

Reznick charged toward the man.

The man fired twice, then fled as Reznick pursued.

A scream from behind. "Jon, I'm hit! Jon! Jon! Help me!" The wails from Elisabeth.

Reznick turned back for a split second. He saw Lauren helping her mother. She'd know what to do. He headed after the fleeing gunman.

A cop appeared from behind a pillar, carrying a machine gun. He fired off a burst at the silhouetted man. But it hit fleeing, terrified people as they tried to escape the mayhem. Numerous bodies fell.

The silhouetted man spun and fired off two shots. The cop fell back behind the pillar. The gunman seemed to disappear in the fog of confusion.

Reznick barged past screaming passengers. His focus was on the shooter. He ran and hurdled over an old man lying sprawled on the ground, clutching his chest. Fire alarms blared as loudspeaker announcements in German called for calm. But it was madness. A hellish chaos.

Reznick crouched down beside the injured cop. The guy was in a pool of blood, eyes blinking, tears spilling down his face. He was dying before Reznick's eyes. Reznick couldn't do anything for him.

So, he picked up the cop's Heckler & Koch submachine gun and tried to find the fleeing gunman. He crashed into a family, fleeing for their lives, sending them to the ground.

The smoke clogged his lungs. He coughed and coughed, eyes watering from the smoke. Maybe a chemical element. Maybe a gas. He panted hard as he tried to get his bearings.

The silhouetted figure was up ahead. He stopped and turned.

Reznick ran in a zigzag pattern toward the shooter, who fired off shots. A man and a woman running past Reznick fell to the ground, blood spurting.

The shooter ran off again, maybe fifty yards ahead.

Reznick was closing in. He headed down a corridor, but the gunman had disappeared from sight. "Fuck!"

He ran on down a maze of corridors as he tried to use his peripheral vision to see better. He needed to gauge where and how the shooter would escape the labyrinthine layout of the Zurich Airport terminal. The man ran down an escalator before he disappeared from sight again.

Reznick barged past more people. "Out of the way! Out of the goddamn way!"

The figures ahead of him screamed, and one ran directly into him, bringing him crashing to the ground.

A woman scrambled and screamed as she extricated herself from Reznick, both sprawled on the floor. Reznick got to his feet and fought his way through the throng to get to the escalator. He saw a door and barged through. His instincts were telling him that the gunman wasn't far. He saw a neon-green fire exit sign. Light streamed in through the door.

He burst through the door and stumbled down a stairwell and smashed through an open door.

Reznick looked around. Thousands of people streaming in all directions. Ambulances with sirens blaring as they approached the terminal, men and women, faces blackened from smoke, collapsing into the arms of paramedics. Onlookers pointed and screamed as an ambulance crashed through a security barrier across a parking lot.

A woman with a backpack by her side lay on the ground, gasping for breath. She looked up and pointed at the vehicle. "Gunman! Ambulance!"

Reznick flagged down a passing police motorcyclist on a powerful BMW, blue lights flashing. He approached the cop.

The motorcycle cop braked hard and flipped up his visor. *"Ja?"*

Reznick pointed the submachine gun at the cop and hauled him off his bike. He climbed on, revved the engine, slung the machine gun over his chest, and accelerated away at high speed.

Fifty-One

Muller ripped off his coveralls, helmet, and gas mask as Sasha sped away in the hijacked ambulance.

"What the fuck happened?" she shouted.

"I got one of them. The wife. The main target."

"You only got one?"

"It all went fucking crazy. It was like a war zone."

"Why didn't you shoot Jon Reznick and the daughter too?"

"Some fucking cop came at me. By the time I had killed him, all hell was breaking loose. I needed to get the hell out of the terminal while I was still alive. But I got her. Two shots."

"You got the wife, definitely?"

"Yes! I got the wife! I would have gotten the other two, but a man appeared out of the smoke, I think it was Jon Reznick, and I got the hell out of there. Then an airport cop appeared out of nowhere, and I had to kill him. It was a shitshow. She was the main one. Two in the chest. So, job done!" Muller was wired. A seething fury had come loose in him. "Happy?"

"You did good."

"Where are we going?"

"Across the border into Germany."

"Where?"

"Laufenburg, just over sixty kilometers away. We'll be there in an hour."

"Then what?"

"Then you are free. Your mother is already in a safe house in Laufenburg."

"How can I be sure?"

Sasha handed him a cell phone and recited a number for him to call.

Muller closed his eyes as Sasha negotiated a few narrow streets in downtown Zurich before they got on the highway.

A frail woman's voice: "Hello?"

"Mother? Are you safe?"

"Yes, I am, Hans. They've been so kind. They say you will be here soon."

"I'm on my way. Take care."

Muller ended the call. A few moments later, the phone rang. It was Sergei.

Sergei was laughing. "One down," he said. "You did it. She was the main target. Complications?"

"Yes. Many."

"You did very well. You didn't get caught. Your identity was concealed. You're in the clear. And you'll see your mother in no time."

"We're going there in the ambulance?"

"Negative, Hans. We'll see you soon. You're about to do a switch."

"What switch?"

"Sasha will explain."

Hans ended the call.

"Once we're in Germany, what's the plan?"

"A private plane will take you to freedom, and your mother will be with you too."

Sasha accelerated through the streets of Zurich, lights and siren on. Cars pulled over to give her more space on the road. She turned a corner, went down a ramp, and drove into an underground parking garage. Down a further ramp to a basement parking zone, encased in concrete, like a catacomb. She screeched to a halt beside a Mercedes SUV. "This is my ride!"

"Where's mine!"

Sasha handed him a set of keys. "The BMW on the other side."

"And I head to the German border?"

"You're Felix Lumberg. ID, passport—all in the glove compartment. A change of clothes in the suitcase. And your mother will be on the other side of the border. You're going to be flown to safety with her, probably within ninety minutes."

Muller got out of the vehicle and pressed the fob attached to the keys. The door clicked open, and he slid into the BMW's driver's seat. He adjusted his seat, pressed the ignition button, and gently reversed the car out of the space.

He lowered the window as he grinned at Sasha, who was opening up her Mercedes.

"Stage one complete," she said. "Now fuck off!"

Muller laughed as he pulled away. He drove up and out of the garage and edged away into traffic. Heart pounding, trying hard not to scream in excitement. He had done it. He had really done it.

Fifty-Two

Reznick opened the throttle and began to push the bike to the max. Head down behind the windshield, he chased the ambulance with its lights flashing across Zurich. He sped past the Grossmuenster—a medieval cathedral—and across the historic Münster Bridge over the River Limmat, but the ambulance seemed to have disappeared.

He continued down the road, then doubled back for a few minutes. He couldn't believe he had lost them so easily.

Reznick saw a sign for a parking garage down a side street. He rode in and checked out all the levels. A security guard with a walkie-talkie in hand approached.

"The people in the ambulance!" Reznick said. "Where did they go?"

"You English?"

"American. The ambulance? Where did it go?"

The security guard shrugged. "I just saw a woman driving the ambulance, in a big hurry." He pointed to the ambulance at the far end of the basement behind a couple of concrete pillars.

"That it?"

"Yes, sir. She got out and drove away in a Mercedes, German license plates."

"German?"

"I thought it was weird too. I wondered if she was just finishing her shift. But how could she afford a Mercedes, I thought? And also, I thought it strange that she was just leaving the ambulance. So, I reported it to the police."

"Did you hear about the shooting at the airport?"

"When?"

"A few minutes ago. The woman driving—she's involved. I need to know where the Mercedes went."

The security guard gave Reznick the license plate number.

"Thanks. But what about a second person, a man?"

"I didn't see a man."

Reznick rode around the basement and the rest of the parking garage again. He needed the guy. His only lead was the Mercedes.

He drove to the very top of the parking garage. He wondered if the car was headed for Germany. The escape route. Not far from Zurich.

Reznick turned and sped out of the parking garage, down a ramp, and to the right. He rode hard along Frankengasse until he saw a sign for the highway. He turned onto a busy approach road headed out of the city, weaving in and out of traffic for a few miles. Then he got on the A3 and headed northwest out of the city, hitting one hundred miles per hour and above. Faster and faster, Reznick rode. Mile after mile down the Swiss autobahn. He was riding the bike like his life depended on it. His mind flashed images of Elisabeth, shot. Her scream. He flashed forward. He wondered why the security guard hadn't noticed a man, Muller, getting out of the ambulance. He had to be in the getaway car, the Mercedes. Had to be. A full fifteen long minutes, darting in and out of traffic. Then he saw it. Up ahead, the Mercedes SUV. The same license plate the security guard had told him.

He rode up fast behind the vehicle. Closer and closer. He saw the back of the driver's head. A woman. Was Muller lying facedown in the back seat?

Reznick edged closer, his freezing left hand on the handle grip. With his right hand, he felt the cold metal of the submachine gun trigger. Then he fired a burst of gunfire at the rear tires. The tires exploded, rubber smoking down to the metal rims in seconds.

The SUV veered violently across the highway, crashed through a metal barrier, and spun over and over down into a snowy field, smoke billowing.

Flames erupted out of the engine, the Mercedes on its side.

Reznick screeched to a halt. He vaulted over the metal crash barrier and sprinted into the snowy field, toward the vehicle.

A woman's shaking arm emerged from a broken window, gun drawn.

Reznick rapid-fired again, raking the side of the car and the bloodied arm. Bullets ripped into the wrist as the woman let out a piercing scream.

The woman crawled out through the broken car window, bloodied, shaking and crying out, cradling her bleeding arm like a baby. "Don't shoot!" The accent was English.

Reznick motioned for her to step away from the vehicle. "On your knees, hands on head!"

The woman complied. She began to cry as blood poured from the terrible wounds.

"Help me, sir!"

Reznick kept the submachine gun trained on her.

"Where's the guy that was in the ambulance you were driving?"

"I don't know what you're talking about. I'm visiting Switzerland."

"Answer me!"

"I was carjacked by him. He had a gun. I had to drop him off. He disappeared. I thought he was going to kill me!"

"Bullshit! Where is he?"

The woman grimaced and moaned.

"You've got a choice. You either tell me where he is, or you die right here, right now."

The woman coughed and clutched her wounds, tears in her eyes. "Why don't you believe me? Call the hospital. I need medical treatment."

"You were identified as getting into this vehicle. So, quit lying, you piece of shit. Where is he?"

The woman bent over and gathered herself for what seemed like a lifetime. Slowly a wicked smile crossed her face, blood streaming from her mouth. "Did he kill your precious wife?" The accent turned Russian. "She was dead for twenty years. And then the bitch dies again." She laughed like a maniac, tears and blood spilling onto the glass-covered snow. "Poor American bitch."

Reznick stared down at her, blood boiling.

"I know all about you, Jon. I know who you are. You're one of the CIA guys—Jon Reznick. A killer. The husband of the sadly deceased again. Poor soul. I guess you arrived too late, Mr. American. The guy you're looking for . . . He's gone. Long gone. So, bad luck, yes?"

He crouched down and grabbed her by the throat. "Where the fuck is he!"

The woman laughed, eyes bulging. "He's here, he's there, he's everywhere!"

Reznick realized in that split second that she was the decoy in case things went to shit. He had been had. He had followed the decoy.

"Who are you?" he seethed, squeezing her carotid artery tight with his fingers.

"Go fuck yourself, Mr. American!"

"Last time. Who are you?"

"I'm a Russian. And I'm proud of it. And I hate your stinking, rotten country. So, fuck you and fuck your bitch of a wife. I'm glad she died."

Reznick got to his feet. He felt an unutterable rage. He reared back and kicked her in the head, knocking her out cold.

Fifty-Three

Reznick ran back across the highway to the police motorcycle he had left on the side of the road. The Russian woman was unconscious, lying in the snow, bleeding out. Cars slowed down as they passed. He picked up the bike and took out his cell phone and called Trevelle.

"Jon, what the hell is going on there?"

"I was hoping you could tell me that."

"What do you know?"

"The shooter and a female accomplice got in an ambulance and ditched the vehicle in a parking garage in the center of Zurich. She sped away in a Mercedes."

"License plate?"

Reznick gave the details of the Mercedes. "Muller must've gotten into another vehicle. I was wondering if you could help me."

"I'm on it. You're fifteen kilometers from the German border. I've checked the footage. Muller—facial recognition has confirmed this—got into a BMW. I repeat, BMW. German plates."

Trevelle relayed the BMW license plate to Reznick.

"Copy that. Was the vehicle stolen?"

"This is all I know."

"Where is the fucker?"

"That will take me a few minutes. I'll need to dig into the Swiss autobahn network systems. Hang on . . . I think I might have something coming up . . ."

The sound of police sirens in the distance. Reznick straddled the motorcycle. "Trevelle, I need to move! You got a GPS location of the BMW?"

"I'm in! Yeah . . . Working on it . . . He's . . . Got it! Muller is eight kilometers north of you, on some minor country road. He's headed in the same direction toward Germany, but avoiding the highway."

"Very smart."

"He's approaching the small town of Marthalen. You need to turn left at the next exit, then get on the road north, Marthalerstrasse. He must be going through all those sleepy fucking Swiss villages before he disappears into Germany. I swear it's him."

"No passport controls at the border?"

"Nothing. Schengen Agreement: free movement and all that between most EU countries."

"Got it. Good work."

"Take care, man."

Reznick sped away from the scene, head down, not caring if he lived or died. He was focused on one thing. He wanted to intercept Hans Muller before he crossed the border. He rode hard down the highway.

He saw the exit as Trevelle had indicated. He turned off and got onto a quiet road to Marthalen. He sped on, opening up the throttle. Faster and faster, snowfields whizzing past.

He headed along the winding, weaving, freezing road for miles, accelerating past dawdling drivers.

Reznick was risking it all. He knew his speed in such icy conditions was dangerous. But he was past caring. He was risking his life as he took bends in the road, riding hard. Past icy fields, small farmsteads blanketed in alpine white powder. Quicker and quicker.

He turned another bend and accelerated fast down a long narrow stretch of road, the rear tire nearly slipping too much. Reznick struggled to contain the power and speed of the bike. He peered over the windshield.

He saw a lone BMW, doing an insipid fifty miles an hour or so, just up ahead.

Reznick revved hard and opened up the throttle to the max, one more time. He felt as if the bike was going so fast it would slide away on the freezing road. Closer and closer. He needed to get to Muller before the border. Then he saw it. The license plate.

It was him.

Reznick felt a full-on adrenaline rush as he tailed the vehicle when it turned onto a narrow country road. The tiny hamlet had a sign. *Meisterhof.* He wondered if this road was another minor route into Germany. The road ahead was clear.

He had to make his move. Now!

His left hand on the motorcycle's grip, Reznick took aim at the BMW's rear window with the Heckler & Koch. He pulled the trigger. He sprayed a deafening burst of gunfire at the car's back window, shattering the glass.

The BMW screeched to a halt.

Reznick slowed and jumped off the bike. He crouched down and raked the rear of the car with gunfire. He kept his head down low as he approached the driver's side door.

He peered in the front window, submachine gun pointed at the driver. A man sat motionless, head slumped forward on the steering wheel.

Reznick had his finger on the trigger, the submachine gun trained on the driver, a young man. Was this *him*? Was this Hans

Muller? He pointed the barrel at the rear side window and fired off more shots.

The young man sat bolt upright, arms in the air. "Don't shoot! *Nicht schiessen!*"

"Hands on head, motherfucker!"

The guy complied, blood streaming from cuts on his forehead.

Reznick gripped the submachine gun in his right hand and opened the door with his left. He reached in and hauled the guy out by the neck, forcing him to the ground, gun pressed tight to his head.

"Please don't hurt me!"

Reznick studied the handsome man wearing a navy suit. He needed to know if this was the Swiss spy. The data thief. Muller. He needed to know for sure. He needed certainty. "Who are you?"

"I'm airport security! My name is Felix Lumberg. I was chasing a suspect! I'm bleeding! My God, I was kidnapped! I'm just an ordinary person."

Reznick took a couple of steps back, gun still trained on the man.

"I swear to God. You are making the most awful, terrible mistake. You scared me. I managed to escape from there. And then I saw you chasing me! Please, what is going on!"

"Bullshit!"

"I was carjacked, but they fled and I managed to escape. Check my ID if you don't believe me."

Reznick sensed a lie. But he had to be sure. "Where's your ID?"

"My inside pocket."

"Reach in, slowly, very slowly, and throw it over here. No sudden movements or you die."

The guy reached into his inside pocket and withdrew a blood-smeared photo ID attached to a lanyard, identifying him as Zurich Airport security personnel. "See? I told you."

Reznick froze. It looked genuine. But he knew deep down that something was still off. He took out his cell phone and took the guy's photo, sending it to Trevelle. He held the phone in his left hand, called his number, and pressed the phone to his ear.

"I need you to identify that photo I just sent."

"Copy that. Stay on the line. Two minutes, Jon."

"I haven't got two minutes." Reznick had his gun trained on the man.

The guy on the ground moaned. "Please, you hurt me. What the hell were you doing? Are you one of them? That's what it is! You're one of them. You've come to kill me. I have a wife and children. They need me."

Reznick pressed the gun to his head. "Silence, fucker!"

The guy closed his eyes as blood streamed down his cheeks. "This is crazy. I'm Felix. I'm a good guy. Who are you? Are you American? I love your country. Why are you picking on me?"

The voice of Trevelle: "Jon!"

"What?"

"I ran the scans. It's a match. Hans Muller. And I'm watching TV footage taken at the airport thirty minutes ago on CNN! Was the guy also wearing a gas mask?"

"Affirmative."

"I just checked the surveillance footage from the airport. The photo you sent is the same guy who must have taken off a gas mask after getting into the ambulance."

"And this is him?"

"One hundred percent certainty. The scans are all in. This is Hans Muller, Swiss IT expert, the guy who took all the data. Zurich Airport has the same ID related to Felix Lumberg. But that's a remote addition to the system."

"And this is the guy who shot Elisabeth?"

"Copy that, Jon. Correct. I went over that footage too."

"I owe you one."

"Anything else?"

Reznick ended the call and put his cell phone back in his pocket. Both hands were on the submachine gun, finger on the trigger.

There was a look of terror in Muller's eyes. This was the bastard who had betrayed his country. The West. This, this sniveling piece of shit?

But it was also the man who had gunned down Elisabeth. He wondered on whose orders.

"What's going on? This is a terrible misunderstanding!"

Far off in the distance, the sound of more sirens.

"You gunned down my wife."

"I swear, this is a terrible, terrible mistake. I'm a security official."

The sirens were getting louder.

"The Russians sent you, didn't they? Why did they send an IT expert to kill her?"

The guy began to smile as he cradled his bloodied, trembling wrist.

"What's so funny?"

"I'll tell you what's funny. I guess you ran out of time, Mr. American!"

"What makes you say that?"

"The Swiss police will arrest you for what you've done. You're so very fucked."

"Good try, Hans."

The smile was wiped off Hans's face. "What did you call me? My name is Felix." Hans blinked away tears. "You have no idea what you're doing. You've no idea what is going to happen to you."

"You shot my wife. You're a spy. How did they turn you? Was it money? Ideology? Hatred of the West? Hatred of our system?"

"I am a victim. You shot an innocent man."

"Explain that to the cops."

Hans began to laugh. "I'll let you in on a little secret. The sirens are not cops."

Reznick realized in that moment that the guy was fucking with him. He was playing mind games even when he was staring into the abyss.

"They're coming to kill you."

"Was it worth it, Hans?"

"Was what worth it?"

"The deception. Selling your soul."

Hans shook his head, tears in his eyes. "You don't know the first thing about my soul."

Reznick pressed the barrel of the machine gun against Hans's brow. "You know what they used to do with traitors?"

Hans blinked away tears.

"They used to be hanged."

Reznick's cell phone rang. He took it out of his pocket, submachine gun still pointed at Hans. "What?"

"Dad, it's Lauren! Where are you?"

"I went after the gunman. I got him."

"Dad, the doctors have found a faint pulse. They're fighting to save Mom."

Reznick felt his throat tighten. He was enraged and wanted to kill Hans and rush to the hospital. "She's in the hospital now?"

"She's lost a huge amount of blood. I'm at the hospital. Zurich."

"Are they operating on her?"

"Dad, I don't know. No one is talking to me. The only doctor who did say a few words told me to prepare for the worst."

Reznick ended the call. He knew Elisabeth's life was out of his control. The surgeons and doctors in Zurich were the only ones who could help her now. He knew she was in the best hands. But he felt helpless. There was nothing he could do.

He was tempted to shoot Muller through the head right now. Maybe he still would. But at that moment, a germ of an idea began to form in his head. He contemplated his next move. He wondered about the logistics of his idea.

Reznick pressed the gun to Muller's head. "We're all alone, Hans. You got any last requests?"

The sirens continued to sound in the distance.

For the first time, real fear appeared in Muller's eyes. The confidence and cockiness that he had exuded a few moments ago were gone. In their place, fear. Fear of death. The final leveler.

"Listen, this is crazy. Why don't we make a deal? You need money? I've got money. I've got a lot of money."

"You shot my wife! You think I'm doing this for money?"

"You're an American! That's what you guys are all about, right?"

Reznick had heard enough. He raised the gun high above his head. Then he brought the stock smashing down hard into Muller's terrified face. His face exploded with the blow. It knocked Muller out, smashing open his mouth, blood pouring from his gums and nose.

Reznick dragged Muller to the back of the BMW, popped open the trunk and bundled him inside. Then he slammed it shut.

Reznick slid into the driver's seat, doubled back down the road. A few minutes later, he was back on the highway.

He hit the gas. He saw a sign for Zurich. But that wasn't where he was headed. At least not now. He took a turn and headed along the highway to Bern. He accelerated and was hitting almost ninety miles per hour, cold wind howling through the rear shattered window, foot to the floor. He ate up the miles. The snowy landscape was draped in a gray, midwinter gloom.

Mile after mile.

Ten miles out from his destination, he made the call.

A somber American man's voice answered. "American Embassy, how can I help you?"

"Put me through to your most senior defense attaché."

"I'm sorry, sir, that's not possible."

"Listen to me, this is a national security issue. You either put me through now or I will drive through your fucking gates! I'm an American citizen. My name is Jon Reznick."

"Please hold, sir."

Reznick felt himself gripping the steering wheel tighter. The sound of banging from the trunk.

"Brigadier General David Herbert. Who am I talking to?"

"Sir, my name is Jon Reznick. Does that name mean anything to you?"

"Yes, it does. This is very irregular, Reznick."

"I do irregular stuff, David. But I have credentials at the highest level. Check if you have to."

"Is this in connection with the terrorist attack in Zurich?"

"I have the shooter."

"I'm sorry, say that again?"

"I have the fucking airport shooter! Do you copy?"

"Copy that."

"His name is Hans Muller. The same Swiss operative who stole classified NATO secrets. He was masquerading with fake ID as Felix Lumberg, airport security. It's bullshit. He's a Russian spy. Now are you listening?"

"Where are you?"

Reznick checked the GPS on the dashboard. "I'm five miles out. I want the gates to be opened, and I need your military personnel to be standing by. I want the CIA station chief to be alerted. I'm bringing him in."

"Now?"

"Right fucking now!"

Reznick ended the call as he entered the capital city. The voice of the GPS guided him through the medieval streets. He turned a corner. And there it was. Armed guards, weapons drawn, covered him as the huge wrought iron gates opened wide.

He drove through as a couple of officials indicated for him to drive to the back of the massive building.

The gates closed behind him, and Reznick pulled up out of sight at the rear of the embassy before he switched off the engine.

A man wearing an impeccably tailored two-piece suit approached. "Reznick?"

Reznick nodded.

"I'm the brigadier general you spoke to, David Herbert."

Reznick got out of the car, and they shook hands. He walked to the back of the vehicle and popped open the trunk.

He reached in and hauled out the bloodied, battered, and clearly petrified Muller.

"I need medical treatment! Under the Geneva Convention—"

Reznick headbutted the traitor, who collapsed in a heap on the ground. He spat on his face. "When this is over, you're going to wish you were dead."

Two armed guards quickly hauled Muller to his feet, hand-cuffed him, and marched him inside the embassy.

"What the hell happened, Reznick?" the brigadier general asked.

"Long, long story."

"You need to get cleaned up. And we'll have to debrief you."

"Not right now. First things first: I need a chopper to Zurich."

Fifty-Four

The chopper touched down on the roof of University Hospital in Zurich.

Reznick was escorted by a couple of nurses down to the sixth floor, where Lauren was waiting. They hugged each other tight. "What are the doctors saying?"

"Mom's in the operating room now. We just have to wait."

Reznick hugged her again as his daughter broke down.

"I'm scared, Dad. I don't want to lose her again. I'm so scared."

"Me too."

Reznick and Lauren sat in silence and began a long wait. Hour after hour, they waited. Time dragged. Day turned to night. Outside, in the darkness of Zurich, snow fell. He checked his watch. He checked his cell phone for messages. It was just after eight p.m. He turned and looked at his daughter. The pain etched on her face. The strain and stress of the events in Switzerland were taking their toll on her. The enormity of emotional highs and lows over the last few days. He reached over and held her hand, squeezing it three times.

Reznick leaned in close. "I want you to know something, honey."

"What's that, Dad?"

"We'll get through this. Together. She's still your mother. She will always be your mother."

"I know that."

"Let's just be thankful we found her again. Found each other. She's your flesh and blood. When I look into your eyes, I see your mom. She will live on, come what may."

"Dad, don't talk like that. I want her to live."

"So do I. Your mother is tough. Way tougher than I ever imagined. Listen, I have no idea what went through her mind all those years ago. Maybe I never will. But sometimes, you know, shit happens. You just need to accept that it's life. Bad stuff happens. But it also means there's good stuff too. Don't forget."

"I want her to live so much. I want her to be in my life. I want a mom. It's all I ever wanted. I want Mom back. I can't lose her again, Dad."

"I know, honey."

Reznick looked over her shoulder.

The surgeon walked into the waiting room and forced a smile.

"How is she, Doctor?" Lauren asked.

"Your mother is still with us. But she lost a lot of blood. One bullet was lodged a few millimeters from a ventricle. The other shattered her sternum. It was a very complex operation."

Lauren blinked away the tears. "Tell us, will she make it?"

"I don't know. That's the best I can do."

"When will we know more?" Reznick asked.

"We'll know in the morning. If she makes it through the night, she might be OK."

It was a long, long night. Waiting. Pacing. Praying. The darkness would never end. But eventually, the first shards of winter sun pierced the waiting room blinds.

Reznick stifled a yawn as Lauren slept next to him with a coat draped over her. He hadn't slept a wink. A couple of Dexedrine kept him going through the night. Not for the first time. A change of shifts. Nurses checking medical notes for patients on the ward. A few doctors taking calls. Eventually, the lead surgeon who had operated appeared.

Reznick woke up his daughter. "Lauren," he said, nudging her shoulder. "It's the doctor."

Lauren rubbed the sleep out of her eyes.

The surgeon smiled. "Come with me, please," he said.

Reznick and Lauren got up from their seats in the waiting room and followed the surgeon through some swinging doors to his office. He sat down behind his desk. "Please." He indicated for them to sit across from him.

Reznick sat down and held Lauren's hand tight as she got comfortable.

"Well . . . Mr. Reznick, your wife was seriously wounded. But you knew that."

Reznick wrapped his arm around Lauren.

"In many ways, she was very lucky."

Reznick said nothing, thinking that was the most insensitive thing the surgeon could have said.

"What do I mean by that? I mean she has had significant blood loss. We would describe her condition as highly critical. She remains heavily sedated and on a ventilator. But she is alive."

Reznick felt as though his head was going to explode. "So, she's being kept alive by a machine?"

"Correct."

"What are her chances?"

"Too early to say."

"If you were a betting man, give me some odds?"

"It's fifty-fifty. And that's generous."

"I'll take those odds. I want to see my wife."

The doctor nodded. "Of course. I must warn you: we can't allow you or your daughter to sit beside her just now. We have procedures here. So, you'll have to look at her through the glass."

Reznick turned to his daughter. "You ready?"

She nodded. "I want to see my mom."

Fifty-Five

Reznick knew all about death. It was the business he was in. He had grown wearily accustomed to the mundane process of assassination. The first contact from a handler. Then the details. And then down to business. But nothing could have prepared him for the sight of his wife—a woman he thought he had lost twenty years before—lying in an ICU bed in Zurich, fighting for her life, every breath provided by a machine.

He needed to be strong for his daughter. He always wanted to be a strong, dependable father for Lauren. He didn't emote. And that's why the tears didn't come. In time, maybe they would.

Reznick pressed himself against the glass as Lauren held him tight. He looked at Elisabeth's hand, the IV tube taped to the back. He felt as if he was standing outside his body. It didn't seem real. How could it be? "Your mom's a fighter. She always was. She's tough. Don't ever forget that."

"I know. I just feel so helpless."

"Listen to me. I don't know how, but I think your mom senses we're here. I don't know why. It's just what I sense. I sense she'll know that we're watching her. Willing her to fight for her life. I know she will."

"I hope so, Dad. I hope that's true."

Reznick's cell phone vibrated in his pocket. He checked the caller ID; he didn't recognize it.

"Yeah, who's this?"

"Jon?" The voice of Martha Meyerstein.

"Martha?"

"Jon, I heard about Elisabeth. I'm so terribly sorry."

"Look, I appreciate your thoughts. But now's not the time for a conversation."

"Forget about that, Jon. I just wanted to say that I just landed five minutes ago."

"Here in Zurich?"

"Yes, here in Zurich. My flight just touched down. I have two American doctors with me. The best we've got."

Reznick felt his throat tighten. "Martha, I don't know what to say. She's getting the best treatment, I assure you."

"I'm sure she is. But I have two eminent trauma specialists from Bethesda Naval Hospital who are here to oversee her medical care, if that's alright with you."

"Whatever it takes, Martha. I just want her to live."

"We'll be with you in thirty minutes."

Reznick felt overwhelmed. He ended the call and told Lauren. Then they hugged.

Lauren placed her hand against the glass and began to cry. "Mom, stay with us. Do you hear me?"

The hours that followed were surreal.

FBI Assistant Director Martha Meyerstein turned up with two of America's top surgeons, alongside the medical director of the Zurich hospital, as CIA agents fanned out around the ICU unit.

Meyerstein informed Reznick that the Agency also had agents located at the hospital entrances, checking those coming in and out. No one got in who shouldn't have been there. Even cleaners were checked, IDs screened. Suddenly it was a security operation.

"I appreciate you helping out," he said.

Meyerstein looked through the glass.

"Did the Director authorize you to head over here?" Reznick said.

"I authorized me to head over here. This is national security, first and foremost."

Reznick touched her cheek. "Thank you."

"You're welcome."

The vigil continued into a second long night. More watching and waiting. Reznick dozed off for an hour at most.

The American surgeons were in and out of Elisabeth's room. Checking her vitals, her medical records, the Swiss medical team's notes about the operation.

Meyerstein sat down beside him and held his hand as Lauren stood at the glass, watching her mother. "Bit of a shock, huh?"

"You're telling *me*," Reznick said.

"I'm not going to ask questions about the why, how, and whatever. What's done is done. I just want you to know that I'm here for you, for Lauren, and I'm also here for Elisabeth."

"I'm assuming you're aware of her identity?"

"I've been made aware of that, on a need-to-know basis from the Pentagon. This is highly sensitive. Hugely sensitive. That's why we're anxious to lock this down tight. Get her better. And get her home."

"What's the plan now?"

"She has to recover sufficiently before we could consider moving her. Then the plan is to fly her back to the States, then make sure she continues to get the very best medical treatment."

"What about after that?"

"After that? I don't know . . . She might have to get a new identity. She might have to disappear, like the last time. I don't know how it'll play out."

"What about us?"

"My concern is to make sure all parties, including you, return in one piece to America."

"I don't know what to say, Martha."

"It doesn't matter. None of it matters. I just want you to know that I'm here for you. Always have been."

Another day broke. The excruciating wait continued.

Reznick asked one of the American doctors, Dr. Rhona Charles, what the latest prognosis was. He was told that they had agreed to wean her off the ventilator throughout the day. A series of tests would be done to monitor her condition. Blood pressure, heart rate, oxygen levels, blood gases. The ventilation tube would be replaced by an oxygen mask.

Reznick needed to sleep. But he couldn't. He was afraid he'd wake up to find her gone for good. But most of all, he was afraid for his daughter.

A few hours later, Dr. Charles emerged from Elisabeth's hospital room.

"Mr. Reznick, there are no guarantees in this business," she said. "I'm afraid it's a watch-and-wait. Again, I'm sorry. We'll see how she performs over the next few hours. Then we'll be in a better place to understand her condition and the outlook."

Reznick felt deflated. He watched his wife as she lay in a deep sleep. The hours stretched before him, no end in sight. Before they knew it, it was night.

"Why isn't she waking up?"

Dr. Charles pulled him aside. "She needs time, Jon. That's the best healer."

Meyerstein tapped the glass softly with tears in her eyes. "I hope she gets better, Jon."

"I hope so too."

Reznick and Lauren were given coffees and sandwiches. They prayed in the small hospital chapel. Prayed that she would live. Prayed that the nightmare would end. Daybreak finally came again.

"Jon!" Meyerstein shouted, motioning him to the glass.

"What?"

Meyerstein pointed through the glass. "Look!"

Reznick held Lauren's hand as they approached the glass. Elisabeth's eyes were open. He smiled at her. She was looking off, as if in a trance, unable to comprehend.

The medical team got to work again. They did another series of tests as Elisabeth looked through the glass for what seemed an eternity. Then, somehow, her pupils constricted as if she was focusing. She caught sight of Reznick and Lauren, hands pressed against the glass. And she smiled back.

Fifty-Six

Three long weeks later, Elisabeth Reznick was back home in wintry Rockland, wrapped up warm, walking on the freezing beach, down from the house that used to be their home. She seemed more frail now, which wasn't surprising. She had been flown home a week earlier, checked over by the same experts who had flown over to Zurich to monitor her. She had been given the all clear.

Elisabeth was able to be debriefed by the CIA at Langley. Now here she was, on heavy duty painkillers, still suffering from flashbacks, but alive.

Reznick helped her toward the sandy cove. Down to the water's edge.

"You remember this place?"

"A thousand lifetimes ago, Jon. It never changes."

"I know. That's the attraction. It's always like this. Just the water and the sky."

Elisabeth stopped and gazed over the icy blue waters of Penobscot Bay. Her short hair was growing back. Strands of gray. The young woman he knew was gone. But the woman who had returned was still the same woman. His wife. "I never thought I'd be here again. I thought Elisabeth Reznick was gone forever." She smiled as she breathed in the cool, fresh sea air.

"What's the Agency say about your identity? Bruckmann, and all that."

"They say that will change. That's the plan. At least for now."

Reznick nodded. "Understandable."

"They say I can't stay here, though."

"Why not?"

"If I'm recognized."

"But it was so long ago."

Elisabeth sighed and closed her eyes. "They said I have to go."

"Go where? What did you say?"

"I told them I wanted to stay. It was a long time ago I disappeared."

Reznick looked at his wife. A few more lines. A few more gray hairs. But she was back. Alive. It was hard to comprehend. He had lost count of the number of times he had walked this same beach, staring out over the water, wanting to die. Now, here he was. Different. They had both been changed by the events. Traumatized. It should all have been so different.

"Why didn't you just come home after 9/11 and tell me you were safe? That's all I wanted to hear."

"Who the hell knows? I think I was relishing my new job, the new role. It was like a secret existence. Then I got the chance to disappear for good. And I took it. I thought it was a higher calling. For country and all that. But I must have been crazy. I put you through something terrible; I can only imagine what it was like. I don't deserve you."

"I'm glad you're back. It's a lot to take in. For both of us."

"Tell me about Martha."

Reznick sighed. "Martha? We're good friends. I worked for the Feds on a number of investigations in the last decade or so. That's how we got to know each other."

"Are you . . . Are you with her?"

"More often than not."

Elisabeth gave a wan smile. "I don't know how you feel about me now. After everything that's happened. But I understand."

"I'm glad you're alive."

"I spoke to Lauren earlier," Elisabeth said.

"How is she? Still kicking ass in New York?"

"Seems like it. She's in the middle of some domestic terrorism investigation in Brooklyn."

"Good for her. She's all grown up. I'm very proud of her."

"Me too. She told me about Martha and you. Said you've gotten closer."

Reznick nodded.

Elisabeth averted her gaze. "Jon, I've got to ask you something."

"What?"

"Do you still want me in your life?"

"Absolutely . . . but . . ."

"But?"

"But as friends. My priorities and focus have changed. I see a future with Martha. A future that's real."

"I thought you might say that. It's fine. Listen, the CIA made me a deal."

"What kind of deal?"

"The deal was that I can stay in America. So, I'm pleased about that. They have a nice place for me lined up in Connecticut."

"I like Connecticut. On the coast?"

"Inland. In the country. I don't know much more. There are conditions."

"Which are?"

"You won't be able to visit. That's a red line for them."

"I understand."

"But if you want, and they're fine with this, I can still visit Rockland from time to time. Once, maybe twice a year, incognito. This way I can see Lauren too."

"I'd like that."

Elisabeth reached out and touched Reznick's cheek. "You have every right to hate me. But you don't."

"No, I don't. I wanted you to live. I wanted you to be here. That's all I wanted, to be with you. And you're here."

"I just wanted to say, for what it's worth, I'm sorry."

"I'm glad you're home. I'm glad you're safe. But I think we both need to go our separate ways."

Elisabeth gazed out over Penobscot Bay. "Oh God, Jon, it seems like yesterday. Lauren was just a baby."

"We were a lot younger."

Elisabeth had a wistful look in her eyes. "I'll miss you, Jon Reznick."

"I'll miss you too."

"Maybe I can write."

"Do people still write letters?" Reznick said.

"I think they do."

"Letters would be nice."

Reznick hugged his wife tight. He didn't want to let go. But he knew he had moved on. He wasn't the same person. Neither was she. He couldn't try and re-create what they once had. But he still felt a sadness, an emptiness, as they held each other.

The waters of Penobscot Bay crashed onto the shore. It was as if time itself had stood still.

Acknowledgements

I would like to thank my editor, Kasim Mohammed, and everyone at Amazon Publishing for their enthusiasm, hard work, and belief in the Jon Reznick thriller series. I would also like to thank my loyal readers. Thanks also to Faith Black Ross for her terrific work on this book, and Randall Klein, who looked over an early draft. Special thanks to my agent, Mitch Hoffman, of The Aaron M. Priest Literary Agency, New York.

Last but by no means least, my family (special mention to my mother, Annie) and friends for their encouragement and support. None more so than my wife, Susan.

About the Author

J. B. Turner is a former journalist and the author of the Jon Reznick series of political thrillers (*Hard Road, Hard Kill, Hard Wired, Hard Way, Hard Fall, Hard Hit, Hard Shot, Hard Target, Hard Vengeance,* and *Hard Fire*), the American Ghost series of black-ops thrillers (*Rogue, Reckoning,* and *Requiem*), the Jack McNeal Thriller series (*No Way Back* and *Long Way Home*), and the Deborah Jones crime thrillers (*Miami Requiem* and *Dark Waters*). He has a keen interest in geopolitics. He lives in Scotland with his wife and two children.

Follow the Author on Amazon

If you enjoyed this book, follow J. B. Turner on Amazon to be notified when the author releases a new book!
To do this, please follow these instructions:

Desktop:

1) Search for the author's name on Amazon or in the Amazon App.
2) Click on the author's name to arrive on their Amazon page.
3) Click the "Follow" button.

Mobile and Tablet:

1) Search for the author's name on Amazon or in the Amazon App.
2) Click on one of the author's books.
3) Click on the author's name to arrive on their Amazon page.
4) Click the "Follow" button.

Kindle eReader and Kindle App:

If you enjoyed this book on a Kindle eReader or in the Kindle App, you will find the author "Follow" button after the last page.